LOVESTRUCK

JULIE CAPULET

He calls me his lucky charm. I call him trouble.

Elias O'Shea is Hawthorne U's starting quarterback and the golden boy of college football. With a winning streak that has the full attention of the NFL, Elias seems unstoppable.

Except for one problem. According to social media, the campus heartthrob is a hopeless romantic at heart. He's searching for true love and he can't find it. Rumor has it, his distraction is starting to throw him off his game.

My dad—who happens to be the football coach—says as long as Elias stays focused, going pro is all but locked in. Which is why Elias noticing *me* is a disaster waiting to happen.

I'm the girl in the paint-flecked clothes who lives for the studio, not the stadium. I'm also his coach's daughter, which makes me strictly off-limits. Obsessing over me is the fastest way to get himself kicked off the team.

Turns out Elias O'Shea is determined. He tells me I'm his endgame and he's calling me his lucky charm.

I call *him* dangerous. Falling for me could cost him everything.

Elias says I'm worth the risk. I only hope he's right.

Because resisting the hot, love-struck quarterback is proving to be downright impossible ...

Lovestruck is a steamy standalone he-falls-first sports romance, starring a hot, hopelessly romantic football hero and the very off-limits coach's daughter who steals his heart. Perfect for fans of Elle Kennedy.

LOVE STRUCK

ELIAS

A loud pounding on my door pulls me out of my own head as I rub a towel over my wet hair. I miscalculated one pass this afternoon—and one pass only—but that's all it takes to change the entire momentum of a game. The season starts in a few short days and I need to play better than I ever have in my life. Everything's on the line and I'm pissed off at myself for the handling error, even if Coach went out of his way to praise my precision. Which is practically unheard of.

"Hey, Chief, two very insistent girls are here to see you," Jake's voice echoes through my door. "They refuse to take no for an answer. It's those blond girls who've been stalking you."

"Which ones?" West laughs, pushing my door open and barging in like he owns the place. "Are you decent,

O'Shea? I need to borrow your charger. Someone stole mine."

"Have you ever heard of the concept of fucking knocking, West?" I finish wrapping a towel around my waist.

"Have you ever heard of the concept of a lock and how to use it?"

"I'll make sure I do from now on." I just stepped out of the shower after a grueling practice. I introduced Coach Fox to my dad's take on an empty set with a compressed bunch formation that used to be one of my dad's favorite plays back in high school, when he was the coach of our team. That was before his health issues got the better of him. Coach was intrigued by the sound of the play and we've been practicing variations of it all afternoon.

"They're on their way up," Jake informs me, leaning casually against the door jamb. "Gabe tried to stall them but he wasn't having much luck."

I got roped into West's plans to hit the town tonight, to check out the first wave of incoming freshman girls. Most of them won't be here until tomorrow but a few have already started moving into their various dorms. The campus was a chaos of SUVs, teary-eyed mothers and their red-faced husbands hauling boxes into dorms. The usual move-in day stuff.

"Why has my room morphed into Grand Central Station?" I mutter. "Out, people."

West helps himself to my charger. "Why, were you practicing some 'self care'?" Using air quotes.

"He doesn't need to," Jake steps aside, making way for the two girls. Gabriel has followed them up. I'm used to being the center of attention but this is ridiculous. I'm standing here dressed in nothing but a towel, still wet, and there are five people practically inside my room.

"Hey, Mandy. Bella," Jake greets them with his signature charm. "Nice of you two to stop by."

"Hi, Jake." One of the girls twirls a long strand of hair around a finger. She blinks fake lashes at me. "Hi, Elias."

The girls seem vaguely familiar. It's possible that I know them. I'm not a bed-hopping player like West or a brooding romantic like Gabe, just a guy who basically won the lottery on a bunch of different levels. I try not to be an asshole or egomaniac about the whole thing, but I'd be a fool not to appreciate the hell out of the hand I've been dealt and run with it from time to time.

I've always been popular. High school was an endless procession of giggling girls trying to get my attention. As for college, my teammates call me the Chick Magnet and I guess it's hard to argue with that. For the first three years at Hawthorne, I made the most of my superstar-on-the-rise status. As the starting quarterback for the Hawthorne Wildcats, everyone on this campus not only knows who I am but seems to want a piece of me. Not that I can complain.

"I hope you don't mind us coming by to see you, Elias," the second girl says as she checks me out. Her gaze wanders down my chest to my abs, and lower, before finally roving back up to my face. "We just wanted to see if you were free tonight before your schedule gets…you know, too busy."

I could have both these girls naked in my bed within thirty seconds if I wanted to. Two years ago—or even last year, who am I kidding—I'd be doing exactly that.

But right now I'm not feeling it. I've been out of my usual carefree groove for a while now and I have no idea why.

Maybe it's the plastic eyelashes, which are seriously testing the limits of their design. Last time, it might have been the overload of cheap perfume. The time before that, I honestly can't remember.

I'm not exactly thrilled about the situation. I should be zeroing in on the usual not-quite-perfect-but-close-enough details that allow me to live my best life. Instead, all I can see are the imperfections. I mean, I don't want to be cruel about it, but it's not just the eyelashes. It's the weird outfit. The watery eyes. The goosebumps on her nearly-blue skin because she's not wearing enough for the cold night. The entire package just isn't quite working for me. Times two.

I don't know why this keeps happening. Standards are a good thing to have but when they start sabotaging my sex life, I've got a fucking problem on my hands.

But I smile and let them down gently. "Actually, we're heading out tonight. But maybe we'll see you downtown."

"Oh." Mandy or Bella—whoever she is—blinks the plastic lashes at me in starstruck disappointment. I'm almost worried about the welfare of her eyeballs. Those things look downright dangerous. "Which bar are you going to?"

"I think we might be going to a party first. Isn't that the plan, Jake?"

"Yeah. TKE."

Mandy/Bella perks up. "Oh, we were thinking of going to that!"

"Great. Maybe we'll run into you later, then. Jake will see you out." It's not the most polite dismissal I've ever come up with, but there's not much point giving these girls false hope when they have no chance.

Plus, I feel strung out tonight. Not just because our season is about to start, but also because the universe keeps cockblocking me. Why can't I just relax and go with the flow like I used to?

Jake escorts the girls back down the stairs and out the door.

"Rude," laughs West, walking out of my room with my charger in his hand. "Not quite getting why you'd choose to turn down a sure thing of a threesome, but your call, QB."

Yeah. I'm wondering the same thing myself. Gabriel gives me a brief once-over, clearly as confused as the rest of us about my new monk-like tendencies, before heading down the stairs.

"Let's go," he calls over his shoulder. "I'm starving."

Within twenty minutes, the four of us are walking across the Green toward the cluster of food trucks that are semi-permanently parked along the edge of campus.

It's cold tonight and my hands are jammed into the pockets of my jeans. I'm wearing a jacket over my t-shirt. It's our first night out in a while. The pre-season is all about training, training and more training. We don't have a lot of downtime.

West is his usual Golden Retriever self, cracking jokes and lightening the mood. "Hey, Elias, are you calling dibs on Bella tonight?"

"Bella. Which one was Bella?"

"The one without the eyelashes," Jake clarifies.

"Ah. No, I'm not calling dibs on either one of them. They're all yours." I don't sound entirely happy about it, and I'm not. Those girls were cute enough.

"You sure?" West punches my arm playfully. "I don't want to break any bro codes." West is a shit-hot wide receiver but we both know I could kick his ass if there was ever any reason to.

"Go nuts, Westie."

"Don't mind if I do," he grins.

"Having a dry spell, Chief?" Gabe jokes, but my friends have noticed that I haven't hooked up in a while.

Tonight isn't the first night of my drought. Not even close.

I dodge the question. "Just focusing on football."

"He's in the zone." I can always count on Jake to back me up. "He's been busy."

It's true. Even though classes haven't started yet, I've landed three new sponsorship deals in the past few weeks, which require meetings and Zoom calls and whatnot. And when I'm not at practice, I'm working out. It's a big year and I'm determined to be ready for it.

Trust West to go for the jugular. "Just don't lose your edge, man. You'll get pent-up if you go too long without."

"I'm not fucking pent-up." But he's right. I'm pent-up as fuck.

Gabriel, Jake and I have been living together since sophomore year. We shared a dorm freshman year and hit it off during football season.

West moved in with us last year. He's from California and looks the part. He has blond hair, blue eyes and the sunny personality of a guy who grew up surfing in Malibu. Which is exactly what he did. His dad is an aging movie star I'd never heard of, but the guy must have made serious bank at some point because his beach house is epic. We spent some time there last summer.

Gabriel and Jake went to the same high school in Virginia and have known each other since third grade. Even so, they're as different as two people can get. Gabe has an IQ of 145 or something ridiculous. He's a business major, minoring in finance and he's already started two of his own investment portfolios, one for himself and one for his friends, me included. He's also a genius on the football field. He's a running back who has a knack for being in the right place at precisely the right time. I don't think football is his passion. It was more of a case of football choosing Gabe than Gabe choosing football. He's just so damn good at it that he can't help but stick around because everyone on his team wants him to.

Jake, on the other hand, lives and breathes football. He's our star linebacker. He's 6'4" and the most laid-back guy I've ever met—except on the field, where his focus is unparalleled. He got a full ride to Hawthorne on a football scholarship, like we all did, but it's safe to say the academics are just a formality to him. He gets by because willing women clamber over themselves to write his essays for him. I've rarely seen him read a book but he knows every football statistic known to humankind.

Jake's usually the kind of guy that nothing bothers but he seems wound up tonight.

All four of us order burgers and fries and sit at one of the tables set up under the rows of hanging lights. We order so much food the guy gives us free cokes. We're part of the reason these truck owners never leave campus. All five mini-restaurants are open until three a.m. and do a thriving business since they're parked between the rows of dorms and fraternity houses. One block further south is the main street where the student bars are located.

A procession of people come and talk to us while we're eating, most of them wondering where we're headed tonight.

By the time we get to the party, the place is packed.

The girls who came to the house are already here. Within five minutes West has Bella on his lap on the couch and the two of them are locked in a full-on make out session.

"Get a room," Jake yells at them.

Gabe returns with four beers. Girls are swarming around us like honeybees. It's the first party of the year, I'm in the best physical condition of my life and the NFL scouts have already started reaching out. I should be celebrating.

I seriously don't know what's gotten into me lately. I swore senior year was going to be different and so far it is, but not in the way I was expecting.

I've spent the past three years in a non-stop bonanza of one, occasionally two and (twice) three-night stands. And had a great time doing it. So I have no idea why I have this sudden craving for something more.

"Hi, Elias. Hi, Gabe." It's Abby Fraser. She's got long dark hair and is vice-president of one of the bigger sororities on campus. I've known her since freshman year. We hooked up one night years ago but never again, because I'd already moved on. West dated her for a while last year but it fizzled out at some point. I think she might have even had a thing with Gabe too, somewhere along the line. "Isn't your sister a freshman this year?" she asks him.

"She's arriving tomorrow," Gabe confirms.

"What's her name again?" Abby asks.

"Isla," Jake answers for him and the tone of his voice is layered. Like he's not sure if he's happy about the sister's arrival.

Hang on. Could *this* be the reason Jake is wound up? He's an easy person to read and he's definitely wired.

"I still can't believe my little sister is a college student." Gabe takes a long, soulful sip of his beer.

Abby's flirting with Jake. "You guys will keep her out of trouble, I'm sure. No one would dare go near her with the entire football team as her protectors."

Jake looks pissed off at her comment. It almost makes me smile, but I feel for him. Holding a secret torch for your best friend's sister is definitely classified as breaking the bro code, if that's what this is. Gabriel doesn't seem to notice. He's distracted by some girls who have just walked in.

Unlike the rest of us, Gabe has relationships. He *wants* to fall in love, he once told us. He tries to, but so far nothing has stuck. We gave him shit for the comment at the time and pointed out that he was playing the field just as enthusiastically as all the rest of us were. Either way, he's not with anyone at the moment that I know of.

The party swirls around me, the music loud, the laughter infectious, but I can't shake this weird feeling of detachment. I wait for enough of a spark to kick in, to pull me toward one or another of these girls, enough to offer to take one of them home.

But it isn't happening.

The sophomore with all the piercings comes on strong and she's abrasive about it. The red-headed cheerleader has a neurotic edge. I recognize the blond from a sneaky exit from West's room early in the morning last week. The one named Penelope laughs at everything I say like it's the funniest thing she's ever heard. It's slightly irritating.

"I follow you on Instagram," she tells me. "I like all your posts."

"Thanks."

"You have, like, *so* many followers."

"I guess so."

"That video you posted a few days ago was…really cool." That nervous titter again.

The conversation stalls and I just can't really bring myself to force it tonight. My chick-o-meter seems randomly stuck on some impossibly high setting. Out of the blue, with no fucking warning, my expectations have shifted.

I'm not sure how to feel about this.

"*Oh my god, it's Elias O'Shea!*" Some tipsy sophomore girls have arrived and they giggle and huddle together, daring each other to come over and talk to me.

They work up their courage and Jake and I make

polite conversation but not one of them is appealing to me on the kind of level I wish they were.

It's all so predictable. "I follow you on Instagram," one of them tells me.

There are only so many people per night I can thank for that.

"You want to head downtown, Chief?" My boy Jake is tuning in on my wavelength, like he always does.

"Yeah."

Some cosmic wind has changed course—and yes, I know what that fucking sounds like but I can *feel* it.

It's like I'm waiting for someone.

Someone in particular.

What the fuck is happening?

West disappears upstairs with Bella. The rest of us go to a couple of bars and town is pumping, but it's the same scenario.

Girls are pushing each other out of the way to get close to me but not one of them is someone I want to spend time with tonight.

Fucking wonderful.

There are a lot of beautiful women here. But not one of them is…*her.*

I seriously don't get this.

Gabriel is deep in conversation with a couple of sophomores, who are hanging on his every word, so we leave him to it.

Jake seems to be mired in his own tortured headspace.

"We're just getting into the mindset we need for Saturday," Jake mutters and I agree with him, but this isn't like either one of us.

It's after midnight when I tell him I'm headed out and he seems relieved.

We get back to the house and Jake disappears into his room, slamming the door like he's as frustrated as I am. His behavior tonight isn't like him at all. I'll find a time to talk to him about whatever's going through his head.

I take a long shower because I'm so wound up I know I won't be able to sleep.

I'm fucking ravenous—not for food but for something else entirely. Hot, take-no-prisoners sex. Which I'm no stranger to, but what I'm craving is lust on a different level. One that digs in and won't let go. One that lasts longer than one night, or two.

One that means something. *Or everything.*

Hell.

I hope Gabriel's broodiness isn't rubbing off on me. I used to be more like West. I *want* to be more like West. Carefree and easy-going. Like I used to be. Instead, I'm losing my mind less than a week before our first game of the season.

Get a grip, O'Shea. Be logical about this.

I'm probably just feeling the effects of the phone call I got this morning from my dad. He called to tell me he's getting more tests done for his heart problem.

Heart failure, he called it. I told him nothing's failed yet, so he shouldn't be using the word "failure." *It's still beating, Dad.*

It's times like these I wish I was closer to home. My mother died in a car accident when I was three years old. I don't remember her at all, but my dad has always kept her memory very much alive with the twenty or thirty pictures he has of her, displayed all over our house. My dad raised me and never remarried, so it's always been just the two of us. I once asked him why he never seemed interested in marrying again, or even dating, and he said he loved my mother so much nothing could possibly compare. He knew from the very first time he saw her, when they were in college together, that she was the one. It's a story he's been telling me my whole life. There she was, standing under her own spotlight at a party, like an angel. *Absolute perfection.* That's how he described her. He fell in love with her on the spot and, according to him, it didn't take much for him to convince her the feeling was mutual.

After she died, my dad basically dedicated his entire life to me and my football career. He was the coach of my high school team until the second half of my junior year, when he had his first heart attack. The doctors recommended he quit then but he was stubborn. Two months later he had another heart attack and ended up having major surgery to fix the blockages, which took him a long time to recover from. He retired because he had no other choice. But he was always there on the sidelines, always there to go through the plays, the analysis, the details I needed to improve on.

He's why I'm here.

I applied to schools all over the country and got into all of them, but I'd been watching the Hawthorne team from afar for years. Coach Fox has been well-known as one of the best in the business for a long time. He has a track record of winning, and honing his players into play-makers who get noticed. My dad insisted that I think about my future more than his. I finally agreed to take Hawthorne's offer, on the condition that he'd agree to let me hire home help and a nurse who checks in on him twice a day.

The way he said goodbye before he hung up this morning was sort of jarring. He told me he loved me and how proud he was of me. How I'm the best son a man could ever ask for and how he wished my mother could see me now. Then he said he hopes he lives to see the day I find the kind of true love he and my mother had. How the piece of her that he could see in me every day was the reason he's lasted as long as he has.

It was sort of fucking heavy.

All right, Dad, go easy, I joked. *You're fine. You're not going anywhere. And I'll be back for Thanksgiving. That's only a couple months away.*

I went home a few weeks ago to check on him but I've been in Massachusetts all summer, taking classes, training and practicing. We all take our toughest courses over the summer semester—in theory, anyway. That way, we can concentrate on football as much as possible once the season starts.

Before I ended the call, I told him I loved him too and I'd talk to him in a few days.

They aren't words we usually throw around.

The whole conversation keeps scrolling through my head.

To be honest, it terrifies me. My dad is the only person I have left. I refuse to lose him too, even if it means chaining him to his recliner, getting him round-the-clock care and forcing him to watch football all day while I work my guts out to make it to the NFL, which is exactly what I'm doing.

Before he dies shadows the thought but I shut it down. I refuse to go there.

Going pro is my dream, of course. It's also been *his* dream, for as long as I can remember. I don't want to say he's pinned his hopes on me because he has nothing else to live for, but some days it does feel that way.

Maybe that's why I'm off my game tonight. I'm worried about my old man. It's understandable.

And I'm craving more than a meaningless one night stand with someone whose not-quite-perfection is something I have to overlook.

I need a distraction from my bleak thoughts but my mind keeps retracing the words.

Absolute perfection.

It's hard to imagine.

Actually, it's impossible to imagine because it doesn't exist. I've met a lot of beautiful women in my time but even so, not one of them could have been described as *absolute perfection.* I guess that's why I never stick around for more than one night.

I go to bed alone but I'm restless.

I close my eyes and try to sleep.

What would perfection even look like?

My addled brain starts to weave together a hazy fantasy.

She'll have perfect pink lips. She'll be curvy and sweet, just for me…mine and only mine.

My heart's pounding in my chest and my cock is huge and hot.

I haven't gotten laid in months. No wonder I'm so strung out.

How long has it been?

The entire summer.

Almost six months, to be exact.

No wonder I'm so voracious. I'm going insane with it, on about a hundred different levels. "Pent-up" doesn't even begin to describe how I feel. I'm almost dizzy with lust and need and rage.

This is crazy.

I'm losing my mind over someone who doesn't exist.

Why?

I lay in the dark and force myself to calm down.

But I can't. I stroke my painfully hard length and imagine what absolute perfection would *feel* like.

Her pussy will be silky-wet and so fucking tight as I—

Jetting cum spurts all over my chest and stomach. I'm practically panting as the surges pulse hotly out of me.

Fucking hell.

Why am I suddenly being tortured like this?

Why am I being forced to get far too up close and personal with my right hand?

And more importantly, *where is she?*

2

———

Zara

TAKING one last look in my rear view mirror, I finally do it. I pull out from the curb and drive away from the only house I've ever lived in. My dad stands there, watching me go, getting smaller in the blurry distance.

Damn it.

This is even harder than I knew it would be.

Tears wet my face and I swipe them away so I can see where I'm going. It definitely wouldn't be a good look to crash and burn before I even get to the end of my own street. I manage to reach the corner of Elm and Main in one piece and, as I'm waiting for the light to change, I press the video call button on my phone, which is perched on its holder on the dashboard.

Hannah answers on the first ring. "Hi, sweetie."

"This is it. I'm really doing it." My sister is basically an extension of my own soul. She's also my grief coun-

19

selor and my best friend, all rolled into one feisty little UCLA film student who hardly ever comes home. Our calls are a necessary form of therapy and have been ever since she moved to the west coast to go to college two years ago. We were going through some pretty heavy grief at the time and we made a promise to talk as often as we can.

"I know what you're feeling, Zee. I've been there."

I've just driven away from my childhood home. I've officially moved out and I'm on my way to start college. "It's so surreal that it's finally happening, this major milestone in my life. I'm feeling it so much."

"Of course you are. And I'm feeling it right along with you."

"It's strange when you're fully aware that you're going through one of these monumental life events that you'll remember forever—and that it's happening to you right now."

"It's a big deal, honey."

I wipe away another tear. "I don't know why I'm even crying. I'm literally moving three miles down the road. I'll still see him all the time."

"It doesn't matter how far away it is. The premise is still the same as if you were moving to the other side of the country. You're leaving, and you're allowed to feel all the emotions that go along with that."

"I miss you, Han."

"I miss you too, Zee. You're going to be fine. You're

about to have the time of your life. It's *college*, girlfriend. It's *so* much fun."

"I know it will be." Still, I'm leaving my dad to fend for himself after everything that's happened. I glance in the rear view mirror before I turn the corner. "Oh god, Han. He's still standing there."

"He'll be fine and so will you."

"This isn't going to be easy for him."

"We can take turns checking in on him every day. It's not like we can't talk to him every hour if we want to."

"I know." I promised him I'd come home every Sunday and make him my specialty lasagna. It's our tradition. But still. My dad and I are close. I have a closer relationship with him than Hannah does, mainly because she lives three thousand miles away. My dad and I have had to live with my mother's ghost more directly. Every corner of our big, rambling house is filled to the brim with her vibrant, beautiful, heart-breaking memories.

Because of that, my dad and I have been each other's rocks for a long time now and leaving him is…a lot.

He loved my mother so much. It was one of those love at first sight stories he loves to tell us. He was a football player and she was a waitress at one of the campus restaurants at Notre Dame. She spilled coffee on him.

When you know, you know, he's always telling me. And he *knew*.

My mother died of a particularly aggressive form of lymphoma almost two years ago. Very soon after that,

Hannah left for California and we were glad she did. She needed that change of scene like a lifeline.

But I missed her terribly, especially since we'd gone from a family of four to just me and my dad at home. The only way I could fill the void was by talking to her often and by pouring my emotions onto endless canvases through my paintbrushes. It's what I do. It's my passion, my outlet and, along with gushing to my sister on a daily basis, my primary form of therapy. It's the reason I decided to major in fine arts, because it's what I spend all my time doing. I figured I might as well try to channel my obsession into a career.

I'm a dreamy, artistic, mostly-introverted and occasionally fun-loving Pisces. But the past two years have been hard. High school was mostly about coping and making sure my dad wasn't falling off the deep-end of his own sorrow.

"Besides," Hannah says, "It's not like Dad's *alone* alone. He's got his friends. Does Jim still come over?"

"Every night." Jim lives next door. He and my dad watch football highlights every evening, arguing happily about stats and plays. They were both briefly in the NFL. My dad was a running back for the Dolphins for three months before a knee injury took him out for good. He's been coaching ever since and got a job as the head coach of the Hawthorne University Wildcats sixteen years ago —which is as far back as my memories go.

"He's also got his assistant coaches," Hannah points

out. Which is true. The NCAA allows him to have like ten of them or something, along with four or five graduate assistants, and they all idolize him. "He's surrounded by what basically amounts to a fan club and entourage. And he's got his football players, of course."

"But it's not the same as having your own *child* who loves you, making sure you're okay, day in and day out." That's the part that hits differently. It's the nights I worry about.

My dad's the toughest guy I know and he's staunch as hell about most things but when it comes to me and Hannah—and especially me—he's a total softie. I know he's going to miss me a lot.

I take a left on Emerson.

It's part of the reason I decided to go to Hawthorne. All the way through the application process, it felt like the right decision. And especially today. I don't say it to Hannah, but I would totally be second-guessing myself if I was boarding a plane to the west coast right now. I got accepted into schools all over the country.

I thought about following Hannah to California, just so I could be closer to her. I seriously considered it. Before everything happened with my mom, I thought I might end up at UC Santa Cruz or maybe Berkeley if I could get in.

But in some ways I'm not even sure why I bothered applying anywhere else. I think deep down in my heart I knew I couldn't be that far away from my dad. He needs me. Even if he tells me he's fine and he'll be too busy with the new season to worry about me, I know he *will* worry about me. It's just wired into my dad's DNA to worry about me. So it's better for both of us if we're close enough to check in on each other.

My sister knows how I feel, of course. She knows why I decided on Hawthorne. "It's a win-win for both of you, Zee. You can get the most out of your college experience by living in the dorm on campus and going to all the parties and so on, but you can still go home once a week. It's the best of both worlds, when you think about it like that. Plus Hawthorne is an awesome school and they have one of the best undergraduate fine arts programs in the country. You're totally going to thrive there."

"I hope you're right."

"You know I'm right. Hopefully you'll meet some super-hunk the first week of school and finally cash in that long overdue V-card."

"Would you stop."

"Did you go on the pill like I told you to? It's a must for college."

"Yes. I did. Are you happy now?"

She laughs. "Of course I'm happy! My little sister is on the cusp of an awakening. I just want you to live your best life, Zee. And hot sex is definitely required."

"For you, maybe."

"For all of us. And don't forget condoms. Keep some with you and absolutely make sure they're securely in place. Two lines of defense are a girl's best friend. You never know…where they've been."

"Okay, boss."

"And make sure he's not a football player. Dad would go ballistic."

"No kidding." While I'm stopped at another light I adjust the angle of my phone. My eyes are red and my mascara is smudged. "God, why didn't you tell me I'm a total mess?" I wipe the smudges away with my fingers. The light turns green. "I'm almost there. I wonder if my roommate has arrived yet."

"Have you made contact with her?"

"Just through Snapchat. She seems nice. She was valedictorian of her high school in Virginia. Very bookish but she also seems down to earth. I hope we hit it off."

"I'm sure you will."

"To be honest, I'm excited to meet some new people who aren't born and raised in Hawthorne, Massachusetts, population 40,000, not including college students. Sometimes I feel like I know everyone in this town."

"You're going to have the best time, Zee. I'm dying to hear about how it goes. And remember Rule Number Two: have *fun*."

"Sure."

"Which means I also need to remind you at this critical crossroads in your life about Rule Number One."

"I know, I know. No football players."

"I need you to follow both rules."

"Of course." I'm suddenly nervous. There's a red and white *WELCOME FRESHMEN!* sign hung over the Hawthorne University gate.

I drive up the familiar campus driveway.

Hawthorne University gets a lot of attention for being a beautiful place. It's been called "the jewel of Massachusetts," the "most picturesque college campus in the East," and "the place you want your kid to go, with all the academic punch of an Ivy League school but with a (slightly) more reasonable price tag."

"I'll have exactly as much fun as I can have while living in one of the two all-girls dorms that Dad insisted on. It's, like, maximum security or something, complete with a front desk guard, high-tech security systems and automatically locking doors." Which feels a little over-zealous, but if it gives my dad some peace of mind then I figured what the hell. "No boys are allowed upstairs."

"You probably won't even spend that much time in the dorm, besides to sleep. You'll be too busy partying."

"Yeah, sure." What I'm most excited about is the art studio. Hawthorne has this amazing arts building called the Whitman Building which is the tallest building on campus, specially designed so that each fine arts major, even freshmen, get their own art studio space with a view. It's modern and has lots of natural light and is basically to die for. "I know I'm going to be living in the art studio practically 24/7. I honestly can't wait to get started. I'll give you a tour of my studio space as soon as I get one."

"I can't wait to see it."

I find a parking space and pull into it. "Okay, Han. I made it. I'm going to sign off for now but I'll check in later to let you know how it's going and introduce you to my roommate. Oh god, I'm actually really nervous. What if my roommate and I don't get along? I mean, I hope we will. I'm sure we will."

"Of course you will. You're the most lovable person I know."

"Even though I'm an eccentric artist who spends most of my time as a solitary hermit with paint-splattered clothes and a messy bun?"

"*Especially* because you're an eccentric, sweet, gorgeous, fun, inspiring and very talented artist with her own unique style."

I blow a kiss to the camera. "Here I go. I'm about to dive headfirst into my brand new life. Wish me luck."

"Good luck, sweetie. Go out there and kill it. Be yourself and make the most of every minute. I can feel it: beautiful, life-changing things are about to happen to you. And you deserve all of it. Say yes, be safe and have fun, Zee." We always end our calls with mini pep-talks. We started doing it when we were both suffering through the worst of our loss and it helped. The habit stuck.

She ends the call and I sit there for a few seconds, just soaking in the enormity of the threshold I'm in the middle of crossing.

I really *am* nervous.

But it's time to grab my new life by the horns and run with it.

I climb out and slide my phone into my back pocket. Then I start loading up with my backpack and a few other bags. My dad wanted to help me move in but I absolutely insisted on doing it myself. He's famous on this campus and the last thing I wanted to do was to advertise my connection to him. Everyone's going to figure it out soon enough anyway. I accept that I'm a nepo baby and I'm getting a free education because my dad is the long-standing football coach with the winningest record in Hawthorne U's 120-year history. Today, it felt easier to say our goodbyes at home and deal with the rest of it as a newly-minted and very independent college student.

I'm ready.

At least I *hope* I'm ready.

I lug one of my three-ton wheeled suitcases out of the back of my car and perch my computer bag on top of it.

There. Easy.

It falls over like it's made of top-heavy concrete.

Shit.

"Need some help?" I turn to see two guys walking toward me. They're huge and wide-shouldered. I'd bet money they're football players.

You can't help but absorb through osmosis some of the details of the game of football when your father's a D1 coach. Unfortunately, that's about as far as my knowledge or interest goes. I celebrate my dad's wins with him and I used to go to the occasional game, but as hard as I try, it's just not really my thing.

Which is part of the reason I've barely met any of the players on my dad's team.

The other reason is that he doesn't let me anywhere *near* his team. Over the years, I've stopped in to see him at work every now and then. But I think he gets sort of borderline traumatized whenever I go near his team. When close to a hundred sweaty, pumped-up college football players are staring at your teenage daughter like lions circling around a fresh kill, I guess you don't tend to enjoy it very much. For his sake, I hardly ever visit him at work.

So I have no idea if these guys are on the team. I have a hunch they are. "No, thanks. I've got it."

"You look like you could use a hand," one of them insists, standing my suitcase up and replacing the laptop bag. He starts wheeling it toward the cluster of dorms. "Where are you headed?"

"I'm fine, really. I don't have far to go."

"We'll help you," says the other one, taking one of the heavier bags that's threatening to slide off my shoulder.

They're both very good-looking, I can't help but notice. Then again, a lot of football players are, just because they're built and athletic by default.

I do happen to know that my dad makes sure his players are tough and resilient on the field but also respectful and good ambassadors off the field. He's talked to me about how important he thinks manners and honor and duty to your team and your community are. He's kicked players off the team for bad behavior more than once.

"I'm West Hawkins. This is Gabriel Dillon."

The names definitely sound familiar. West has sandy-blond hair, blue eyes and a mischievous grin. Gabriel's hair is dark and he has a more serious, stormy vibe, like if Heathcliff was a football player.

"You're really beautiful," West comments. Those dimples are something.

I don't mention that flirting with me could potentially get him kicked off the football team.

I guess they're waiting for me to introduce myself. Which I don't really want to do. My first name is unusual and most likely the Wildcats players have at least heard of me. We're close to the dorm now. "I can take it from here. Thanks for your help."

"Is this one your dorm?" asks West.

"Yes, this is it. Carrington Hall."

"My sister's in this dorm," says Gabriel. "She's a freshman too. We helped her move in a few hours ago."

"Really?"

"Her name's Isla."

Isla Dillon. It's my roommate's name. "Wow. She's my new roommate. I haven't met her yet."

"You're Zara?" Gabriel and his sister must have talked about me. Which means he knows who I am. "Coach Fox's daughter?"

"Um…yes."

West looks slightly horrified. "Oh shit. *Please* don't tell him I just told you how beautiful you are."

I smile because he's so full of remorse. "I promise I won't."

Gabriel holds out his hand. "Give us your keys, Zara, and we'll unload your car and put all your stuff inside the lobby of your dorm. We'll lock up the car and leave the keys at the front desk."

West puts his hand on his heart, dramatically. "I swear we're trustworthy. You have nothing to worry about. We're basically oversized Boy Scouts. We'd take every-thing up to your room for you but we're not allowed up there. Coach would have a major meltdown."

"Are you sure you don't mind?" It would actually be nice to have the help, especially since it'll take them about five minutes to do what might take me an hour or more.

"We'd be honored," West grins. "And that way I can make it up to you for complimenting you when it was completely out of line."

"It's fine."

"We won't even take the Toyota for a joyride," West jokes.

"Go for it if you want. Have fun reaching its top speed of fifty."

West laughs and I give Gabriel my keys.

"Thank you," I tell them. "I'll let my dad know how gentlemanly you were. I really appreciate it."

"The pleasure's ours," West winks at me. He's got a streak of mischief a mile wide, that one.

Gabriel elbows West, as though to keep him in line. "We're meeting up with Isla for dinner tonight so maybe we'll see you then. Either way, I'm sure we'll see you around."

"Yeah. Thanks again."

They head back toward my car and I make my way inside. The young woman behind the front desk introduces herself as Kit Peyton. "I'm a senior and one of the RAs here at Carrington. You must be Zara."

"Yes. Nice to meet you."

"Your dad just called to let me know you'd be arriving any minute and to open the door for you."

"Yeah, that sounds like him."

She laughs. "Don't worry, you're not the only one. Here's your room fob. You're in 433. Your roommate just finished moving in. You'll like her," she adds. "I think you two will be a good match."

I thank Kit and wheel my suitcase into the elevator.

When I get to the fourth floor, I follow the signs to room 433.

The door of the room is open and Isla is sitting on one of the beds, reading a textbook. She looks up as I walk in.

"Hey, roomie. I'm Zara."

"Hi, Zara. I'm Isla." She gets up off the bed and after a second of hesitation, we hug. I can immediately tell we're going to hit it off. She's cute, with dark blond hair and little round glasses. She's slim and we're around the same height. I can see the family resemblance between her and Gabriel in the shape of their eyes and their cool, intelligent vibe, but in every other way, they're very different. "I hope you don't mind me claiming the bigger desk. Your closet is bigger."

"No, that's fine. I ran into your brother and West in the parking lot. They introduced themselves. They're moving all my stuff into the lobby."

"Oh, that's good. When I told Gabriel who my roommate was, he said he'd never met you. Had you met West?"

"No. Believe it or not, I don't really have a lot to do with my dad's team."

"West is fun. He and Elias have come to visit us in Virginia a couple of times."

"Elias." The name Elias O'Shea is definitely one I've heard. "He's the quarterback, right?"

"The very *hot* quarterback. You haven't met him either?"

"No. I've never been much of a football fanatic and my dad is sort of overprotective. He doesn't like me mingling with that much testosterone."

She laughs. "I don't blame him. So you're an art major?"

"Yeah. And you're a business major?"

"With a minor in finance. Following in my brother's

footsteps, for better or worse. Math was my thing in high school. Ugh." She smiles, like she knows that's a rare thing.

Isla definitely comes across as a bookworm, but as I get a better look at her, she's seriously gorgeous. She's got fine, petite features and her hair is long and braided down her back. She's got a few freckles across her nose and, behind her glasses, her eyes are amber-colored with long, blond-tipped eyelashes. It's sort of striking, how her golden eyes perfectly match her honey-blond hair. She's wearing skinny jeans and a white t-shirt. Almost the same tom-boyish outfit I'm wearing.

"Better you than me," I smile. "I don't have a mathematical bone in my body."

Even though she's obviously studious, there's a rock-star edge to her. I don't know why I say that. She's got a quirky sense of humor and you get the feeling that, even though she's shy, she's not easily intimidated. My guess is that my new roommate has a wild side and for some reason I love this about her.

"Let me help you bring your stuff up. Then I'm supposed to meet Gabriel for dinner and probably at least one of his teammates. You should come."

"I guess my dad will just have to get used to me being around a few of his players from time to time."

"My brother is overprotective too. And so's Jake. He's Gabe's best friend. I've known him forever. But I've already told them they're no longer allowed to make any decisions for me whatsoever. They're a little overbearing. It's annoying but I knew that would be part of the deal if I came to Hawthorne. I hoped we could spend one year together on this campus without driving each other crazy. And I really wanted to come here. Hawthorne was always my first choice."

"Mine too. What position does Jake play?"

"Linebacker. He's really good. All four of them are like the stars of the team. And they all live together."

"Wow." I place a few of my bags on my bed, checking out the space. "This is a cool room."

"Yeah, it's bigger than I was expecting. I think we got one of the better views on campus."

The room has a large window seat that looks out over the Green. My bed is next to the window and there's a built-in desk under a few bookshelves. Isla's bed is against the far wall, next to her own desk and more bookshelves, which are already full to the brim with books and framed photos of her family and friends. Her laptop is on her desk, along with a speaker and more books.

Over the next half hour, Isla helps me carry my stuff up to the room. Gabe and West made quick work of unloading my car and everything is already piled high in the lobby. Kit hands me my keys.

I get everything moved in and we talk about Isla's hometown in Virginia and our hobbies. Isla's were chess club, studying and reading. And going to football games. "You must be glad you'll be close to home and close to your family," she says. "At least you'll get some home-cooked meals."

"It's just been me and my dad for a while now. My mom passed away two years ago and my sister's at school in L.A."

"I'm so sorry to hear that, Zara. Losing your mom must have been really hard."

"It was. But we got through it. Life has to go on."

I sit on the window seat and look out over the fall colors and the picturesque campus. Our room is cozy and Isla already feels like a friend. The moment feels profound because…I *did* get through it. I'm here and a brand new chapter of my life is beginning. Life *does* go on and, right now, I'm ready for the newness of it all. "I better call my dad and let him know I'm all moved in. He'll be waiting to hear from me."

"My parents were the same. I ended up talking to them for almost an hour because they had so many questions. I'll leave you to it. I'm going to take a quick shower before dinner."

We share a bathroom with the other double room across the hall but our suite mates haven't arrived yet.

I bring up my favorites list and press the call button. My dad picks up on the second ring. "Hi, honey." I can picture him in his favorite chair with the TV on, watching replays. He would have muted it on the first ring.

"Hey, Daddy."

"You got there okay? How's the dorm?"

"It's great. I'm all moved in and my roommate is really nice. You won't believe this but her brother is on the team."

"Oh yeah?" He doesn't sound thrilled about this. "What's his name?"

"Gabriel Dillon."

"Gabriel's my rising star running back. One of the best I've ever seen."

"I ran into him and West as I was getting out of my car. They offered to move all my stuff from my car to the lobby of the dorm. They were very polite."

He pauses for half a second and I already know what he's about to say. "Good to hear. And now you need to stay far, far away from both of them. Those boys are both trouble for girls like you."

"Girls like me?"

"Girls who are too young for seniors who play more than one field."

"Dad, it's very likely that I'm going to see, talk to and possibly even hang out with some of your players from time to time since I'm at the same college as they are. You're going to need to get used to that."

I can practically feel him shudder at the thought. "As long as that's all you're doing. You know the rule. No football players."

I've had it drummed into me since I hit puberty that I was not allowed—under any circumstances whatsoever—to date a football player. He makes sure they have standards of behavior, but he also knows the tendencies of college football players, especially the ones at the top of their game. They're usually popular, promiscuous and cocky. They know they can have the pick of almost any woman they want. My dad has—and will—make it clear to everyone concerned that that won't include me. This is going to be the downside of going to college here at Hawthorne, but I always knew that and it wasn't something I minded all that much.

Anyway, I've always pictured myself ending up with someone artistic, like myself. I've never really been into jocks. It goes without saying that I've never dated one, but I've never really dated anyone else either. My high school experience was more about surviving loss, making sure my dad and my sister were coping, and honing my artistic style. It takes a lot of work to produce paintings that don't look totally derivative of someone else. I finally feel like I'm getting closer to developing a style that's uniquely my own.

Plus my dad literally keeps a sawed-off shotgun in his gun safe. Living alone with him for the past two years has meant my romantic life basically has tumbleweeds rolling through it.

"Are the doors of the dorm locked? Do you feel safe there?"

"Yes, Dad, the doors are locked. It's an all-girls dorm with high-tech security and RAs on duty twenty-four seven, which you already know. Don't worry about me."

But it's nothing new. If my dad got his way, I'd be wearing an armored suit and be locked in a fortified castle with SWAT-team guards. "I'll be home on Sunday afternoon to cook you dinner, like I promised," I remind him.

"Have I told you how proud of you I am, sweetheart?" He hardly ever calls me that, not since I was a little girl. But today is a big deal and our emotions are closer to the surface than usual.

Isla comes back in. She's changed into a pair of black jeans and a blue sweater. She's brushing out her long hair, which is still wet.

"We're going to go get some dinner now." I don't bother mentioning who we're going with. There's nothing for him to worry about and giving him too many details would definitely stress him out. "What are you having?" I made him a week's worth of meals and left them in the freezer. "Did you defrost some of that chicken parmesan I made for you?"

"Sure did. I'll put it in the microwave."

"I'll see you in a few days, then. We can talk tomorrow if you want."

"I'd like that, honey. Oh, and a letter came for you today."

"What letter?"

"It's on the table in the kitchen. Do you want me to see who it's from?"

"It might be about those paintings I submitted to a few galleries, remember? I told you about it."

I can hear his footsteps as he walks into the kitchen. "It's from the Sea Glass Art Gallery."

"Really?" I sent the pictures out on a whim, after reading an article about a few new, emerging artists who have landed major exhibitions at some big name galleries. And the Sea Glass is one I've been watching from afar for a long time. I never really expected to hear back from any of them, and especially not that one. They're basically the pinnacle of galleries. Exhibitions at the Sea Glass almost always completely sell out for crazy prices. And they put their artists on the map.

"Do you want me to open it?"

"No, it's okay. I'll wait." It's not the kind of thing I want to do over the phone. I want to open it when I'm alone. In case it's my wildest dreams coming true or just another rejection. But I don't know if I can wait until next weekend to find out. "Dad?"

"Yeah?"

"Can you bring it to work with you tomorrow? I could come pick it up after your practice."

"Sure. We finish at six. Why don't you come at six fifteen."

"Okay. I'll see you then. Make sure you have some salad with your dinner."

I can hear his low chuckle. "And you make sure you stay out of trouble."

"I will," I assure him. "Go have a beer with Jim. I'm

only a phone call away. Just text me and I'll come home whenever you need me to."

"I'm fine, honey. Don't worry about me." But there's a husk to his voice that I'm very familiar with. "Have fun in your new dorm, okay?"

"I will."

"Not *too* much fun," he sort-of jokes, but there's a sorrowful, over-protective edge to it. My dad's a big teddy bear of a man—when it comes to his family, at least. On the football field he's more like a tactical grizzly bear. He's direct and strict, as he needs to be. Like a general leading his troops. Which is his job, of course. But when it comes to me, he's the kindest person I know.

We end the call and I know we're both feeling the separation. But we're ready. We have to be ready. It's life, and we need to get on with it.

3

Zara

So far, the best thing about college is Isla.

I've never fallen so easily into a friendship with someone who's going through the exact same thing I'm going through *as* I'm going through it. We're completely on the same wavelength. I already know she'll be my best friend for the next four years and quite possibly for the rest of my life and it's an amazing feeling.

"I'll warn you now," Isla tells me as we walk across the Green toward the restaurant in town where we're meeting Gabriel. Her arm is linked through mine. "My brother and his friends are going to attempt to be totally controlling and act like they're your own personal overlords. It'll probably be almost as bad for you as it is for me, since you're their coach's daughter and my roommate. But I've already told Gabriel that he and his teammates are no longer allowed to be my over-protective bodyguards. This is college and if I want to make my own mistakes, then I'm going to. From now on, I refuse to live by anyone's rules but my own."

"Exactly. We're hedonistic free spirits. We do whatever we want."

"No more parents. No more rules." She glances over at me, realizing how that might have sounded to me. "Zara, I'm so sorry about your mom. I can't even imagine."

I shrug a little. "I've grieved as much as it's possible to grieve. For years. I'm ready to do something else now. My sister told me I'm only allowed to concentrate on the present and future from now on. And myself. Even my therapist told me it's time to step out from under the weight of my past and all the tragedy. That's how she said it: 'step out from under the weight of it.' So that's what I plan on doing."

"I'll do it right along with you," Isla says. "Do you have any other siblings?"

"Just my sister. What about you?"

"It's just me and Gabriel. My parents are still mostly-happily married and living in the same house I grew up in, near Virginia Beach. My parents are both very Type A. My dad founded a bank and my mom's a lawyer. My parents wanted me to study law but I refused."

"Majoring in business is just as good though, isn't it? You'll be a CEO instead of a lawyer. That's not too shabby."

"You'd think so. My mom thinks law is more of a career path and business is more of a crapshoot. Businesses fail."

"So do law firms."

She scoffs. "Not Eastman & Dillon Law, where my mom's a senior partner. She was hoping one of her kids would take the firm over one day. She wanted a protégé. It's been one of her biggest disappointments in life that she won't get one. But she's finally beginning to accept that neither of her children are going to carry on her legacy of being one of the top prosecutors in the state of Virginia."

"Wow." I'm starting to get that Isla and Gabe's parents must have put a lot of pressure on them to succeed. From what I know about the two of them so far, they're insanely successful already. "They must be so proud of you both."

"They are, but there's always this edge to it, like we could be doing better if we were more like them and if we'd made the decisions they wanted us to make, instead of our own. My dad thinks football is a waste of time. If it doesn't make money, then it's not worth doing, according to him. My dad thinks Gabriel should quit football and concentrate more on his investments."

"There's huge money in the NFL, though. Crazy money. Do you think Gabe will go pro?"

"Gabe is already making a lot of money through his

portfolios. I don't know if he'd even want to go pro. Oh, look, there's the restaurant."

The main street of Hawthorne is quaint and looks like a postcard of an idyllic New England town. It's starting to get dark earlier now and the street is lit by the rows of old-fashioned street lanterns and the golden glow of the many bars and restaurants. It's busy with returning students and there's an air of excitement. We're not the only ones who are here to have a good time and discover ourselves. "Here's to being free birds together. Masters of our own destinies."

"That's us, roomie," she grins, leading me toward the door that has *Hawthorne Steakhouse* etched into the glass of the door. "This is it."

I'm a little nervous to be meeting more of Gabe's friends. I finger the silver arrow necklace at my throat, the one my mother gave me on my fifteenth birthday. I've hardly taken it off since. It's a habit, touching it when I feel out of my depth. But I remind myself that I belong here, just as much as anyone else does.

The restaurant is bustling. Walls are decorated with Hawthorne sports memorabilia dating back at least two generations. Even though I grew up in Hawthorne, I've never been to this restaurant, mainly because it's where the football players hang out and my dad was never much of a going-out-to-restaurants type, especially if it was where his players were partying.

Walking into the crowded scene now, it feels good to

be a part of something bigger than myself. Traditions being made in the here and now. I can't help but feel a flicker of excitement as we make our way to the table where Gabe, West and another guy are already seated.

I glance at Isla and she's feeling it too. Her cheeks are pink and her golden eyes are bright. I can't help wondering if there's more to it than just the coolness of the night air.

The guys see us coming and Gabe stands from his chair, giving Isla a hug. "Hey, Pix. Hey, Zara. Glad you could make it."

"Hi, Gabe. Hi, West." I'd forgotten how freaking *big* they are. Then again, it's not surprising. They're football players. They have to be big. And fit. And muscular as all hell. I mostly see them on screen and I'm not used to the sheer up-close-and-personal physicality of them.

Isla is released from her brother's bearhug. She introduces me. "Zara, this is Jake Bowie. Jake, Zara Fox."

Jake is the tallest of all of them. He has mink-brown hair, green eyes and an observant, laid-back vibe. "You're the coach's daughter?" I have a feeling I'm going to be getting that question a lot, but I don't mind it. It gives me a buffer from worrying about any of them getting any ideas beyond being friends with Isla's roommate. I'm completely off-limits and it's a relief in some ways.

I haven't really had a lot to do with boys—or men. Partly because my dad is so protective. But even more than that, I coped with my mother's decline by basically retreating into my own headspace. My room is the attic of our house and takes up the entire fourth floor. It's both my room and my studio and is, at this point, full to bursting with my art. Possibly not entirely healthy to live as an art-mad hermit, but it's got cozy nooks and good light and it provided a sanctuary for me at a time when I needed it.

While most of the girls in my high school were trading make-up tips, flirting with football and hockey players and staging their Instagram shoots, I was trying to figure out how I was going to survive losing my beautiful mother while also making sure my dad was able to remain stable enough to keep his job and his sanity.

I've always been an introvert anyway, and it gave me an excuse, maybe. *Sorry, I can't go to the movies with you on Friday because my dad's dealing with a lot right now and I think he needs some company. Maybe another time.*

It never felt like a hardship. None of the boys in my high school really interested me. Their hobbies and banter seemed a million miles from the world I was occupying.

I didn't expect people to understand. How could they? Their family units were whole. Their Thanksgivings and their Christmases hadn't been ravaged by tragedy. Their worlds were still intact.

Mine wasn't, and it almost made it worse to hang out with people who were more carefree than I could relate to or deal with at the time.

I'm as over it as I can be, and at this point I've trained myself to be upbeat and as outgoing as I'm capable of. But I can still sometimes feel that degree of distance.

So these huge, strapping football players are a little intimidating.

But Isla pulls me into the booth next to her. She falls into easy conversation and I start to relax a little.

"Where's Elias?" Isla asks. "I thought the four of you usually traveled in a pack."

"He's got a meeting about one of his new endorsement deals," West says. "Our boy is in hot demand. He'll be rolling in money before we know it."

"He already is," Gabe drawls.

"Elias gets mobbed wherever he goes," Isla tells me.

"Oh." Of course the star quarterback would get mobbed. I've heard my dad discussing his players over the endless replays he and his assistants are always discussing when they come to our house. I never really took a lot of interest in the conversations they were having about football because I was too distracted by other things.

But Elias O'Shea is a name that comes up a lot and it's usually handled with a certain amount of awe. He's very good: that much I did pick up. A prodigy, my dad once said about him. A once-in-a-lifetime kind of player for a coach.

"He lives with these three idiots," she says, elbowing Jake playfully. He elbows her back.

The quarterback always gets talked about like he's

practically a mythical creature and especially Elias O'Shea, but everything I know about him has been background noise. I don't even think I've seen a photo of him. The few times I've watched clips of him playing football, he was wearing his helmet.

Isla picks up Gabe's beer to take a sip but before she can, Jake takes it out of her hand.

"Don't even think about it, Pixie," he scolds her. "You're underage."

"So?" she protests. "I'm about to become the biggest party animal on campus and there's not a damn thing you can do about it."

"Try me." His reply is surly. I'm trying to get the gist of their connection. They've known each other forever, Isla told me, and it's obvious they have a bond. He's protective of his best friend's little sister. But I can't help wondering if there's more to it than that. Her cheeks have those pink flags and his eyes haven't left her.

"We call her Pixie," Jake explains to me, "because, when she was little, she was this tiny blond-headed omnipresent thing, with her round little retro glasses, her hair sticking up and this cheesy gap-toothed grin. She would flit around us all the time, asking a million questions and insisting on following us wherever we went, like an annoying little pixie. The name stuck."

Isla pretends to be offended. "You can call me Isla now, Bowie. I'm not a tiny little gap-toothed girl anymore."

"You're still tiny." Compared to him, anyone would be tiny. "And just as annoying." But his teasing isn't heated at all. In fact, there's a depth to his gaze that's more than affection.

Interesting.

I can already read the dynamic. Gabe is oblivious. And when it clicks for him, neither Isla nor Jake know how he'll react.

I'm watching them for clues but I can't actually tell if they're even aware of the spark that's simmering between them. Maybe their friendship is so ingrained they don't realize they're practically flammable. Or maybe they do but their default is to suppress it.

It'll be interesting to watch how it all plays out. I've only known Isla for a few hours so it feels too soon, but since we're living together, I'll be waiting for her to tell me more when she's ready to.

A waitress comes over to take our order. "The usual for you guys?" she asks with a flirty smile, especially for Gabriel. I don't think anyone can blame her for crushing on Gabriel Dillon. With his dark hair and darker eyes, he's striking to look at. His moody charisma and cool confidence have the waitress practically drooling. "My friends and I have front row seats to Saturday's game, Gabe. I can't wait to watch you play."

He grins at her, but it's lightly dismissive. "Three cheeseburgers with extra fries. Zara? Isla? What do you two want?"

"Cheeseburger for me too, please," Isla says. "And a Coke."

"I'll have the same."

Time slips away in the cozy restaurant. By the end of the night, Gabe, Jake and West feel like old friends. They're easy to be with and their fun camaraderie is infectious. They refuse to let me pay my bill no matter how much I protest.

We all stroll back to the dorm together.

"So, Zara," West nudges me. "What do you paint?" Isla mentioned to them that I'm an art major.

I always have trouble describing my style. It's abstract close up but from a distance it looks almost impressionistic. "All kinds of things."

"Do you ever paint people?"

"Sometimes."

"Do you need a nude model?" He cracks up at his own joke. "Oh, shit, did I just cross a line again?"

"For fuck's sake, West," groans Jake. "Would you cut that shit out?"

Jake slings his arm around West's shoulders and puts him in a headlock. "Sorry, Zara. We've tried training him but he can't help himself."

I laugh. "He's fine."

West tries to break free of the headlock Jake has him in. But he's not giving up easily. "Because that would definitely be a masterpiece, just sayin'."

The two of them are practically wrestling. Jake pins West to the ground on the grass.

"Don't mind them, Zara," Gabriel says.

We're close to the dorm now. "This is us, guys," Isla says.

"Thanks for a fun night," I tell them.

Jake finally releases West, who lays on his back for a second, groaning and winded, before climbing to his feet.

We say goodnight to the three of them and make our way back up to our room.

And as I lay in bed, staring out at the full moon that hangs low in the sky, it takes me a long time to fall asleep.

Tomorrow I'll go to my first classes and I'll get assigned my new studio space. I'll see my dad in the afternoon so I'll be able to get a feel for how he's handling things. I'll find out if I have a shot at getting my first exhibition—in New York, of all places. I know it's wildly unlikely but it's nice to know that there's a tiny chance that maybe, even if not now, somewhere along the line, the possibilities are endless.

I've got new friends. I love my roommate.

The night feels sparked with possibility, like new beginnings, the fuses of the fireworks of our futures, are just waiting to be lit.

4

———

ELIAS

I PASS TO GABRIEL, who juggles the ball before getting a secure hold, finishing the play with the kind of precision he's become known for.

To catch a defense like the Northeast Falcons unprepared, you have to hit them with something new every single time. They're one of Hawthorne's oldest and fiercest rivals. Faking the ball to the running back and dumping it to the tight end is predictable. So's a screen pass on 3rd and long. These plays have been run so many times that even high school defenses are prepared for them. Which is why we're practicing a throw-to-run concept from empty.

Purists might cringe but my dad used to insist that this was how the game is evolving. Football is being played in space these days and the passing game is king. Brute force still has its place, of course. But it's been overtaken by speed, pace and spacing. The scheme we're working on follows this trend. And receivers like Gabe and West are dangerous.

"We'll finish here for today." Coach Fox looks at his watch again. "It's almost six."

That's the third time he's looked at his watch in the last few minutes. It's not like him to finish early, but tonight I'll take it. We were up at five for strength and conditioning training. It was the first day of fall semester and classes went from nine until three, at least for the players. We schedule our classes around our football schedule.

Then we got taped for practice and have been working non-stop on our formations all afternoon.

The four of us are basically carrying this team and it's a worry to Coach. Reggie Grayson, our best tight end, was injured a few weeks ago in a waterskiing accident. He'll recover but it doesn't look like he'll be fit for play until mid-season. Our defensive line is weaker than it needs to be. And some of our younger players, like Noah Booth and Mitch Logan, both sophomore wide-outs with huge potential, are fast but they both have issues securing the ball. They underperform whenever they're under pressure. Which is why we've been throwing them to the wolves all afternoon, putting them in situations where they have to act fast, and faster, without losing their focus.

Usually Coach would keep us late to pore over the replays but he seems distracted tonight.

Fine by me.

We head into the locker room. I shower and change, and when I get back to my locker, Gabriel is dressed, packing up his stuff. "You want to grab something to eat, Chief?"

"Yeah, I'm starving."

"So…" No one else is close by and he seems to be taking the opportunity. "What's going on?"

"What do you mean?" My game has never been better.

"I mean, why are you suddenly living like a fucking monk, Elias? This has been going on for a while now. What's the problem? You got a girl back home or something? Did you meet someone on the sly you're not telling us about?"

Gabriel and Jake go way back, but both of them have just as close a friendship with me as they do with each other. Jake is my wingman, loyal to a fault, the one I'm most likely to go out and have fun with. Gabe is deeper. We have conversations every now and then that are like mini therapy sessions for both of us. He's the smartest person I know and he *gets* things no one else would ever even think about even trying to get.

I can admit things to Gabe I wouldn't admit to Jake, and definitely not to West. West is a good friend but everything's a joke to him.

I check to make sure no one else is within earshot. "I don't know." I shove some clothes into my bag. "I don't seem to be able to relate to any of these girls at the moment. Something's missing each and every time. Do you think it's true that pheromones or whatever are the reason we're attracted to people? Because my detectors seem to have fucking shut down lately."

"Pheromones are oxytocin," Gabe says. "They trigger the limbic system, where the amygdala is located. The amygdala is responsible for the release of dopamine and norepinephrine, which make us feel giddy, energetic and euphoric—what we feel as emotion and arousal. Which is simplifying things, but you get the idea."

"Fuck." Despite what we're talking about, I laugh. "I forgot I'm talking to Einstein."

Gabriel shrugs. "There's a science to attraction. None of them are triggering your amygdala, that's all it is."

"I don't know about my amygdala, but I do know my dick suddenly has ridiculously high standards."

"Or you've just been distracted by football. We all know it takes a lot of focus to memorize the formations. Plus you're spending a lot of time working with the younger receivers. A lot of quarterbacks wouldn't go that extra mile. And our first game of the season is only a few days away. The stress of the game is real."

I can definitely agree with that. "True enough."

"I think you just need to bang the angst right out of your system," Gabe tells me philosophically.

I glance around again to make sure we're not being overheard. "The thing is, I *can't*. My dick won't let me."

"What do you mean?"

"I mean I'm just not feeling it. No one's living up to my fantasies lately. It's a fucking problem."

"It happens to me too."

"It does?"

Gabe eyes me thoughtfully. "Yeah."

"How long does it last?"

"I basically have to force myself to get back in the saddle. I override the situation by pretending whoever I'm with is my dream girl. Like I did on Saturday night. Which I now regret. Maybe that's why beer was invented."

I exhale something close to a laugh, but there's no humor in it. "Yeah, maybe I just haven't been drinking enough."

"Either that or you're more of a romantic than you give yourself credit for. Maybe you're getting tired of bed-hopping. Maybe you've fucked the thrill of meaningless one night stands out of your system and now you're looking for something more. Maybe you're looking for The One."

I don't bother admitting I've had those exact thoughts myself. This is what I mean. I sometimes think Gabriel can read minds. "What if I don't *want* to be looking for The One? What if The One doesn't exist?"

"She fucking better." He's checking his bag for something. "Shit. I left my gloves out on the bench."

"We can go out that way."

He slings his bag over his shoulder. "There's nothing wrong with waiting for the real thing, Elias."

I shake my head a little and sigh more deeply than I have in a while. "I don't know if that's what I'm doing. I'm losing my fucking mind, that's what I'm doing."

He smiles sort of ruefully, like he gets it. "Come on. Let's get the fuck out of here."

So we make our way outside to the benches. Coach is still talking to Noah and Mitch, no doubt either making their life a living hell or giving them a pep talk, or some combination of both.

Gabe finds his gloves and we start walking along the sideline toward the exit to the parking lot. "You want to hit the food trucks? Or head into town?"

"Food trucks works for me." Most of the team are gone by now, either home or to the training center, where they have food for the players after every practice. It's usually only the freshmen and sophomores who eat there. The food is free but basic and two years of eating egg salad sandwiches is more than enough.

There's also academic assistance for the players, if they need it, which some of the guys go to, to keep their grades up. Coach insists on it. The tutoring isn't something I've needed to use very often. Gabe, not at all.

Someone's walking this way and my gaze slides over

her. She doesn't look like a cheerleader or part of the team's physiotherapy cohort.

She's small and petite. She's wearing baggy jean overalls with a white, tight-fitting long-sleeved t-shirt under it. Definitely not a cheerleader. Her hair is wavy, different shades of light brown and blond, pulled up. Long, curled strands that frame her face catch the late afternoon breeze. The sun-bleached ends of her curls are almost white-blond. Her overalls are speckled with paint. So are her white sneakers.

I'm weirdly mesmerized by the way she moves. It's not quite a walk and not quite a skip. It's like she's happy about something. Excited to get to wherever she's going.

As she gets closer, I can see her face more clearly.

She's cute but also…gorgeous. Stunning. More than that. Angelic. She's radiating this sweet, dazzling glow that's quite literally lighting up the stadium.

Our eyes meet as she approaches us but then she sees Gabe and she smiles like he's familiar to her.

He knows her? She's happy to see him?

Why? How? In what way?

This enrages me in a rush of some red-hot emotion I don't even recognize. It might be…jealousy? Whatever it is, there's so much of it I have to stop myself from doing something reckless. Like throttling my own best friend.

I can't pull my eyes away from the girl long enough to glare at him.

I'm too riveted.

"Hey, Zara," Gabe says.

Zara. Where have I heard that name before?

"Hi, Gabe."

She has to be new here. I'd have noticed her before. She must be a freshman.

Her eyes are green. Not just green but emerald-bright. Long eyelashes blink at us and what I find myself thinking is: they're perfect. There's nothing fake about her.

The pinkness of her lips and her clear, golden skin are hitting me right where I live. Her expression is sweet but also sassy, and both details spin me into a kind of frenzy of fascination. The light scent of her is of sun-warmed lemons, tropical flowers and, barely, fresh paint. Everything about her is reminding me that I haven't hooked up in far too long.

I *should* be hooking up.

I *need* to hook up.

Very, very badly.

With her.

THIS IS THE GIRL I WANT.

That's how it lands in my head. Not just my head. My body. My heart. Like a demand that carves itself onto the granite of my absolutely-must-haves list—which, at this point, only has one thing on it and here she fucking is— and won't take no for an answer. It's shockingly sure of itself.

I want to kiss those luscious lips. I'm so fucking hungry. I need to taste her like I need air.

I'm stunned. Much more than that, I'm fucking slayed.

One side of her overalls is unbuttoned. Her little t-shirt hugs tightly to the shape of her body, showing off the swell of her breasts. I can barely make out the highly perched, lightly raised swell of her nipple.

Holy fucking hell.

I'm suddenly—and severely—suffering the hellish consequences of going too long without. My chest feels tight and my heart's pumping fast. But most of my blood rushes south. My cock—*fuck*—goes instantly rock hard.

Elias. Calm the fuck down.

Her sweet, hot, completely-unaware-of-it cuteness is quite literally hitting me like a runaway freight train.

"Zara, this is Elias. Elias, Zara."

"Hi, Elias." Her voice is soft with the slightest smoky edge to it. Just insanely alluring.

I want to lie in bed with her and bask in her dazzling glow. I want to feast on her sweet beauty and listen to her tell me about all the reasons she's so lit up.

"Zara," I manage to huskily repeat. I'm completely, hopelessly starstruck.

Gabriel is watching me. His gaze slides from me, to her, and back to me again. He's reading the situation and it's almost funny to him, but not quite. He lightly elbows me, but it does nothing to tone down how spellbound I am. "What he means to say, Zara, is that he's very glad to make your acquaintance."

She smiles up at me and I have to remind myself to breathe. She's so damn *beautiful*. And so much smaller than I am. Her little white teeth are neat and there's a feisty defiance behind her shyness, like even as she takes in my build, my height and my face, what she's thinking is *no way*.

No way? We'll see about that.

"Nice to meet you too, Elias."

I can't think of a single word to say to her. I'm too beguiled by how incredibly flawless she is.

Absolute perfection.

I'm vaguely aware that Mitch and Noah are walking past us.

And that Coach is coming over to us and he doesn't look particularly happy.

The girl flits over to him, standing on her toes to give Coach a kiss on the cheek. "Hi, Dad."

Dad?

Holy fuck.

No.

No.

She gives us a little wave and follows Coach inside.

I watch her until the door closes behind her and she disappears from view. With her glow gone now, the stadium seems darker. It registers that the sun is in the process of setting.

Gabriel is giving me a look. "No way in hell."

And I'm giving him a look. "My amygdala is officially on overdrive."

"Elias. Absolutely not. Be reasonable."

I'm fucked and we both know it.

Gabriel sums it up perfectly as I glance back once more. "Oh, fuck."

ALL THE WAY back to the house, Gabe continues his attempt to talk some sense into me. He reminds me of how much is at stake this year. How my chances of going high in the draft are all but assured if I can play like I've been playing. How important it is that I keep my focus razor-sharp.

Like I don't know all of this already.

My mind is a blur, retracing every perfect detail of her while at the same time fully realizing that I have far too much to lose to even think about going near her. I'm the starting quarterback for a championship-winning division one team. My dreams of going pro, which I've been working toward my entire life, are about to become a reality.

And there's no doubt in my mind that Coach Fox will kick me off the team if I so much as breathe in his gorgeous little daughter's general direction.

The slam of the door surprises me. I slammed it. I'm not usually the kind to lose my cool, but this is something else entirely. My brain is stuck on a loop. Of Zara Fox standing there in her tight little t-shirt blowing my mind and looking like she just materialized out of all my wildest dreams.

During my late-night fantasies, I never managed to draw a picture in my mind. I couldn't have created a more perfect vision if I'd tried.

She's real and she's here, taunting me with her existence.

West is at the kitchen table, cramming food into his mouth while leafing through a playbook. The tension between me and Gabe is easy to read and it gets West's full attention as soon as we walk through the door.

"What's up?" West says with a mouthful.

"We have a huge fucking problem on our hands, that's what's up." Gabe announces. Which seems sort of melodramatic but the "we" doesn't escape me. These guys are my brothers. My team. They've got my back and it's what I love most about them. Social media calls the four of us the "Hawthorne Band of Brothers" because the four of us are so in sync when we play football.

But it's just as true off the field. We're in this together. They won't let me fuck up my future, not only because it's their future too but also because they genuinely care about me.

But damn, the temptation of Zara Fox is like being hit by a wrecking ball. I've been stranded in a wasteland of a drought the likes of which I've never known, all summer long, and she's the most glorious oasis I've ever fucking seen.

My mouth feels parched. My raging lust is almost unbearable and I can feel my new obsession digging into me. Heat pumps through my veins at the memory of how stunning she was.

Those bright green eyes.

That perfect pink mouth.

The shape of those soft nipples.

Fuck, I'm jonesing so fucking bad.

For her.

I need more.

Jake walks into the kitchen, dressed like he's getting ready to go out.

"Where are you going?" Gabriel asks him.

"To a freshman party," West answers for him. "I can't figure out why my boy here wants to go and hang out with a bunch of freshmen, but I'm going along for moral support."

Jake grabs a taco from West's fully loaded plate. "Hey —" West protests.

"Freshmen orientation week," Jake grins, taking a bite. "Come on, Westie. You know it sounds like fun."

"Looks like we're going to the party too, Gabe." I honestly don't mean to rile him but there's no question I'm going, and I know he'll insist on supervising me.

"You think this is *funny*?" Gabriel seethes, setting our bag of food on the table. We stopped by the food trucks, deciding to get it to go since Gabe was lecturing me the whole time about how I need to ignore the whole amygdala thing and concentrate on football. A total 180 from our earlier conversation in the locker room, I pointed out, which only pissed him off more.

"No. I don't think this is funny." I open the bag and take out some fries and a burger. "I don't tend to be entertained by my own doom."

"Doom?" West is watching our back-and-forth like he's enthralled by a tennis match.

"All you have to do is practice some self-control for a few months and distract yourself with someone else," Gabe tells me.

Sounds easy enough. But I already know my fate is sealed. It's a weird feeling, when the two things you want most out of life are suddenly at war and you know there's really only one you'll sacrifice.

But I play it cool. "I don't know why you're getting so worked up. I've literally said one word to her."

"Exactly. You can't make a judgement that fast."

"Her?" West's eyebrows shoot up.

"Oh, I can make a judgement that fast. You're the one who said it. 'There's a science to attraction,' I think were your exact words. I can't fight science." I take a bite of my burger.

"Can someone please tell us what the fuck you two are talking about?" Jake goes over to the fridge, pulling out four Rolling Rocks and setting them on the table.

"Our starting quarterback thinks he's got a thing for the coach's very off-limits daughter," Gabe says, "less than a week before the first game of the season."

West grins despite himself. "No shit."

Jake takes a sip of his beer. "Zara?"

"Yes," Gabe confirms grimly. "Zara."

Even the sound of her name makes my chest ache.

She'll be at the freshman party. I'll see her again tonight.

Jake's watching me, reading my mind. "That would be a very bad idea, bro."

"Tell me something I don't already know, Jakey."

"She *is* cute as fuck," West offers, standing up from his chair and patting my shoulder empathetically as he downs half his beer.

Slowly, I grab the front of West's shirt with my fist. "Yes she is. And if you go anywhere near the mother of my future children I'll have no choice but to make your life extremely painful."

All three of them are staring at me like they don't recognize me.

I don't recognize *myself,* come to think of it.

West finds the humor in the situation, as always. He holds his hands up like I'm an old-time bank robber. "Did you just say mother of your future *children*? Fuck. This is *bad.*"

"Chief." Jake takes my fist and unclenches it. "We're going to need him in one piece on Saturday. And we're going to need our quarterback to *not* get kicked off the team." He looks concerned.

I'm concerned. I'm *very* concerned.

"Dude," West says, with actual seriousness in his tone, "You definitely can't even *think* about saying 'mother of my future children' to anyone outside this room. Ever."

I rub my hand across my jaw. "Fuck. You're right."

"You need a distraction," West says. "We'll find you someone else. To tide you over. To keep your eye on the ball. Literally."

I don't want to be tided over. I want the real thing.

My mind is racing. How do I throw this pass without getting sacked? *How do I make the girl of my dreams mine without fucking up my entire career?*

"Wait a minute," says West. "You saw this girl once, said one word to her and now she's the mother of your future children?" He laughs. "That doesn't make any sense."

"I know that," I growl.

I *do* know that. Things like that don't happen.

The first time I saw your mother, I knew she was the one. There she was, standing in her own spotlight like she was made for me, just as pretty as anything I'd ever seen. She was absolute perfection. I knew nothing could ever compare. She ruined me for anyone else from that very first time.

I shove the thought out of my mind. So what. My parents fell in love within the first five minutes of meeting each other. It doesn't mean it can—or has—happened to me.

Gabriel's right. I need to focus on football. I need to put the girl out of my head.

Unfortunately, she's the only thing *in* my head. That stunning vision of her with her bright smile and the face of an angel. Not to mention the sweet little body that's threatening to resurrect the raging hard-on that suddenly has a mind of its own.

"What do you say we give the freshman party a miss," suggests Gabriel darkly.

"You can do whatever you want, Einstein." I finish my beer, thumping the empty bottle on the table. "I'm going. Jake? West?"

Jake is contemplative. "Obviously, the coach's daughter is off the table. Our plan of attack is to find you someone who can take your mind off her. We'll go to the party, scout out the freshmen girls and you'll take your pick. Thirty-five thousand people go to this university and a quarter of them are freshmen, half of which are women. That leaves…"

"Four thousand three hundred and seventy-five," Gabriel finishes for him.

"Exactly," Jake confirms. "And that's just the freshmen. No doubt there will also be sophomores and upperclassmen there. Our mission is to find someone to distract you from Zara Fox."

Damn it. Just the sound of her name makes my blood run hotter.

West grabs his jacket. "This shouldn't be hard. Any one of the entire freshman class would kill to get up close and personal with the dreamy star quarterback."

"Fuck off, West," the three of us say in unison.

Gabriel shakes his head and they follow me out the door.

5

———

Zara

Earlier in the day…

As I WALK toward the Whitman Building, my heart's beating fast.

This is it. The first day of the rest of my life. This is where I get to start my career as a working artist. It's the only thing I've ever wanted to do.

I know my mother is probably beaming down on me from heaven right now. Or at least I hope she is.

Here I go, mom. Wish me luck.

She used to give me my own little canvases and paint palettes when I was small, to keep me from getting in her way while she was painting her masterpieces. I was just as obsessed as she was. My sister used to joke that if either one of us cut ourselves, we'd bleed oil paint.

There's not an item of clothing I own that doesn't

have the telltale sign that I got caught by inspiration in the middle of something else I was supposed to be doing. Like now. I'm wearing my favorite pair of overalls that are dotted with a couple of random splatters of paint. Today I might as well be prepared to get dirty.

The faculty at Hawthorne includes a few major artists and some of the best fine art teachers in the country, but this building is also one of the reasons the art program here is so popular. It's made almost entirely of glass. Steel framing gives the place a modern, futuristic feel, setting it apart from the classic New England architecture of the rest of Hawthorne. It's the tallest building on campus and sits on its own little hill.

I pull open the huge wooden door and step inside. I've been here before, on tours and for exhibitions, but it's no less breathtaking than it was the first time I saw it. Huge windows offer amazing views out over the campus. The walls are decorated with artworks that have been gifted by now-famous alumni over the years.

There's a Fergus Worthington, with its bold primary colors.

A Romeo Jones, with its off-center geometric lines.

And an Adelaide Fox.

My mother's style might be described as photo-realism with a twist. Sections of her paintings look like photographs, but mixed into the composition are more expressionistic swirls, like the two styles are at war.

When she burst onto the art scene in her twenties, my

mother's pieces were considered new and original. By the time she was thirty, her exhibitions were selling out and she was making real money out of it. By the time she was thirty-five, she'd made an international name for herself.

One of the most memorable days of my life was when we went to New York City after one of her paintings had been bought by the Museum of Modern Art. I was seven years old. Even being so young, I knew it was a huge deal. The painting looked so impressive on that big white wall under its own spotlight. It was surrounded by other masterpieces but, to us, it outshone all of them. The museum people took us all out to dinner at the fanciest restaurant I'd ever been to.

Now, I love that a part of her is here, where I'm about to launch myself.

Or at least try to.

I don't bother trying to compete with my mother. There's no point. Our styles are so different, it would be impossible to ride on the coattails of her legacy, not that I'd want to. *Your style is nothing like your mother's*, they comment. I get that a lot. Then they often say, *but it's good.* Like they're surprised.

If I'm going to make it as an artist, it's going to be purely off my own steam. And if I don't…then I don't.

It's not that I'm not ambitious.

I am.

I'm also sort of content to be the daughter of Adelaide Fox. I've always known that I might never be able to outshine her talent. You don't grow up with a famous parent without coming to terms with the fact that you might always be second best.

I'll try to be as good as I can, of course, but there's also a part of me that doesn't want to obscure her memory with my own ego.

It's confusing.

I loved her so much. I miss her. It's hard to think about how to evolve without her.

"Welcome," a woman greets me. She's holding a coffee mug in one hand and a stack of papers in the other. "I'm Gwen Hartley, chair of the art department. I'll be teaching the freshman painting class this semester."

"Nice to meet you. I'm Zara Fox."

Ms. Hartley smiles, studying my face, looking for similarities. She has riots of curly red hair barely contained in a bun. Strands have come loose and frame her face. "I was impressed by the portfolio you submitted with your application, Zara. You're definitely forging your own style."

"Thank you." In other words, I don't paint like my mother, which I already know. With my dad as the university's football coach and my mom's reputation as an artistic genius who died too young, I have some work to do to carve out my own identity.

I guess that's what I'm here to do.

Ms. Hartley nods toward the interior of the building. "Let me give you the grand tour. We've got the shared studios and the main exhibition space on the first floor. Classrooms are on the second floor and the individual studios are upstairs. And of course, the most important part, the coffee maker is in the foyer. Just over there."

I relax a little. "I'm excited to see everything."

She consults a list as we make our way to the staircase, which rises alongside the wall of windows, looking out. "Your studio is room 312. It's one of the bigger studios, with a view of the pond. I chose it for you myself."

I'm a little surprised by this. "You did?"

"I was a huge fan of your mother's work. I never met her but if there's anything I can do to help you, Zara, I will. I can't show favoritism but your studio space was something I didn't want to compromise on. I've always thought it's the room with the best view."

"Thank you. That's really nice of you." I follow her up to the second floor open-air classroom, where some of the other students are talking and setting up easels.

"We have a few minutes," Ms. Hartley says. "I'll show you 312 now and give you a chance to get settled."

I follow her up another flight of stairs and she leads me to my studio. I literally gasp when I see it.

The space is painted a dark grey and has a wooden ceiling. It's furnished with a chair, an easel with a blank canvas already perched there, a stack of several more canvases behind it, a table with paints and paintbrushes laid out, and a jar for water. There's a raised window seat that's as wide as the room, with pink and orange squashy cushions and a throw blanket. The large window extends all the way to the ceiling, bathing the room in light and offering a view of a pond with a fountain. Beyond it, rolling hills are dotted with trees that are already starting to turn shades of red and gold. "Wow."

"This will be your studio for the year," Ms. Hartley tells me. "Feel free to personalize the space however you'd like. Here's the key fob to the room and the front door of the building so you can access this room anytime. Some of our students tend to work at night, some during the day. It's entirely up to you." She glances at her iWatch. "Class starts in fifteen minutes in the main studio on the second floor. Anything else you need before I leave you to it?"

"No, it's absolutely perfect." I almost feel emotional about how much I love this space. It's sleek and inspiring and completely mine.

Ms. Hartley reads my thoughts. She places her hand gently on my arm. "Part of our work this semester will be unshackling ourselves from our pasts and our influences. Everyone has them. Finding your wings as an artist is all about freedom. We want you to follow your own path, Zara, and no one else's."

She gets me. That's her job, I guess. Maybe my past and influence are more obvious than most, but she's right. And I appreciate what she's telling me. "Thank you, Ms. Hartley."

"Call me Gwen. We're pretty relaxed here at

Hawthorne. Most of the professors in the art department go by their first names."

"Ok. Thank you, Gwen."

"I'm excited to see what this workspace inspires, Zara. See you in fifteen."

After she leaves, I sit on the window seat for a few minutes, just taking in the view and forcing myself not to, first, freak out because I finally feel like my destiny is being realized after a long time of wondering if it ever would. I'm also tempted to squeeze some of the paints onto a palette and lock myself away in here for days on end.

But I have all year to do that.

Tearing myself away from the view and the blank canvas, I make my way back downstairs to the open plan classroom, which looks out onto the same view as my studio. Easels have been set up with canvases, and placed in a large circle that faces the center of the room, where Gwen is arranging some items on a table covered in a navy blue velvet tablecloth.

A few other students are just arriving. Some have already claimed their spots and are talking and setting up their supplies. There are around thirty of us.

"Take any seat you'd like," Gwen says.

I find an available easel and set my bag down next to it.

The guy sitting next to me looks up from his phone. He has dark brown hair. He's wearing black-rimmed glasses and a Star Wars t-shirt. "Hey," he says. "I'm Christopher."

"Hi, Christopher. I'm Zara."

"Zara Fox?"

Great. Everyone knows who I am. "The one and only."

"I'm sorry for your loss."

"Thanks."

"That must feel like a lot of pressure, being the daughter of such a famous artist."

"Yeah, sometimes. But I just try to do my own thing. What about you? Where are you from? Any Picassos hanging over your backstory?"

"Nope. I'm from Boston. Every single person in my family is a computer science nerd. My dad's pissed off I'm not attending MIT for coding or something equally nightmarish."

I give him an empathetic smile. Everyone has things going on in the background of their families and lives that aren't particularly easy.

"Welcome to Intro to Painting," Gwen begins, and everyone quiets. "I prefer to call this class Freedom to Explore because that's what you'll be doing this semester. Your job is to find your artistic voice. It's to throw off the expectations of others, to climb out from under the influences that limit you, and to explore the unique vision that stems from your very personal experiences, inspirations, emotions and style. There is only one of you. Only you can create a Christopher Beck. Or a Violet Warner."

The girl on my left goes pink.

And I wait for it. "Or a Zara Fox."

I feel the rush of heat on my face as everyone turns to stare at me.

But I'm not the only one. "Or a Jameson Hyde."

"You'll be *wishing* you could paint a Jameson Hyde," says a blond guy wearing a muscle shirt. He pumps his fist in the air and everyone laughs.

"Of course we will, Jameson." Gwen lowers her glasses, peering through them at the still life. "Now, you'll notice that I've set up a collection of objects here in the center of the room. Your goal will be to capture the essence of the composition using the medium of your choice. You can choose to paint with oils or acrylics, which are both at your workstations. You'll also notice that there are dividers between each of your easels and screens you can lower. Which means you can't see what your neighbors are working on. Your job is to think carefully about what makes *your* style unique. You're going to channel your inner muse, ignoring all influences. You're going to stay very true to how you feel in this moment. Express yourself without boundaries. Without limitations. Paint *your* painting and no one else's."

There's some murmuring around the room.

"You have ninety minutes to complete this painting," Gwen continues. "All of you work at your own pace, and they'll all be different. Some of you work more slowly than others. Some would prefer to take a week. Some, a month. But not today. Today you'll *complete* this piece in ninety minutes. Don't try to paint a masterpiece. Try to paint an expression of how you *feel*. Any questions?"

"What if we can't finish it in ninety minutes?" Jameson asks.

"Then you fail the course." Gwen's laughter echoes through the large room. "Just kidding. Do your best, Jameson. Make it your goal. To complete the painting, even if it means filling in space with a single layer of color. Artists, your time starts…now."

We all start squeezing paints onto our palettes. I reach for a paintbrush.

And I start to paint.

My style isn't realistic. It's hard to describe. Splotches of color that are layered and arranged until they mimic the shape of the object I'm painting. For most of the process, it looks like a mess, but by the time I'm done, it looks surprisingly (to me, at least) true to life. My paintings have a lot of texture and a lot of depth.

I mix some blue with a swirl of red. I capture the gleam of sunlight on the glass vase and the purple shadows pooling under the bowl of ripe fruit.

As for how I *feel*, I feel like I'm exactly where I need to be. My nerves fade away and I'm fully in the zone. It's where I'm happiest.

Time slips away. There's music playing on a low

volume. Some of the other students talk as they work but I'm focused on one thing only. The light and the shadows, the colors and blends, the curves and the straight lines.

Gwen calls time. "Paintbrushes down," she commands.

I blink and look up. Everyone in class seems to be having the same reaction. Jameson Hyde mutters, "Dude, it's not enough time."

But Gwen breezes past the murmured protests. "When an hour and a half feels like ten minutes, *dude*, you know you've found the one thing you're supposed to spend your life doing. Now, lower your screens. You can prop them up so they don't touch the wet paint. Then you're free to go. I'll see you all back here tomorrow morning at nine. When you come in, the canvases will be lined up in a row, but not named. We'll discuss the works you've all created—anonymously, to begin with. Until then, this room will be locked. You all have unlimited access to your studios. See you tomorrow, people. Have a good first day, everyone."

We all make our way out into the foyer.

Christopher walks with me. "Did you finish yours?"

"I could've done more but it was close enough."

"I wish we could have had more time. I still had sections that weren't even filled in." Christopher slings his backpack over one shoulder. "Zara, do you want to grab a coffee later, after your classes are done for the day? We could meet in the student café."

He seems nice enough. But I don't want him getting any ideas about…well, anything. I don't want distractions. And I already have plans. "Sorry, I can't. I have to go see my dad after my last class."

"Isn't your dad the football coach?" He says the word "football" like it leaves a bad taste.

"Yeah." Just a guess, but it seems sort of obvious: "You're not a football fan?"

"I'm a vegan libertarian Gemini art nerd." He adjusts his glasses. "Football players hate people like me."

I don't really even know what that means, but I smile and try to be diplomatic. "I'm sure that's not true." Christopher is lanky and very slim. After hanging out with Jake, Gabriel and West last night, I can see why someone like Christopher would be intimidated by guys like them. He takes up a lot less space than they do.

"How about you?" he asks. "You must go to all the games."

"No, not at all. I used to go sometimes, but I haven't been to a game for a few years. I don't think I inherited the football gene."

"I bet you inherited the art genius gene though."

"We'll see, I guess."

"Self-belief is the most powerful inspiration there is," he tells me. "You can manifest your own success if you unblock your chakras."

"Oh…well, I hope you're right. Except that I'm not

sure what a chakra even is. And I wouldn't have the first clue how to unblock one."

"Then I definitely need a raincheck on that coffee." Christopher's looking at me intently, like he's visualizing my chakras. Which I'm really not sure I want him to do.

"Yeah. Sure." But I don't want my chakras—whatever they are—messed with. Especially by Christopher. I don't see a future in which our chakras will be getting anywhere near each other. Side by side easels is going to have to be where I draw the line. "See you tomorrow, Christopher."

"See you, Zara. I'm really glad we're in the same class."

"Yeah, me too." I make my way outside and across campus, soaking in the sights and sounds of the students spilling out of their classes.

The sunlight is warm but the breeze gently carries a scattering of falling leaves. It'll be another few weeks until peak foliage but there are already a few splashes of color dotting the emerald carpet of the Green, like Mother Nature is showing off, easily outdoing us all.

The rest of my classes go well and the day passes quickly.

When my last class finishes, I head toward the stadium, which sits at the far end of campus.

Hawthorne University is a D1 school and has a stadium to match. It's one of the largest structures in the town of Hawthorne and is a hub for concerts and other major events. We're lucky it's here because all the A-list musicians pass through here on their national tours. There are also a lot of events and festivals. It adds layers of culture and fun to the entire area.

But most of all, the stadium and everyone in it celebrates the football team. It holds around seventy-five thousand people and it's full to capacity every single game of the season.

The stadium was originally built in the 1950s but had some major upgrades done a few years ago and is now recognized as one of the best college football stadiums in the country.

Next to the newly re-paved parking lot sits a modern annex to the stadium that's entirely dedicated to the players and coaches. Like most D1 schools, Hawthorne treats its football players like superstars. They get state-of-the-art gym equipment, a team of personal trainers, physiotherapists, "mindset" coaches (an assistant's idea a few years ago that my dad begrudgingly realized was ridiculously effective so they've stayed in place), academic tutors, a "chill zone" (another assistant, who'd previously worked at Google, insisted it was useful for team building and morale boosting and he was right). They even get social media consultants, who help the players with publicity if they need it. The whole facility cost something close to a hundred million dollars.

Ever since the NCAA changed its rules about college football players being allowed to make money off their own name, a lot of them are doing exactly that, and making small fortunes. Even my dad admits it was overdue and that the publicity adds another layer of fame and adulation for the team in general.

He never complains when the stadium is full.

My dad's office sits near the players' entrance, just past the trophy room. But I'm a little early. It's not quite six yet so chances are he'll still be on the field.

I go in the main entrance, showing my ID, which always gets a reaction at Hawthorne, and make my way through to the back.

It's busy. There's a concert tonight. They're also getting the place ready for the first game of the season this coming weekend. A lot of people are milling around and it's a lively atmosphere.

Making my way down onto the field, there are still a few players warming down but most are gone now. I spot my dad at the far end. Arms folded, he's talking to two players, with a look of fierce concentration.

A pang of affection hits me. My dad is tough with his players, like he has to be, but he's also well-known for being fair. And really good at his job.

I'm glad to get this chance to check in with him. I want to see how he's holding up after his first night solo in his empty nest. I'm weirdly high on life today and it's a good feeling. So many of my days over the last few years *weren't* good days. They were hard. And oppressively sad.

So I notice the difference in myself. I'm excited. I feel

optimistic. New things are happening that are going to change the entire course of my future.

As I get closer, two football players walk out onto the field from the players' entrance and make their way along the sideline toward me. Even from a distance, they're huge and broad-shouldered.

And I can make out now that one of them is Gabriel.

I wave. It's nice to *know* someone, even though it's only my first day.

The guy he's with is an inch or so taller than Gabriel. He has thick dark hair with a slight wave to it, where it gently flicks around his ears. He's wearing jeans and a Wildcats t-shirt that hugs his shoulders and chest.

Wow.

He's built like a Greek god.

Really, Zara? A Greek god?

But he is. He could be Ares or Apollo or at least some demigod. He'd fit in just as well up there on Mount Olympus as he does down here with us mortals.

All wide shoulders and swagger, he's just ideally, beautifully buff. This is the body of a natural athlete who's honed every muscle into its optimum for peak performance.

God, would you listen to yourself? You sound like a football coach's daughter.

But it's true. He's about as perfect as anyone could be.

His eyes, as he gets closer, are watching me with a crazy, magnetic depth and I can't tear my gaze away from them. They're blue. Not just blue. They look like starbursts, with different shades of lighter blue glinting through the sapphire, like his superpowers are visible. They're framed by dark lashes that are unfair on a man.

They're the most beautiful eyes I've ever seen. Which is a very weird thing for a football player to have.

His face is rugged and gorgeous, his expression almost stern.

Wow.

"Hey, Zara," Gabe says, breaking my trance.

He's a football player, I remind myself. Rule Number One: No Football Players. A piece of me feels a little bit heartbroken but I'm not sure why.

Because he's freaking beautiful, that's why.

"Hi, Gabe."

"Zara, this is Elias. Elias, Zara."

Wait, *this* is Elias O'Shea?

No wonder his reputation is practically mythical.

When you live in a football-obsessed world, quarterbacks tend to do that: they exist in a zone of their own. In some ways, they *are* gods. They control the success or failure of thousands of people's hopes, dreams and in some cases, entire identities.

I happen to know that, after a difficult first year, Elias O'Shea has been on an unbelievable winning streak that's made him a national superstar. I've picked up bits and pieces about his rise to stardom from overhearing my dad's phone conversations and from the constant stream of assistants who use our house as one of their headquarters. I wasn't always paying attention, but somehow a lot of it stuck. And now, the best football player my dad has ever coached is gazing down at me like I just flew in on my unicorn.

"Hi, Elias," I manage to say, and my voice sounds breathless. Which is understandable. He really is gorgeous. And even though I'll never consider going there—and I don't know where I'd *go* even if I wanted to—it's impossible not to appreciate the outstanding specimen of athletic masculinity that's standing right in front of me.

"Zara." His voice is deep and low. There's a question in it. He's heard my name before but he can't remember where. He continues to watch me, his eyes taking in every detail of me until a blush warms my cheeks.

Gabriel nudges Elias with his elbow, a mixture of amusement and something else in his expression, as though there's something about the way Elias is acting that's out of character. "What he means to say, Zara, is that it's a pleasure to meet you."

I smile at him. "Nice to meet you too, Elias."

Two other football players walk past us and I glance over to where my dad is standing. He's still in his gruff coach mode but I can tell by his eyes he's happy to see me—even if that emotion is co-existing with his rising temper over the fact that I'm currently in the same stadium as several of his players.

My dad walks over and Gabe and Elias seem to take

this as their cue. I stand on my toes to kiss my dad's cheek. "Hi, Dad."

Glaring at Elias and Gabe for a short moment, dismissing them, my dad drapes his arm gently around my shoulders, as though to shield me. "Hi, honey. Come to my office. I brought your letter. How was your first day?"

"It was fantastic," I say honestly. It *was* fantastic. I glance back once to see Elias still standing there, still watching me with those dark eyes. I can't quite decipher the intensity of his gaze. And I'm not about to analyze it.

Maybe he's just one of those strong, silent types.

Either way, I'm hardly going to complicate things by fixating on Hawthorne U's star quarterback, along with every other girl on this campus and hundreds more across the country. Especially when doing that would get *me* into deep trouble and quite possibly jeopardize *his* entire career.

Forcing myself not to look back at him again, I follow my dad into his office.

"So your classes went well? You're not regretting enrolling here at Hawthorne?"

"I definitely feel like I've made the right choice."

"That's great, honey. I knew you'd be happy here." He pauses for a few seconds, as he often does when he's thinking about my mother. "So, how was it, attending art class at your mother's alma mater?" It was always going to be a thing I'd have to deal with.

"I like it. It's kind of comforting."

"I'm glad to hear that." He finds my letter in a stack of papers on his desk and hands it to me. "Here you go."

I check the sender's address. *Sea Glass Art Gallery. Mercer Street. New York City.* It's where a lot of my idols have had their first exhibitions. The gallery has a knack for finding new, emerging artists who go on to make huge splashes in the art world, partly because the trend-watchers take the Sea Glass's selections as gospel. Getting exhibited there is rocket fuel for an artist's career. But it's really, *really* hard to get accepted. "Thanks, Dad. I'm not getting my hopes up. I'm going to open it later."

"You sure?" His expression softens from gruff football coach into supportive dad.

"Yeah, I have a ton of homework already and there's a party tonight for freshmen. Part of orientation week. Isla texted me earlier and told me she'd be waiting for me."

"All right. You go on and have some fun. Remember that there are a million galleries and you're only just getting started."

"I know." He's giving me moral support in advance in case it's a rejection—which it very likely is.

"I'm proud of you, sweetheart. And I'm glad you're here."

"Thanks, Dad. Me too."

"Even if it is jarring as hell to see you mingling with my players," he adds, only half joking.

"We're at the same school, Dad. And there are a lot of them. But I'm going to be spending most of my semester in my art studio, so you can relax."

He folds his arms and leans back in his chair. "Good."

"You holding up okay? How was last night?"

"It was just fine, honey, like we both knew it would be. Don't worry about me."

I go over to kiss him on the cheek. "See you Sunday, then."

"Stay out of trouble, kid."

"I always do."

He chuckles as he watches me go. After leaving his office I head back across campus. Dusk hangs heavily now but the campus is lit. The party on the Green is already pumping, mostly with freshmen but there are some older students there too.

A band is playing a Harry Styles song and there are already a few people dancing. Food stalls are dotted around, along with tables, chairs and strings of lights. It's warm tonight and the campus feels alive with laughter and music. Students are mingling and enjoying their newfound freedom. I spot Isla talking to a group of people.

"Roomie," she calls out to me. "There you are. I've been looking for you. Come hang out with me."

She gives me a hug and hands me a travel mug. I can tell she's already tipsy. "Lauren and Mollie and I made some cocktails before the party," she whispers. "They're our new suite mates. They got here this morning and they're *so* nice. They went to get some food but when they get back I'll introduce you."

"How were your classes?" I ask her.

"Amazing. They let me into the 200-level classes for macroeconomics and differential calculus because I took some 100-level online classes in high school and also because of my internships, but I've already read some of the textbooks they're using so my professors are going to give me some extension work to do. I can't wait."

I laugh at her enthusiasm. "I've never known anyone so excited by economics and calculus," I tease her.

"Oh, shit, look who's here. I told them not to hound me. *Or* you."

I turn to see who she's talking about and…*oh no*.

It's Gabe, Jake, West…and Elias O'Shea.

6

——————

ELIAS

WE HEAD TOWARD CAMPUS. All of us are in a mood. As we get closer, we can hear the party's loud music and thumping bass line.

"Remember the plan," Gabriel says. "Elias, you've worked your entire *life* to get to the position you're in right now. Think logically about this. With your brain."

"Yeah, Elias," West adds. "Not your dick."

Gabe ignores him. "You're *so* close to getting everything you've worked toward since day one, man. Fame. Fortune. The best shot of any of us at the NFL."

"Hundreds of millions," Jake muses. "That's how much the top quarterbacks are pulling down in their extended contracts, Elias. *You* could reach that level if you stay focused. You're *that* good."

It's nice of him to say.

Gabriel backs him up. "Going high in the draft is basically a sure thing if you stay the course. That's all you need to do. The hard work is mostly done. Keep the distractions to a minimum and ride that train all the way to the station."

"Choo choo," West laughs at the description, then adds, "Unless you fuck everything up by lusting all over the coach's nubile freshman daughter."

I give him a shove. "Don't call her that."

West almost stumbles but recovers, grinning insolently at me. "Call her what? You don't like me calling the mother of your future children 'nubile'?"

"Not if you want to continue to live."

He finds this hilarious but at the same time he takes my warning seriously when my fists involuntarily clench. "Okay. I'm sorry. Dude, don't kill me."

Jake asks, "Can't you wait to make her the mother of your future children until *after* the draft picks?" Unfortunately, it's a good question.

"Trust me, I don't *want* to fuck up my future. I also can't risk anyone else going near her. She's mine."

The three of them give me another one of those looks. Like I'm losing my mind.

Maybe I am.

"Who are you and what have you done with our quarterback?" West jokes.

"Well, that's a possible solution, then." Gabe's tone is

more upbeat. "We somehow get the message out that she's off-limits. To everyone."

"How would we do that?" Jake has to ask it loudly because we're close now. The music is loud.

"*I'll* do it," I growl.

"Maybe the chance encounter earlier this afternoon was just a fluke," West suggests. "Maybe when you see her again, you'll realize that it was the slant of the sunlight or something. Maybe she's just an average girl and your obsession isn't really a thing."

"There's nothing average about her." I shove my hands in my pockets, wishing I could somehow tone down the rage. *The need.* To see her again.

A group of people watch us approach. They stop talking, riveted by us. We tend to get attention.

I don't recognize anyone in the group but West goes straight up to them. "Hey, are you guys freshmen?"

"Obviously," mutters Jake.

"Oh my god, aren't you West Hawkins?" a girl asks breathlessly. When he grins, she says hopefully, "I'm Heather. This is Elle."

I hear the whispered gasps nearby. "*Holy shit, it's Elias O'Shea.*"

"*And that's Jake Bowie and Gabriel Dillon.*"

West takes the adulation in his stride. "Elias, come on over here and meet Heather and Elle."

I'm not in the mood for West's games, so he makes

conversation with the girls as I scan the scene, searching for her. "How are you liking Hawthorne so far?" he asks them.

"It's *so* much fun." The redhead is nervous and whole-some-looking. The other one has dark hair and dark eyes. Details I barely notice. It's like trying to show interest in a couple of dim sparks when all you want to do is stand next to the bonfire that's burning you from afar with its perfection. Especially when you know she's real and she's here, somewhere close by.

Where is she?

"My brothers are really into football and they watch you guys play all the time." The dark-haired one steps forward and I take a step back before she can get too close to me.

Fuck off, I feel like growling. *I'm taken.*

"We're coming to your game tomorrow," one girl tells us.

"Great," West replies.

The red-haired girl is staring. "Hi, Gabe."

"We might see you around," West tells them, as I make a break from the group and head deeper into the crowd.

My wingmen follow me. Their idea of distracting me with other women has backfired. All it's done is remind me that no one lives up to the impossible standards Zara Fox has somehow imprinted on my life in the shining thirty seconds I spent in her company.

I'm looking for her in the sea of freshmen.

There she is.

In the distance. She's still wearing her jean overalls and her white top and I wonder for a second if she's cold. She must not have had time to go back to her dorm after seeing Coach.

Her hair is down. It spills halfway down her back in golden waves that catch the light of the hanging lanterns.

She's talking to a group of girls but there are guys closing in on their circle. This is unacceptable to me.

I head straight for her.

And I feel a hand on my arm. "Chief," Jake practically pleads. "*Think* about this. She's extremely off-limits. You know that. Come on, be realistic. You can't have her. Not now."

But that's when she sees me.

Her eyes sort of light up and I can see the colorful greenness of them from here.

And I know in that moment that there's nothing they can do to stop me.

There's nothing I can do to stop myself.

She's without a doubt the most beautiful thing I've ever seen in my life.

I'm one hundred percent fucked and I can't even bring myself to care right now. My need to get closer has become everything about me.

Heading toward her, I barely hear my team's tactical plan.

I'll get Isla to take her back to the dorm.

Let's make this as inconspicuous as possible. We're a group socializing with their group. Do everything you can to keep this from becoming a spectacle.

She smiles shyly as I get close to her and *I am so fucked.*

7

—————

Zara

THE SIGHT of Elias O'Shea is more than mesmerizing. He exudes confidence and charisma, just like he did in the stadium, but it's worse here and now. We're at a party. There's no buffer. I'll have to talk to him.

Even though there are hundreds of people in this crowd, Elias O'Shea's eyes land directly on me. His gaze locks with mine.

Holy shit.

My heart races.

He and his friends are walking over to us.

"It's *Elias O'Shea*," some girl gasps.

Yes, it is.

And he's far more gorgeous than any human being has any right to be. Tall and athletic, with that thick, slightly unruly dark hair and those denim-blue eyes, he's magnetic. Every single girl is watching the four of them and especially him. His cool confidence fits him like a glove. He doesn't have to work at it. He's not cocky about it. There's something almost regal about him.

Girls are literally swooning as the four of them walk past.

A strange mix of curiosity and caution tugs at my emotions.

The saner side of my subconscious tries to talk sense into me. *You can't have him—even if there was the remotest chance of him wanting that to happen. He's a senior and a football god. The entire country knows who he is. Legions of women are obsessed with him. He's also at the very top of the list of your no-go zone, as we've already discussed a number of times. You know this.*

But the little devil on my other shoulder, who for some reason I picture as a sassy little mermaid who wants to play, still wet from her swim in the crystal clear turquoise water of the Caribbean (which I've never seen but she has) and holding her tiny pink pitchfork, is reacting to Elias O'Shea like he's already mine. *Would you* look *at that guy? He's freaking perfect. Every urge you own is simmering, waiting to be unleashed. By him. Isn't that what you came to college to do? To break free? To grab everything life has to offer with both hands? Grab* him. *He'll feel better than anything ever has.*

I shut her down, but I'm riveted.

I didn't know it was possible for anyone to be so beautifully…in proportion. He's the ideal combination of athletic, tall, lean and buff. Just completely hard-bodied and sculpted. He's still wearing his Wildcats t-shirt and jeans, now with a leather bomber jacket that's open. He could be a cover model for both GQ *and* Sports Illustrated. Then again, maybe he already is.

Time seems to stand still as Elias and his friends approach us. The connection, as his eyes stay locked on mine, is extreme. I bite my lip, torn between wanting to run and wanting to allow myself to feel the outrageous pull of him.

"I told you not to stalk us," Isla scolds them.

"Good luck with that, Isla," West tells her, his voice dripping with mischief. "My house is obsessed with you people."

You people? What people? I have no idea what he means. Why would they be?

These boys—okay, *men*, like seriously—have the presence of gladiators. Which I guess in some ways they are. They're emitting clouds of hundred-proof testosterone that's roughly equivalent to crack for every female with a heartbeat.

The crowd circles them from a distance. Some of the bolder girls move closer.

"Westie-e-e," a blond girl teeters up to West in her full-length dress and sky-high heels—which can't be easy on the soft grass—and practically wraps herself around him. "Why didn't you call me back last week? I gave you my number but I didn't have yours. You promised you'd *call* me!"

Anyone else might find this awkward. She's basically

announcing to everyone that he blew her off. But West's blue eyes twinkle with humor and also a chivalry that makes a few girls sigh as he slings his arm around her. "That's because I lost it. Come dance with me." He pulls her toward the dance area and she follows along, unsteady but clearly ecstatic.

"Do you remember my name?" I hear her ask him as he leads her away.

I can't really blame West or the others for making the most of being the most desirable men on campus. They're young, they're hot and they're superstars. Of course they're going to live life to the fullest and jump into bed with whoever they want. They can literally take their pick.

I wonder if Elias does.

Of course he does. Look at him.

Gabriel's cool about his stardom. He's the Tristan to Elias's King Arthur, a knight with a MENSA member-ship, maybe. The four of them are handsome in different ways. Gabriel's the mysterious dark-horse with a percep-tive edge. West is the fun-loving and sunny Gawain (I saw that movie a while ago, the version with Clive Owen and I was sort of obsessed by how those hot, tough-guy men cared so much about each other). West is the golden retriever who always sees the lighter side of life and keeps his friends from taking things too seriously. Jake's the Galahad, loyal and steady and all-American. You get the feeling he would take a bullet for any one of his friends.

And Elias is the leader. The alpha. The absolute A-list of everything biology has to offer.

Would you stop? You have no business even going near *anything biological.*

Still burning under Elias's gaze, I take a sip of the drink Isla gave me. It's some kind of punch that tastes like it might be half lemonade and half tequila. Yikes. She wasn't kidding when she said she's ready to let loose.

Jake reaches for the cup Isla's holding but she twirls away from him and tips back the rest of it, drinking all of it. Not that there was much of it left.

Shit. My girl's going to need supervision to make sure she doesn't do anything she'll regret by morning.

And Jake is not pleased.

But she laughs and pulls me toward the dance floor area in front of the band. I don't really want to dance but I go with her anyway. "What are you doing?" I ask her. "This drink is *strong*, girlfriend."

"I told you, I'm ready to have some fun."

Jake is watching her like a hawk. "Are you doing this just to rile…him?"

She glances over to where he's glowering at her. "Who, Jake? No, of course not. Jake and I are old friends. He's just having trouble letting go of the little sister image he's always had of me. He'll get over it."

Okay, so they're still at the stage where they're not admitting to themselves or each other what seems sort of obvious to me. "Go easy, roomie," I tell her. "I don't want to have to carry you back to the dorm."

"Just get Jake to do it," she laughs. "I'm joking. But he would. He'd do anything for me. Grumpily, sure—but literally anything. Oh, here they come!" Two girls walk over to us and we move to the edge of the dance area so Isla can introduce me. "Lauren, Mollie, this is my roomie and new bestie, Zara."

Our new suite mates are nice and I can tell the four of us are going to get along well. Lauren is a dance major, with dark brown hair and the petite, toned body of someone who's spent half her life in pointe shoes. Mollie is curvy and has a short blond bob that curls at the end. She hasn't decided her major yet. The two of them have been best friends all through high school.

The football players stand around a high table with stools placed around it. A waitress arrives with a pitcher of Coke and some glasses. People swarm around them and they're joined by people they know. Everyone is gawking at them.

Elias O'Shea is still watching me. He crooks a finger, making a *come here* motion.

Wow, he's beautiful.

Slowly, I shake my head. It's a bad idea.

Slowly, he nods.

Don't do it, girl.

I do it anyway, my feet carrying me toward him like they're staging a mutiny over my sane mind.

"Hey, Zara."

"Hey, Elias."

"Imagine meeting you here. Twice in one day."

"Yeah, imagine that."

"How'd your day go?" he asks me.

Am I really making small talk with my dad's hot star quarterback? Apparently so. "It was good."

"What classes did you have?

"My first class of the day was Introduction to Painting. That's my major. Painting. Well, fine arts." Am I rambling? I tend to do that when I'm nervous.

The corner of his mouth quirks but his eyes are smoldering. "You're an artist. I should have guessed from the paint."

"Yeah." I look down at my overalls. "It's a dead giveaway. What about you? Besides football?"

"I'm a business major."

"Like Gabriel." I glance toward the group, where Isla, Mollie and Lauren are talking to Jake, West and Gabriel.

"I figured it would be a good fallback. In case football doesn't work out."

"Sounds like it's working out pretty well." My tongue touches my bottom lip and he watches the movement with rapt attention. "You probably won't need a fallback."

"What did you paint today?" Like he's genuinely interested.

"Oh. A still life. Tomorrow we'll have our paintings

revealed to the class and we'll be talking about whether they're any good or not."

His slow smile is basically like staring at the sun. "I'm sure yours will be the best one."

I can't help smiling. He says it like he already knows it as fact. "I'm definitely not sure about that. We were only allowed ninety minutes to finish the whole painting. I usually take a lot longer than that."

"What made you get into painting?"

"My mother was an artist. I sort of followed in her footsteps."

"Actually, I remember that about her. And I know that you and Coach lost her. I'm sorry."

"Thanks."

"I lost my mother too, a long time ago. I don't even remember her."

"I'm so sorry." My heart hurts for him, and for me. It's a bond we share and it provides an unexpectedly powerful link. I feel so *much* for him, that he never even got to know his mother, or have any memories of her at all. My urge to comfort him is so strong I have to stop myself from reaching out to him and doing something crazy. Like giving him a hug.

I can't help but notice his teammates are watching us and it's easy to read the concern. They shouldn't be concerned. We're having an innocent, heartfelt conversation. We just randomly bumped into each other, which is bound to happen from time to time. We're acquaintances now. But that's as far as this will ever go. It has to be.

Besides, someone like Elias O'Shea probably has a harem of women at his beck and call. No doubt he plays the field to his heart's content. It's one of the reasons my dad's rule exists, of course. Because athletes at the top of their game tend to leave a trail of broken hearts wherever they go.

"Do you ever sell any of your paintings?" he asks.

"No, not yet. I actually sent some out to a couple of galleries a while ago." I'm not sure why I'm even telling him this. Maybe because he's so enthralled. He's watching me like I'm the most fascinating person he's ever met.

"How'd it go?"

"Actually, that's why I went to visit my dad just before, to get a letter that came to our house. It's from a gallery."

"What did it say?"

"I haven't opened it yet. I haven't been brave enough."

"Do you have it with you now?"

"Yes."

"Open it."

Bossy much? But I guess that's to be expected of a quarterback. The Alpha and all that is bound to have a take-charge kind of attitude. "I was planning on waiting until later."

"Go on. I'm right here for moral support."

A huff of laughter escapes me. I'm not sure what's

funny. Maybe it's just that he's so damn cocky. "I want to be alone when I open it, in case it's a rejection like it usually is."

"It might be a win this time. I think you should open it."

His eyes really are amazing, with their different shades of blue, like there are embers burning behind them, lighting them from within.

Something about his riveted, manly interest gives me courage. So I reach into my back pocket and pull out the sealed envelope. "This gallery is in New York. It's called the Sea Glass. It's where a lot of new artists get their first break. It's kind of what they're known for. Launching newbies. Everyone who gets exhibited there becomes an instant sensation."

"All right then. Let's see what they have to say."

Damn it. I'm really doing this. I start to slowly rip the seal. But I can't do it.

"Do you want me to open it for you?"

"No, it's fine. I'll do it." So, under the laser beams of his encouragement, I rip open the envelope and pull out the crisp single piece of paper. Special paper. The kind people make themselves, with colorful threads baked in. "'Dear Ms. Fox," I begin, my heart sinking. My eyes are faster than the words I'm reading. But I keep reading anyway. "Thank you for your recent submission. Unfortunately, we have not selected your work to exhibit at this time but please feel free to send more of your work in the future. Thank you again for your interest.'"

Damn it. Why the hell did I agree to open the letter in front of *Elias O'Shea,* of all people? It only makes the humiliation that much worse. He's the most successful person at this school. And I'm…not.

Elias notices my disappointment. "Hey. You know what?"

"What." My voice sounds flat. I'm disheartened, of course, but not surprised. *How did I ever think I'd be as good as my mother?*

"I don't nail every pass," he says. "Not even close. But I keep trying. I keep practicing all day every day, memorizing the formations, working like hell until it becomes so instinctual I barely even have to think. And then I do it again until I land another one. Not just land it but feel the flow of it, like a dance almost. When I nail one, I know I've nailed it before it even leaves my fingers. But none of them are easy. Every single one of them takes blood, sweat and tears to get right."

His little speech almost helps. "I guess so."

"You're just getting started. It's your very first week of school. You can't expect things to happen overnight."

"I've been painting for a long time," I point out.

"And I've been playing football for a long time. But I still miss. All the time. The trick is to keep going. Feel your own power, stay true to it. Only you can do what you do. Keep working and keep getting better. That's the only way you'll ever hit the mark." Then, like he's reading my mind. "Besides, who cares if you don't hit the same targets your mother hit. That's not something you should try to do. You'll hit different targets. Better targets. Targets that are meant for *you* to hit, not her."

It's true. "Maybe you're right."

"I'm always right." That smile—*holy hell he's gorgeous.*

"Of course." I find myself smiling back. "You're the quarterback."

"I have to be right. Let me see a picture of one of your paintings."

"No…I mean, I'm still finding my style."

"Show me your favorite painting that you've ever done."

Damn him. But what the hell. He already knows about my crash and burn at the Sea Glass. Showing him a painting at this point can hardly hurt.

I pull my phone out of my back pocket and pull up a photo. He holds out his hand and I give him my phone. He zooms in on the painting.

"That's one of my favorites," I tell him. "It's a self-portrait but it also turned out to look almost exactly like my mother. I didn't even mean to do that." I immediately regret showing him. "I haven't shown my work to many people before. Most of it is still stacked in my room in the attic of our house. Not even my sister or my dad has seen this one."

"So I'm the very first person to see it besides you."

"Yeah."

Elias is quiet for a few seconds as he studies the painting more closely. It's the strangest thing but I feel like he's absorbing some of my sadness—which is mostly gone now but it still has the power to creep up on me and cast its dark shadow over everything—just with his patience and his empathy. Maybe because he *gets* it, I don't know. But the invisible current between us is connective. "It's the best painting I've ever seen."

"You don't have to say that."

"I mean it." His glance slides to my face, like he's genuinely impressed, before returning to the photo. "You're insanely talented. This is really, really good, Zara."

"Thanks." It's a nice thing to say.

He takes his time with it. "You and your mother must have looked a lot alike."

"Yeah. We both have the same color hair and eyes. Or we did. Anyway, I like how the painting seems to capture some of both our personalities. It was the first time I ever felt like I could do that with my art."

"Can you send this to me?"

"What do you mean?"

"Can I text myself a screenshot?"

"No." I laugh a little, reaching for my phone, but he protects it with his strong-looking hands. "Why?"

"So I can look at it when I want to feel inspired."

I watch him studying the photo, a little bit heartbroken by what he just said. In a good way. He's not just saying that because it's what he thinks I want to hear. He's too self-secure to do something like that. I mean, he's the freaking quarterback, he doesn't need to feel inspired.

But he's real. I don't know if I've ever met anyone who's so completely…themself. He's not fake or pretentious or putting on any kind of front. It's hard to describe it, but he feels fully realized.

It's also basically the nicest thing anyone's ever said to me.

He glances up at me. "Can I?"

"Absolutely not." But I smile. "I don't know why you'd want to."

"Because it's my new favorite thing. I want to be able to look at it whenever I want."

"If you're trying to flatter me, you're pretty damn good at it."

"I'm sending it."

"Oh, fine then." I shrug and he sends himself the photo as a text message.

Isla weaves her arm through mine. "Hey, roomie. We're heading back to the dorm. I've been instructed to take you with me and I'm not allowed to take no for an answer. See? They can't help themselves. They think they own this campus and everyone on it."

"It's fine. I need to get back anyway. I already have homework due tomorrow, believe it or not."

Elias still has my phone.

And it just occurred to me that he now has my phone number.

There's a spark of triumph behind his blue-on-blue eyes.

"Don't even think about it," I tell him.

"Think about what?"

I reach for the phone and take it from him. "You need to stay away from me," I whisper.

"I wish I could," he whispers back.

Isla doesn't overhear our low conversation because she's telling Gabriel and Jake, "No, we do not need you to walk us back. Thank you, but there are four of us. We're fine. Good night, ya'll."

Isla pulls me along with her.

I follow her willingly but I glance back at Elias. "Bye, Elias. Good luck on Saturday."

He watches me in that way he has, like he can't believe I'm real. And like he has no intention of waiting until Saturday.

There's a weird feeling of emptiness in my chest that's new, as we walk away and I don't look back. Against my will, *I wish I could stay and talk to him all night, and drink in all that beguiled, blue-eyed enchantment.*

This is bad.

This is very, very bad.

Then why did it feel so good?

8

Zara

"Moving on to our next and final painting," says Gwen. "I've saved the best for last. Once we've discussed this one, I'll reveal to the class whose paintings belong to who. I think some of you might be surprised."

We've been going through the paintings from yesterday, commenting on each one. I'm amazed by the talent in this room.

The last painting is mine. Gwen has just said she's "saved the best for last," which, at one point in my life, might have made me burst into tears. With happiness. But I hardly ever cry anymore. Somewhere along the line, all my tears dried up.

You belong here, is what that comment suggests and I can feel that. It's ridiculously energizing to be part of a group of like-minded people who thrive on artistic expression as much as I do. Until now, I've only ever painted alone, as a kind of knee-jerk reaction to grief and existing through difficult times. It's refreshing to step out of all that, like I can finally look forward.

"This painting," Gwen begins, and I brace myself for the commentary, "is a style I might call Millennial Impressionism with a very original twist. With the artist's permission, I'd like to include it in our freshman exhibition coming up in October, along with the first piece we discussed."

Wow.

"Who do you see as this artist's influences?" Gwen asks the class.

I wait for it.

But, to my wild relief, no one says Adelaide Fox.

"Matisse," says Christopher. "Obviously."

Matisse does happen to be my favorite artist. But… obviously? He hardly needs to emphasize it like that. It's almost as if he's accusing me of being derivative. I've spent the past four years working like hell *not* to be derivative of anyone or anything, so it stings.

"I can almost see the influence of Basquiat," says a girl with pink hair and a lot of piercings. "In the neo-expressionism of the color blocks." I've learned during the discussion that her name is Maeve and she's nice. She's kind about what she says and she's well-informed. Like me, she obviously studies art history and reads all the latest art magazines.

The class discusses my painting and most of the

comments are encouraging. But I'm glad when the critique comes to an end.

Once they've finished, Gwen attaches a name tag to each of the paintings and there's a lot of murmuring. Gwen's right: I am surprised by some of them.

Jackson Hyde is all about hyperrealism.

Maeve paints like a seventeenth century Dutch artist. Which I wouldn't have expected, with her pink hair, her tattoos and her punk rocker vibe. Of all the artists in the room, she might be best. Hers was the other painting Gwen mentioned she'd like to include in the freshman exhibition.

Christopher's painting is the one that looks like a Mondrian with graffiti painted over it. It's cool but, secretly, I don't think it's wildly original. I would never say that, of course. And he obviously feels the same way about my painting.

Anyway, it hardly matters what we think. Like anything, you can never tell what's going to strike or which trend is going to hit some kind of tipping point. We all know luck and hard work play just as big a role in success as talent does. That and—I'm hoping—sheer grit.

"We'll take a five minute break before the second half of the class," Gwen tells us. "Your next assignment is going to be a life drawing. In paint."

A life drawing.

It's something I haven't done a lot of.

We all head back to our easels to start setting up and there's a commotion near the door. I hear several people gasp. Including Maeve.

I look up to see—*holy shit.*

It can't be.

But it is.

Elias O'Shea.

Gwen clasps her hands together. "I got the email from the registrar this morning and I was very surprised to see your name there but of course we're thrilled to have you in the class, Mr. O'Shea." *Mr. O'Shea?* I guess he does command a certain amount of respect. "There are some extra supplies over there in the corner and you can set up your easel wherever you'd like."

What the hell? He's joining the class?

Everyone's talking in hushed, excited whispers.

Elias's eyes find me instantly and if I'm not mistaken, the hot quarterback looks almost guilty. And even more gorgeous and impressive in this familiar, everyday setting than he was out there in the open air.

He grabs an easel and a canvas and walks over to me. To Christopher, he says, "Hey, man, move along, would you?"

At the sound of his low, commanding voice, my nipples bead into tight little peaks and the tiny hairs on my arms stand up. *Holy shit.*

Christopher glares at Elias but considering the size of

Elias, he seems to reconsider protesting and he slides his easel to the left, making room for Elias to set up next to me.

"Do you mind telling me what you're doing here?" I can't quite keep the accusation out of my question. The last thing I need is…*him. Here.*

"I decided I needed to reconnect with my artistic side." The deep huskiness of his voice does the strangest thing. It touches me like a physical force. *There.* In the most secret…*soft, wet* place imaginable. *God.* "I feel like I've been neglecting it for too long."

Blue eyes watch me. Which isn't helping me concentrate. "I hope—" I can't bring myself to say it.

"You hope what?" That guilty mischief. "That I'm not stalking you?

"Exactly." I put my paintbrush down. I'm actually kind of mad that he would do this. But then, he can't be here just for me, can he? Maybe he's failing one of his classes and needs an easy A. Not that this class would necessarily give him that. And I remember overhearing somewhere along the line in the football discussions that are constantly going on in my house that Elias O'Shea gets mostly straight A's.

"I thought we agreed to…" What to say? *Hey, star quarterback, I thought we agreed to stay away from each other. Which would imply that I'm suggesting that you somehow want to not stay away from me. Which would mean that I think you're somehow interested in being around me.*

Help. He's flustering me. My mind is tripping over itself.

I try not to stare but it's impossible not to.

It's so strange to see him in this setting. He's huge. And just so freaking beautifully…put together. His powerful thighs are filling out his jeans like nobody's business. His lean hips taper up to that broad chest and those perfectly sculpted muscles. His neck is tanned and corded. His almost-black hair has that ridiculously sexy wave to it, curling around his ears and flicking softly against the back of his neck.

I'm grateful when Gwen distracts me. "I'm sorry to say that I'd arranged for a model to come sit for us during the second half of the class, but she just texted me to tell me she has a flat tire so she isn't going to make it. So I'm going to let you work in your studios for the remainder of our time this morning. Unless…someone wants to volunteer? We're going to be painting the shoulders, neck and head, so it'll require the volunteer to be comfortable wearing something fitted enough for us to do that. A t-shirt is fine."

I look around. Nobody volunteers, so I raise my hand. "I don't mind. I can do it."

Elias watches me as I take off my sweater. I'm wearing a white tank top underneath it. It's hardly that revealing. I wear this kind of thing all summer.

"Wonderful." Gwen is placing a chair in the middle of the circle. "Thank you, Zara."

But Elias does something I'm not expecting. He takes off his jacket and wraps it around my shoulders. "No way in hell."

9

ELIAS

So this is how I find myself sitting in a chair in the middle of an art class as thirty freshmen paint me.

I honestly don't give a fuck about that. Or them. Or what they're doing.

There's only one thing I care about.

Her.

The girl of my dreams.

She's mad at me. Her face is pink and she's shooting little daggers out of her green eyes at me that are edged with questions. *What are you doing here? Are you here for me? Why? You absolutely can't be. Are you crazy?*

So I shoot a few back. *Of course I'm here for you. Yes, I'm crazy. Crazy with relief because you're perfect and now I know how it feels to* know. *To absolutely know.*

I'm entranced, fixated, obsessed. Her hair is wild today, pulled up into a messy bun with strands escaping it, giving her a wavy, blond-tipped halo. She's wearing skinny jeans that hug every insane curve and make me wonder not only how she got them on in the first place but also how I'm going to get them off her later.

No. I hear my teammates scolding me from afar. *She's forbidden to you.*

I'll take it slow, if I can.

She shrugged off my jacket and has put her sweater back on. Which is a very good thing because if she was sitting there in her little tank top with her nipples barely visible, I'd have had to scoop her into my arms like a caveman and carry her the fuck out of here.

I still might.

A few people are murmuring. They're wondering what the quarterback is doing here. They're probably also noticing that I'm staring at her. Of course I should do something about that. I should try to hide it. Make it less fucking obvious that I'm starstruck, so it doesn't end up all over social media or, much worse, somehow getting back to Coach Fox.

I genuinely try to, but it's the most difficult thing I've ever tried to do.

I literally can't tear my eyes away from her.

She's too damn beautiful.

I'm absurdly captivated as she dips her paintbrush and touches it to her canvas, concentrating on her work between loaded glares.

This gives me a chance to watch her.

Her golden skin has a dewy freshness to it that makes my chest ache.

The fitted pink sweater hugs her body, showing off the feminine curves that are quite literally blowing my mind.

I'm in love with the shape of her. And the colors. The green of her eyes and the pink of her lips. The whiteness of her teeth. As she concentrates, she loses some of that feisty anger. She forgets about how I shouldn't be here and instead hones in on painting me. She can't help herself. She's like me, when I'm playing football. She's in her zone and I love this.

Every now and then she remembers and our eyes meet. The light flush returns to her face.

An entire conversation passes between us.

Don't stare at me, Elias.

I have to.

You can't.

I know. But I am. I'm so damn hooked.

You'll get us both into trouble.

I'm already in trouble. I don't care about trouble.

You should. You absolutely should.

Trouble has a different meaning to me now, angel. I can handle trouble as long as you're a part of it.

Her lips are a shade of pink that reminds me of cotton candy at a fair on a Fourth of July weekend that stays with you for life. A perfect day. They're full and naturally plump. Bee-stung. Lightly puffy and ludicrously appealing. I want to lick them so badly it hurts.

So I concentrate on that pain. I let it dig into me, like a thirst I can't quench until I taste her.

How long can I hold out?

How far will I go to have her?

All the fucking way.

How much will I have to lose to make her mine?

10

Zara

Staring at Elias O'Shea for forty-five minutes straight is forty-five minutes too many. The guy is like some kind of drug, capable of melting hearts and panties merely by emitting his super-powered pheromones—or whatever they're called. All I know is that there's no way in hell a mortal girl like me could resist such a thing as whatever it was that just stormed into my art class.

And it still doesn't answer the question as to what he's doing here in the first place.

The class ends and Gwen goes over to talk to Elias. I take my opportunity, packing my bag and making a run for it.

My next class doesn't start until noon so I head for the stairs, trying to be as inconspicuous as possible as people are milling around, packing up their stuff, having hushed conversations about—of course—Elias O'Shea.

The name is one I've heard too often over the past few days.

I don't want to see him, talk to him or be anywhere near him. He's pure Kryptonite and it's too much. My dad would kill me. More importantly, the entire university and possibly the entire country would hate me because *I* was the reason the beautiful and talented star quarterback got kicked off the team.

And here I go again, thinking that Elias is here for me.

Why would he be? I'm a nobody. A freshman. An introvert with an art obsession.

I don't look back.

I run up the stairs, reaching my studio and unlocking it with the little fob I've hooked to my backpack. Once I'm inside, I close the door, leaning up against it.

Thank you thank you thank you. For this room and this door that locks.

It's something I do.

It was some lady I didn't even know very well, some acquaintance of my mother's at the funeral. She was a seasoned New Yorker, you could just tell by the stylish cut of her black clothes that you'd never find anywhere else, by the world-weariness that's cooler than you'll ever be, by the raspy voice of a nicotine habit she still hadn't quite kicked, by the old-soul eyes. I'm sure she was an art person, maybe a curator at the Met who'd lived on the upper east side for forty years, who knows. She looked me straight in the eye and she said, *it won't make any sense to you today, or maybe even a year from now. But one day it will. Remember this word: gratitude. If you practice gratitude, for having her, for all the years the two of you spent together and for all the memories you shared, she'll feel closer to you. Gratitude is powerful. All you have to do is say thank you three times in a row and you'll have all the fortune the universe can possibly provide. It's as simple as that.*

It was an intense little speech on a very heavy day in the pouring rain and it definitely stuck with me.

Ever since then, I do it all the time. At least a few times a day, it helps in a thousand little ways. I find some random thing that I can appreciate and I say it. *Thank you thank you thank you.*

Sometimes it's for something as mundane as the beauty of a patch of dappled sunlight in the late afternoon. Or the sound of my dad's gruff laughter when I hadn't heard it for a while. Or the feel of my favorite paintbrush in my hand and the comforting glide of smooth paint on rough-textured canvas.

For a while, the daily barrage of grief, shock and anger really were more than I could bear. But it's been a long time since that day.

I've found that there's such a thing as empathy fatigue.

I have empathy fatigue. For *myself.* There's a limit and I reached it a long time ago.

But I still use that little mantra when I'm feeling closer to the edge than I want to be.

So I find something to be thankful for.

My brand new studio. It's filled with early September light. It's got a window seat with bright cushions that's big enough to sleep on if I want to. Which I will when I want to work late into the night. It's a little creative haven and has an awesome view—*BANG BANG BANG.*

It's more of a pounding than a knocking and it startles me.

Go away, I'm thinking. *I need time.* I'm not used to this extroverted lifestyle of spending all my time with a lot of people.

I hope it's not Christopher. I'm annoyed that he practically dissed my painting. The whole *"Matisse, obviously"* comment pissed me off. Okay, yes, it's sort of true, but it's not like his paintings are all that freaking original either.

I know it's not Christopher. Or Gwen. Or Maeve, even though I feel like we're destined to become friends.

I open the door.

Why is he playing with fire? It doesn't make any sense.

I sigh deeply, like this was inevitable, and take a step back from the doorway, opening it for him. I knew he'd come.

Elias O'Shea walks into the small space and I don't know why I close the door behind him but I do. Something about us is already linked. I guess I was hoping he'd run away from it and do the things common sense would tell him to do.

He hasn't. Obviously. Because here he is.

All 6'4" of more perfection than anyone has any right to own.

I allow myself a few seconds of taking it all in. The height of him and the sheer amount of space he takes up.

He's got *presence*. The kind that insists you notice it. The wide, sculpted shoulders. The muscular chest. The thick dark hair with its ridiculously appealing wave to it that your fingers crave to just bury themselves in. I wonder how many women have run their hands through that hair.

The dark blue of his eyes—*okay, would you stop staring? You're making it obvious.*

So I drag my gaze away from him and walk over to the window seat, where I sit in a ray of sunshine.

Thank you thank you thank you.

Not for *him*. For the sun. For burning up its helium or whatever and sending its warmth in my direction. "Do you mind telling me what you're doing here?"

"Thanks for the warm welcome." He's peaceful about it though, like he's got all the time in the world for this and I'm entertaining him with my insolence. He checks out the small space unhurriedly. The art supplies I spent time yesterday setting up. Then his eyes meet mine. "I think you know what I'm doing here."

"Honestly, I don't. And don't say you're channeling your inner artist." I don't want to sound rude, not at all. But I need some kind of barrier between us and I already feel it crumbling. He's the human equivalent of a super-strength magnet, pulling at all the cravings I never knew I had until now. "We both know that's something you made up."

"I thought of it last night when we were talking at the party," he admits. "I couldn't stand the thought of not knowing when I might see you again. This way, I can see you whenever I want to."

"This class is three mornings a week," I point out.

"Gwen gave me my own studio. It happens to be right across the hall from yours."

I glare at him and it's basically like trying to stare at a superhero. You can't do it, is what I'm finding, because they can match your stare with beams of intensity that are far more powerful than the courage you try your best to project but don't always succeed. "Why, Elias?"

He comes over, taking all the time in the world, and leans a burly shoulder against the frame of the window seat. "Because. The first time I saw you I couldn't believe you were real. I still can't."

"Stop doing that."

"Doing what?"

"Saying the nicest things anyone's ever said to me."

"It's true."

"But what does it even mean?"

"It means you're perfect."

I can feel my eyes narrow for a second. "Can you stop that, please? I'm definitely not perfect. Not even close. I'm also a freshman who happens to be your football coach's daughter, remember? It's a very bad idea for you to even be here right now."

"I know." No remorse though. Not even a hint of it.

"You *know*? Then why are you here?"

"Because I've been…" He pauses for a second, like he's not sure how to explain himself. "I've been looking for you for a long time. I was starting to think I wouldn't find you."

"How can you have been looking for me, Elias? It doesn't make any sense. I only got here a few days ago."

"Exactly."

"Exactly?"

"I've been looking for you since before you even arrived."

Here he goes again, speaking in riddles, acting like this whole forbidden thing between us is either pre-destined or a joke, I can't quite figure out which.

"I've been tormented. *Tormented*," he says again, for emphasis. "Ask Gabriel if you don't believe me. I was all fucked up about it."

"About what?"

"Thinking you didn't exist. Then I looked up and there you were."

God, he's infuriating. "There I *was*? You mean when I was going to see my dad at the stadium?"

"Yes. You looked so fucking beautiful I couldn't believe it. All the light in that stadium landed on you, like you were some kind of mythical creature created just for me. You can't expect me to just ignore that. Especially since I've been waiting for you to show up for so long."

I'm not sure what to do with this. I mean, yes, it's nice. It's almost heartbreakingly flattering. I've never really thought of myself as beautiful before. In fact I haven't spent a lot of time worrying about or even thinking about my looks, to be honest. I'm the kind of introvert that basically can't do social media because the thought of putting my photo all over the internet for other people's approval makes me cringe and practically have a panic attack. Which isn't exactly a recipe for creating a gigantic platform (possibly part of the reason I haven't been picked up by a gallery, because they expect that of artists these days). But to hear it gushed like that, from *him* of all people…"Elias—"

I freeze when he takes a loose strand of my hair between two fingers, twirling a ringlet around one of them. "Zara."

I can smell his scent and it should be illegal to smell so good. Like fresh air, leather, sunshine and pure male energy. "Yeah?"

"Do you ever check your messages?"

"Um…"

"I sent you some. You didn't answer them."

"Oh. I don't really go on my phone that much." I might be the one person on the planet who's not addicted to my phone. I sometimes wonder if there's something wrong with me because I don't get the dopamine hits everyone's always going on about. "I don't really go on social media that much because it always seems a little…I don't know. Staged. Fake. I'm not that interested in other people's staging of their own lives. I find it all kind of… boring."

He's watching me, like what I've just said is the most enthralling thing he's ever heard.

"So I've turned off all my notifications except for messages from my sister and my dad."

"Makes sense, if you don't want to be distracted. But you're going to need to add me to the list."

"Elias. No. Seriously. This is crazy. Please. You need to leave now."

"I am. I have another class, then football practice. But I'm going to be back later on tonight and we're going to talk about what we're going to do about this."

"This? What this? There is no *this*. There can't be."

He looks down at me patiently. He's so freaking good-looking and also annoyingly…genuine. "Oh, there can be."

Slowly, I shake my head.

Slowly, he nods, holding my face gently and guiding my movement so I'm nodding too. *God.* He's touching me.

His hands are so warm. So strong and so sure. "If you'd bothered to check your messages you'd know by now that…shit. Don't get mad when I tell you this."

"Why would I get mad?"

"I posted your painting."

"What painting?"

"The one you sent me. The one I sent myself."

"What?"

"Before you panic, I didn't put your name on it or any identifying information at all. I can take it down whenever you want. But I think you might want to leave it up for a while. People are going crazy over it."

"What people?"

"I have a lot of followers."

"What? How many?"

"I don't know. Seven million or something like that."

"Seven *million*?" I try to tone down my panic. "Elias, are you crazy? What if my dad sees it?"

"Is your dad on Instagram?"

"No."

"Does your dad even know what Instagram is?"

He's got a point. "Not really."

"You said you'd never shown him the painting. Even if he did see it—and the odds of that happening are practically non-existent—he wouldn't know it was yours anyway."

"Elias, it's a *self-portrait*. Give me your phone."

His smile is smug, damn him. "It's *abstract*, Zara. It's

not like it's photo-realism or anything. You said you haven't shown him or anyone else many of your paintings at all and that you keep them hidden away. You and I both know your dad is so distracted most of the time by his job, the very last thing he's going to be doing is scrolling on Instagram. Even if he did he wouldn't know the painting was yours."

He's right, but I'm hardly going to admit that to him. "It doesn't matter, Elias."

"Of course it matters. You might not find it *boring* that it already has two hundred thousand likes," he says.

"Two hundred *thousand?*"

"People are asking who the artist is. They want to know if it's for sale. They're making offers. There's a bidding war." One of his eyebrows lifts—and it's not fair that he's so freaking beautiful. "What if the Sea Glass sees it? Isn't this the kind of exposure you want?"

"Take it down," I insist.

Of course he's bossy about it. "I think we should leave it up there at least until tonight. I'll be back here later on and we can take it down then, if you still want to."

I watch him for a few seconds, trying not to be distracted from the disturbing news he's giving me by how gorgeous he is. Or how big. Or how his brawny shoulders and buff chest strain against the thick cotton of his t-shirt. He must have left his jacket downstairs.

"You wouldn't be sending your work out if you didn't want to get noticed, Zara. But you're never going to get noticed if you lock all your paintings away in your attic and refuse to show anyone."

"It's not really your business," I grumble churlishly.

"Here." He pulls his phone out of his pocket and unlocks the screen, taking a look before holding it out to me. "It's up to four hundred thousand likes. Delete it if you want. But first, look at some of these comments."

I take his phone and—wow, he's right. 412,327 likes. As I watch, the number continues to climb at a dizzying pace.

I can't help noticing not just the comments about the art.

Elias, I want to have your babies! Please call me on 7728441234!!!

Elias, I love you so much!

Please follow me, Elias. You're the hottest football player everrrr!!!!

Marry me, Elias xxxx

There are hundreds of them. But there are other comments too.

Wow, this painting is amazing!

Who's the artist? Is it for sale?

I'll pay $1000 for this painting

$2000

This is worth way more than that. I'll bid $10K

Tell us who painted this!

I NEED THIS PAINTING

I'm an art curator in Chicago and I'd like to reach out to this artist. Please give us more info

$40K

$50K

50K?

It's now up to more than 450,000 likes.

Holy shit.

My painting is going viral.

11

ELIAS

The afternoon sun throws long shadows across the football field. I'm so in my element I might as well have been born out of this green grass and this blue September sky. These chalked lines and this singular concentration that can only be found here, inside the pocket. Everything about my life has led me to this place. This play. This season. It will define my entire future and I'm here for it.

But the *future* suddenly feels sparked with so much more than just football, the championship, the draft, the career, the success. All the things that have hung over my head for as long as I can remember. All the things I've been living for, breathing for, planning for and working toward. Now is my moment to realize them. What I wasn't expecting was for all those things to take on a completely different shape since the second I saw her.

They're all for her.

Somehow, the little freshman nymphette with the sparked eyes and the shy smile has taken over my entire outlook. She fucking *owns* it, just like that. I don't know how she swanned into my life, batted her sweeping eyelashes at me once and managed to hook herself deep into my beating heart.

It's like she's watching me from my peripheral vision, a soft, dizzying distraction in this world of aggression and competition.

I make the pass and the ball soars, the spiral cutting a decisive path through the air. It lands securely in Gabriel's arms as he sprints toward the end zone, using a perfect pass to finish a perfect play.

Jake jogs over to me. "Play like that on Saturday and you'll be able to name your price, Chief. You're on fire, man."

He's not wrong. Fire doesn't even begin to describe what's happening to me. My new obsession is forging in my blood, fine-tuning my focus into something that feels almost supernatural.

I want to win for her.

"Damn, O'Shea," West chimes in. "That art class really must be inspiring you."

Gabriel lobs the ball in my direction as he makes his way back this way.

Reflexively, I catch it. "Careful, Hawkins, my aim is exceptionally good."

"He's just expanding his playbook, boys," Jake jokes.

"Some of us use words, some use art, and some, like West, use tacos."

"Hey," West protests, "never underestimate the seductive power of a good taco."

Coach's whistle blows, signaling the end of practice, and I feel the weight of his gaze even before he dismisses the others and calls me over. His arms are crossed over his chest and he contemplates me as I walk up to him, pulling off my helmet. I'm at least a head taller than he is but the guy has a staunchness to him I'm very familiar with. I don't want to piss off my coach and I wish I didn't have to.

He takes his time, waiting until the others wander off toward the locker room. "I've been informed you've added another class to your schedule. A freshman art class. What the hell for, O'Shea? You've got more important things to be concentrating on right now."

"I'm only auditing the class, Coach." I've already planned how this conversation might go. I've prepared my reply. "I thought, since it's my last chance, I'd take the opportunity to broaden my horizons. My grandmother once told me I had a painter's soul. I wasn't sure what she meant by that at the time, so I wanted to see if it was true." It sounds cheesy as fuck, and borderline disrespectful. So I add, "She was my mother's mother. She used to visit every summer so she could get to know me since she lived in Oregon. We'd spend two whole weeks doing paint by numbers. It was our thing." It happens to be true, even if it's not the reason I'm taking the art class.

He glowers up at me, not mentioning Zara, even though he's bound to know she's in the class, like he's afraid that stating that fact out loud might somehow confirm his worst suspicions. "It's in your best interests to drop the class, Elias. Immediately."

"It's purely for self-enrichment and academic exploration, sir. I'll only go when it doesn't interfere with my football schedule."

More glaring. But his tone is laced with fatherly advice under his steely delivery. "You're smart, Elias. And you're on the cusp of greatness. My suggestion to you, as NFL scouts watch your every move between now and January, when we both know you'll be invited to the Combine if you continue to play like you're playing, is to keep your eye on the ball. Whatever game you're playing, you need to rethink your strategy and pronto."

"I'm not playing any other game besides football, Coach." It's true. I have no intention of playing games with Zara Fox. I'm a hundred percent serious about getting her to fall in love with me. But I'm not about to tell that to her father. Not yet, at least.

"I think we also both know that scouts are rarely interested in players whose coaches have issues with them," he tells me. "My feedback plays into their decisions, as you're well-aware. If any information comes across as negative, then more often than not those players are removed from the value boards. Am I making myself clear enough?"

"Crystal, Coach."

It's a threat, obviously, but there's a silent plea behind it. He needs me. This team has chemistry and I'm the driver, the play-maker, the commander who brings it all together. We both know that. There's no way in hell this team has a shot at the playoffs if I'm not here to guide us. "Good. Then I don't want to hear any more about the art class. If you've got that much time on your hands you can schedule an extra session with the training team."

I don't confirm or deny. Okay, so I won't go to the class. But I still have access to the studio. Which is directly across the hall from Zara's. *Which is where I'm headed directly after practice.*

I know I'm playing with fire. I don't *want* to fucking play with fire. But I'm completely consumed by the hold she has over me. I can feel the pull of her even now, like a sweet, sassy lure that's already hooked itself savagely into my deepest desires.

"See you tomorrow, Coach."

He gives me the side eye as I walk away. I salute him, to keep the tone light. He almost smiles, shaking his head.

As soon as I reach the locker room, I hit the shower and get dressed.

Then the inquisition begins.

"He's already on your trail, boy-o." West claps a hand

on my shoulder. "Don't you dare get kicked off this team."

"I don't plan to."

"I'm making tacos for everyone tonight. It's the best cure for anything that ails you."

"There's only one cure for what ails me, Westie."

"If it involves your neglected manhood getting anywhere near the—"

"Shut the fuck up, West." Gabriel's low warning silences a grinning West. Mitch and a couple other guys are still changing nearby.

"Tacos *again*?" Jake complains, deftly changing the subject. "Dude, you need to learn another recipe."

"You're coming back with us, right, Elias?" Gabe slings his bag over his shoulder.

"I've…got other plans tonight."

They're not happy with me, of course. The three of them try to talk me out of it on our way out, but there's no way I can stay away from the little green-eyed angel. The only assurance I can give them is that I'll be as careful as I can.

It's dark by the time I make my way to the art building. I let myself in and take the stairs by threes.

The door of her studio is closed but the sliver of light underneath it tells me she's here. My heart hammers in my chest.

I knock, not so loudly this time.

She opens the door and—*holy fuck*—I'm so far gone

already I feel half-devastated by the risk I'm already resolved to take and half-feral with a need I've never experienced before.

"Elias?" Again that question we both know the answer to.

Why are you here?

Because I can't stay away.

She feels it too, I can see it in her eyes as the dark pupils leave only thin rims of bright green. Her gaze drops to my mouth. She licks her pink lips.

"Zara, we need to talk." In fact we need to do much more than talk, but it's a start.

I have everything to lose. But for Zara Fox, I'm willing to play the most dangerous game of my life.

12

Zara

ONCE AGAIN, against my better judgement, I let him in.

Elias walks in and closes the door behind him, brushing past me like a huge bear in the small space. Once again he takes his position on the window seat, where he pulls a small, dog-eared notebook out of his pocket. But he doesn't open it. All his attention is on me.

He's relaxed, even if his cocky male perfection is so deeply ingrained in him, he might not even be aware of it. He wears it like a second skin. He's not showy, but this off-hand self-assurance is one of the most pronounced things about him. That, and the formidable size. The graceful way he moves. The powerful physicality of him.

Not to mention the bluest eyes I've ever seen, ringed by that thicket of black lashes that blink at me.

Wow, he's gorgeous.

Elias O'Shea emits a kind of sparked, charismatic

energy that has the ability to leech into me like it's more than just atoms and ions or whatever. It feels substantial and connective, feeding me a weird kind of comfort and also a low, electrifying thrill.

With Elias in my small studio, I become much more aware of my own body. A lightly-tingly physical excitement takes me off guard. It centers in the tips of my nipples…and much lower. *There. Where I've touched myself late at night, to see what would happen.*

Not much did. But it is now. Radiating little pulses are warming…my *pussy*, as my sister always calls it.

Whoa.

It's true that in those few times I've…explored, I never got to the point of figuring out what all the fuss is about. Hannah once offered to lend me her—"trusty" she even called it—vibrator to ease whatever tension I was having at the time.

The conversation still lives rent free in my head.

First of all, Han, I'm not using your vibrator. That's just gross. Second of all, I wouldn't even know how.

Well, Zee, maybe it's time you learned. It's not that hard. And it's the best kind of stress relief there is.

I don't need stress release.

Bullshit. Everyone does. I'm talking about the orgasmic variety of stress release, not the hide-away-in-your-attic-morosely-as-you-paint-your-angst-onto-every-canvas-you-can-get-your-hands-on kind of stress release.

Whatever.

It would do you a world of good, Zee. You need it. I'll buy you your own vibrator if you want me to.

Would you stop? I'll get my own.

You should. Trust me, you won't regret it.

I never got around to buying my own but I secretly… experimented. Nothing really happened. I thought about following my sister's advice. But where does a person even buy something like that? The thought of ordering one online and having my dad sign for the package made me cringe. So I haven't ever…*gotten myself off.*

And all of a sudden I want to know what it feels like.

Elias's presence is literally lighting my body up. I'm suddenly hyper-aware of all my basest urges.

I got an electric shock once, when I was nine years old. I knocked over an old lamp and the wires were exposed. I tried to put it back together before anyone noticed I'd broken it, accidentally touching the naked wires. My sister heard my scream. She also heard the sizzle of the jolt as it knocked me several feet across the room.

Being around Elias O'Shea feels like that. Like there's a buzzing electric current swirling through me that's attached to him. It feels like it's entwining itself around us both.

I can feel it inside me. Where I once put my fingers.

Elias shrugs off his jacket. He's wearing a blue shirt and a pair of jeans that fit him the way hot guys' jeans fit. Fascinatingly, because men are built so differently and so *masculinely* it sometimes has the power to take you off guard. He looks gorgeous and all-American, like an Abercrombie ad, with his white teeth, his suntan and his colorful eyes.

Is it warm in here?

My studio is a little sun trap for the late afternoon sun. I went back to my room to change after lunch because I knew I'd be working late and I figured I might as well be comfortable. All I'm wearing is a flouncy little mini-skirt and a pink tank top. I took off the tights and hoodie I was wearing earlier because I was getting too hot.

And I'm aware right now that I'm not wearing much. But it can't be helped. If he's going to barge in on me mid-creative-flow, that's a risk he's going to take.

His thick dark hair flicks against the back of his neck, which is strong-looking, corded and brown. His hair is longer than I might expect from a quarterback, I'm not sure why. His arms are gently muscled, his shirt clinging to the sculpted shape of his shoulders and the hard contours of his chest.

I remember something my dad was talking about to some of his assistants once, that most quarterbacks don't bench press. Something about how the increased tone in pectoral muscles can cause an internally rotated shoulder, which doesn't allow for a wide enough range of motion. A quarterback's shoulders need to be pliable. In other words, they can't be overly pumped-up.

It's true he doesn't have the physique of a gym junkie. He's tall and strong. Lean and perfectly proportioned, a living, breathing artistic masterpiece.

It's strange that his brute, masculine power excites some deeply-buried feminine instinct in me. His hotness is extreme and romantic, go figure.

"How was practice?" I ask, just to break the bubble of intensity we're locked inside of. I pick up a paintbrush. "Are you ready for Saturday?"

"We're ready. But Coach gave me some shit about my new interest in art."

Our eyes meet. *Yikes.* My dad knows Elias came to my class.

I wonder if I should ask him to leave. I *really* don't want Elias to get kicked off the football team because of me. "What did you say?"

Despite the danger, we seem to have a silent agreement that we're somehow going with this…whatever *this* is. I don't think either one of us can resist how good it feels just to spend time together and to explore this sparked promise that's gaining momentum. "I sort of agreed not to go to the class anymore. But I've got my studio, even though I'm only auditing the class."

"Have you even been inside your studio yet?"

To this he smiles. Not a full smile, just a playful half-smile that touches his eyes. Butterflies erupt inside my stomach. *God.* "No," he says. "I like this one better."

I nod toward the notebook he's holding. "What's that?"

"My playbook. I have to live, sleep and breathe this thing before Saturday. I can't make any mistakes."

"Sounds like you hardly ever do."

"I do, believe me."

"Have you always played football?"

"Yeah. For as long as I can remember. In fact one of my first memories is catching the toy football my dad threw to me. I was three, maybe. My dad was a football player when he was younger. He's basically a lifelong fanatic. My first love was baseball though. I played both when I was a kid, through junior high. But then when I became the starting quarterback as a freshman in high school, my dad wanted me to focus exclusively on football."

"Sounds like we've both spent a lot of our lives making sure our dads were happy."

It's a few seconds before he answers. "Maybe it's time for us both to make sure we're making ourselves happy too."

"Maybe it is." I make a point of not being completely starstruck by how freaking gorgeous he is in the fading light as the sun starts to set outside the window. The sky is lit with shades of red and orange, like it's doing its best to highlight his magnificence.

I can admit that Elias O'Shea and I somehow seem to

click. Nothing about this is awkward or weird. The small silences feel comfortable. He's easy to be with and I find myself enjoying his company. Which is sort of a new feeling for me. I never really made friends all that easily, not in high school at least.

But something about his presence feels like—and I don't want to use this word lightly because it feels too soon and too strong but it's the feeling that comes to mind: *Elias O'Shea feels like home.* Except that I don't know how he could. I hardly know him.

Then again, I've been hearing about his stardom and tactical prowess for three solid years. "I actually know a lot more about you than you'd think," I admit, trying to keep this light as I squeeze some blue onto my palette and dab some onto my painting.

He's doing that thing again where he watches me like I'm the most compelling person he's ever met. "Yeah?"

"I never thought I was paying close attention when the football coaches hung out at my house, talking about the plays and the players non-stop. But I guess I picked up more than I thought."

"Like what?"

"I know that your passing style is unique. You sometimes lob the ball instead of throwing it. You're creative. You take risks that pay off and it's hard to predict what moves you're going to make."

"You *were* listening." Like this pleases him. "My

passing style is unique because I've played so much base-ball, at least that's what the analysts say. And the critics. I've been told I sometimes throw the ball almost like I'm throwing a baseball. That's why I can nail the shorter passes just as well as the longer ones. You're right that it's hard for the other team to predict what I'm going to do. So we design our plays with that in mind. We mix it up."

"Do you love playing football?"

He thinks about this for a few seconds, as though he wasn't expecting the question. "Yeah. I guess so. It's been so much a part of my life for so long, it's hard to think about doing anything else. My brain must be shaped like a football at this point."

I steal a glance at him, resisting the urge to gaze at his outrageous hotness sort of dreamily before returning to my painting.

"I got you a box for Saturday," he tells me.

This information causes me to look up, and I smear the blue further than I meant to. "Oh. I don't usually—"

"I need you there."

I pause, meeting his eyes levelly. "Why would you need me there?"

"I'll play better if you're watching me."

"Why?"

"Because."

I need more. "Because isn't a reason. Tell me why."

He leans his head against the wall of the window seat,

folding his burly arms across his buff chest as he props his long legs against the opposite side of the window seat. "Because you're my dream girl. If I know you're watching, I'll play out of my skin."

Okay, wow. "Please," I scoff, but it breaks my heart a little, that he's so beautiful and also that he's got a knack for saying the nicest things to me that anyone has ever said. "How can I be your dream girl? You met me yesterday. You have no idea what I'm even like. What if I'm secretly a psycho? What if we have nothing in common?" I'm teasing him—I think. This is new territory for me.

"I'm pretty good at reading people." He's relaxed with that edge of playful charm that's—as if the rest of the package wasn't enough—hypnotically alluring. "I can tell you're not a psycho."

"How?"

"You're too gorgeous to be a psycho."

It's hard not to melt under all this sweet talk. "Psychos can be gorgeous."

"Your beauty is half physical and half spiritual. I can just tell. That sparked light in your eyes makes you the exact opposite of a psycho. It's the light of a creative genius who's basically perfect in every possible way."

God. I almost laugh. "Would you stop?"

"Stop what?" All innocently.

"Stop telling me I'm perfect."

"But you are. I mean, *look* at you."

This is getting out of hand. If I don't do something—like protest or kick him out—I might end up falling for him before I can stop myself. "You might be surprised by how strange I am. I'm an awkward introvert, a hermit and a person who avoids the spotlight at all costs. Not like you, the superstar. We're complete opposites."

"You're not strange, Zara. You're sad. You've suffered."

God. He just nailed all my vulnerabilities and summed up years of my life in one off-hand comment. "We've all suffered. I definitely don't have a monopoly on grief."

"You're going to be okay. You've got me now."

There's a sting behind my eyes that I haven't felt for a long time, since the day I stopped crying after basically crying myself out. I don't even trust myself to reply to that. He just beat his own record at saying the nicest thing anyone's ever said to me.

His eyes flash a little at my silence, like he's tuning in to deeper levels of me, protectively. "You can treat college as a new beginning. You're going to be a huge success, you'll see. And as for having things in common, we have tons in common."

"Like what?"

"We've both grown up around football. We're both close to our dads—too close, maybe, and it's cost us in some ways. We've given up certain things about ourselves to make sure they're okay."

I shrug a little, wetting a sponge and trying to concentrate on fixing my mistake. I'm hiding it but he's killing me with his super-powered perceptiveness that's so accurate he's stirring up emotions that I'd buried, along with new ones too. "My dad warned me about people like you." I start out meaning it as a joke, but by the time I get to the end of the sentence, it doesn't really come out that way.

"But not me specifically."

"His warning definitely included you."

He's not fazed in the least. "It might have. Before."

"Before what?"

"Before I knew you were real."

I sigh more heavily than I mean to, taking a minute. "So…" I have to ask it. "You don't play both fields, then?"

His tongue presses down on his bottom lip as he contemplates me. "I used to. I spent all of high school and the first three years of college playing both fields. But then I realized something."

Okay, I'll bite. "What did you realize?"

"One day I woke up and I was just…over it. Nothing meant anything anymore. All I was doing was making myself feel miserable. Depressed. Lonely as fuck. Because none of them were the one I was looking for."

And you are.

It's hanging in the air between us with all its surreal outlandishness.

But I'm not quite ready to let it touch me. It's too new.

Too unbelievable. Too bright with possibilities that might kill me with both pleasure and pain, probably at the same time. "That's tough."

He smiles at my response. "I know what you're thinking."

"What am I thinking?"

"That I can't know already. That I'm crazy. That I'm telling you what you want to hear."

"I do think you're crazy. And I don't think you can know already. I'm not even sure what it is you think…you *know*."

"I knew the second I saw you."

I glance over at him, then lightly roll my eyes. "What did you know?"

He's all masculine lines and vivid colors, with his eyes almost violet against the sunset. I kind of love that he's got layers. There's a deepness to him, but it's spliced by a playful sense of humor that's melting all my inhibitions. "That you were the most beautiful girl I've ever seen. Ever. Anywhere."

This stops me for a few seconds. "So it's…the way I look?" I wish I hadn't said that. Now I feel awkward. I'm a girl who spends most of my time in overalls and sneakers, hair pulled up, no make-up, lost in my own headspace of art swirls and junglescapes. It's true I've hidden away for a lot of the past few years, so I haven't had much exposure to this kind of thing. But I never thought "the way I look" is something that would stop a guy in his tracks, especially a guy as hot as this one.

He's grinning at me and I'm in awe again, that anyone can be *this* good-looking. This kind of bone structure should be illegal. "That's part of it," he confirms, his voice husked with both amusement and sincerity. "You're a jaw-dropping, heart-stopping kind of beautiful. But that's not the only reason. It's the way you move. Like your soul is dancing. And the way you blink your eyelashes at me. Underneath your shyness there's this fun, fiery little wildcat I want to get to know. I can tell we'll make each other happy, which isn't something I've ever even thought about before. But there it was. And the shape of your mouth is just…perfection, that's the only way to describe it. And the colors of you. Your pink lips and your eyes with all these different shades of bright green. And the way the sun catches the gold of the curls at the ends of your hair. Your cute, gorgeous angel's face just about killed me the first time I saw it. The sound of your voice basically reached inside my chest and grabbed my heart the first time I heard it. And don't even get me started on the rest of you."

Just…wow. "All this…within the first ten minutes of meeting me?"

"It was more like ten seconds."

I'd almost say he was fucking with me if he wasn't so damn sincere about it. "Wow."

"I knew right then that we're destined to be together."

I'm almost glaring, but then I huff a light laugh. This hot, buff Adonis is too much. I almost feel tempted to pinch myself. No one can be *this* gorgeous and this…stubborn—in a completely random direction that seems to imply that me and the superstar quarterback are somehow soul mates. "I think it's too early to know anything along those lines, Mr. Blue-Eyes Elias O'Shea."

"No you don't." That slow grin could melt the panties off a nun. And this is coming from someone whose panties have never melted before. I've actually never met a nun either. "You can feel it too. I can see that." Hardly pausing, he adds, "Isla and your other two friends have already agreed to come to the game, by the way. Fully catered. Right on the fifty yard line. Best seats in the house."

We both know Isla will drag me along to that box with her, kicking and screaming if she has to. "It's a nice offer, thank you. I'll see."

Low laughter warms his husky voice and the sound touches the triangle of points he seems to have secret access to. *Damn it.* My nipples are almost painfully taut and sensitive. I know they'll be clearly visible in my skimpy top. And I can almost hear my sister's voice in my head. For some reason the nail filing emoji is right there alongside it.

Finally, girl!! For the first time in your life you're experiencing the effects of a seriously hot beefcake who's obviously interested in getting you naked and cashing in your V-card for you exceptionally thoroughly, possibly right here and now. Let him give you your first orgasm, Zee. Find out if he feels as good as he looks! No one else has to know.

I mentally close the door on my sister's tirade, but I'm flustered. I can feel the blush warming my cheeks. *And the light trickle of moisture on the high skin of my thigh.* My short skirt and the minuscule G-string I'm wearing under it don't feel like enough at this point.

"What are you painting?" he asks.

"A panther."

"A panther?"

"Yes. A black panther. Rousseau is my second-favorite artist. I have a whole series of jungle-themed paintings. They're some of my favorites."

He gets up and walks over to where I'm standing to get a better look at the painting. Okay, he really is…tall. And sort of…amazingly…*built.*

Holy hell.

There's a knowing heat in his blue eyes. A person could really get lost in those eyes if they let themselves. "You painted a wildcat."

I didn't even realize it until now. My subconscious painted *him.* He's literally a Wildcat. He definitely has the vibe of a jungle cat, with his thick-silk, off-black hair and his vivid, magnetic eyes. It's there in the way he moves. The dark, animal grace and the coiled strength.

He's standing too close to me and I can smell that scent of him, of fresh air and woodsmoke. He smells like full sun on a fall day. And something else. Some elusive man-scent that's ludicrously appealing.

Instinctively, without even meaning to, I barely lean in, wanting—*needing*—more of it.

He notices. And he takes this as his cue.

Elias's hand eases around the nape of my neck. The roughness and warmth of it raise all the tiny hairs on my body. "You're so damn pretty," he whispers with hushed awe.

I feel his potency like a drug, slowly spreading its warmth like honey, wetting me and turning me on like nothing I've ever known. He's so tempting, so big and so freaking *male*. I don't know how he can do it so easily, but he's stoking every primal urge I didn't even know I possessed. I can feel them all throbbing and converging intimately, driving me crazy.

He coils his finger around a loose ringlet that's escaped the messy bun I pulled my hair into hours ago. He pulls the tie loose so my hair spills down over my shoulders in unruly waves. "You're so much more beautiful than my lame imagination could have dreamed up. You're seriously blowing my mind right now."

I don't know about destiny or soul mates. What I do know is that…I want him to kiss me. So badly. That scent of him is deliciously enticing. All I want in this moment is more of it.

Elias leans closer, brushing his lips against mine.

I gasp lightly, feeling so much.

The truth is, I've never kissed anyone before. There was the spin the bottle incident at a party I went to in ninth grade, before things in my life badly imploded. It was some boy I barely knew. I can't even remember his name. The bottle pointed to me and we went into the closet and his lips landed awkwardly on my chin for a split second—not even on my lips—and that was it. It was slightly wet, a little bit gross and the whole thing convinced me that I had no idea how to kiss and wasn't good at it.

This kiss is something else altogether.

It's like striking a match.

Elias eases my mouth open, parting my lips with his tongue. The taste of him, like his scent, is crazily, insanely irresistible. I'm a little shocked by my response to him. His tongue slides over mine, feeding a sweet surge of lust into my entire body like a heady flood. I open to him willingly, needing more.

"Fuck, Zara," he groans. "You taste so fucking good. You're mine. You have to be. You can't just show up like this and not give me everything. I can't take how perfect you are."

This feels bigger than us, like the universe is storming around us, pulling us together through cosmic forces we're powerless to resist.

His kiss turns wilder, more demanding and aggressive than I know what to do with. Elias's iron-strong hands pull me against the dizzying hardness of his body. I've never met anyone so *hard*—everywhere—as this big, lusty quarterback.

My urges uncoil, opening to him. I reach up to weave my fingers through his thick hair. It's the only soft thing about him. He makes a low, tortured sound, lifting me and carrying me over to the window seat.

"Elias," I whisper. I don't know if I'm trying to slow this down or if I'm pleading for more.

"You're mine to take care of now. Let me make you feel good. I'm going to give you everything you've ever wanted. All of it. The lust and the love and the happy ever after. Everything. We'll get to know each other along the way."

Goddamn him.

The level of intensity screams at me to be careful.

He's off-limits. And totally in tune with the thoughts whirring through my head right now, it seems. "When you spend as much time as I have looking for the girl of your dreams and you think maybe you'll never find her and it keeps you up at night and messes with your game, and then she walks into your life one random day when you're least expecting her and her cute, hot, sweet beauty hits you like a fucking freight train at full speed, trust me, you *know* and you're going to give it every damn thing you've got."

"This is *crazy*," I whisper, but it doesn't sound like a protest.

He lowers us onto the window seat, placing me on his

lap so I have to straddle him. One of his hands sinks into the hair at the nape of my neck, gripping tightly. He gazes into my eyes, challenging me. "Yeah, it is crazy," he murmurs back. "Crazy good. Crazy insane that you walked straight out of my wildest fantasies and into that stadium. And now that you have, angel girl, there's no getting rid of me."

Oh fuck. How am I supposed to resist this guy? "Are you sure you haven't had one too many concussions?"

His low laugh raises goosebumps across my skin. "It's very possible."

He kisses me and I don't have it in me to do anything but fall.

So here I am, making out with Elias O'Shea, half in love with him already while I sit on his lap in this cozy, private little haven. My legs are spread and my wet, softening pussy is pressed up against the *gigantic* ridge inside his jeans. My only barrier between us is a very wet, very almost-non-existent G-string.

Girl, you're breaking Rule Number One! You hardly know him! You have no idea what you're even doing! Are your forgetting you've never even kissed anyone?

The thing is, as Elias O'Shea kisses me hotly and almost worshipfully, gripping me with those strong fingers, I feel like I do know what to do. *I know how to touch my lips to his, like this, and suck gently on his tongue until he groans.*

It's wildly intimate. His free hand slides up my bare thigh, under the hem of my skirt. He palms my ass, growling as he feels bare skin, pulling me harder against his—*freaking huge*—hardness. I moan into his mouth as my body instinctually angles toward him, grinding lightly.

We should stop. It's too fast. It's too much.

Clinging to my last shred of sanity, I break the kiss, practically panting.

Elias blinks at me gently. I can literally see the steely resolve behind his patience that tells me he'll listen to my hesitations but he'll also break through them, with alpha male praise and glittering promises. He licks my top lip. "You like me, little angel." Like he's reminding me. "Kiss me again. As slow and sweet as you want."

I like the way he says that. It makes it sound manageable. It makes me want to do it.

So I do. I lightly hold his face in my hands and I kiss him slowly. Softly. He tastes better than anything ever has.

The kiss turns greedier. Slippery and hot. There's a barely-controlled hunger in him as he grips me.

I don't know if it's the sheer size of him, the hardness of that huge, hard ridge inside his pants that I'm sitting directly on top of, the adrenaline pumping through my veins or the wild curl of pleasure that's starting to build where I'm pressed up against him, but every rational thought disappears.

I don't care how off-limits he is.

He's hot as fuck.

I want him.

He thrusts against me as he presses me more strongly

against him. All I can do is hold on to him and take it. I moan again.

I swear I didn't think this would happen when I let him in here. I thought we might talk for a while, then he'd go home or over to his studio and we'd resist because it's what we're supposed to do.

But now he's nipping at my mouth, licking into me, feeding me his lusty flavor as he kneads my ass against his hardness in a measured, deliberate rhythm. I'm melting into a puddle of pure need.

My legs fall open a little wider as I squirm against him.

"I don't know how to do this small, baby girl. Do you know how fucking gorgeous you are?"

Baby girl.

Are these lines he's feeding me?

Do I care?

It's hard to worry about it either way when a deep, low wave of excruciating pleasure is building exponentially with each press of his hands and his body, threatening to tip me over into some parallel universe that's so full of bliss it's going to change my life.

"I'm breaking every rule, angel, because I fucking *need* you."

My breasts are practically spilling out of my top from our hot, grinding exertion. All I'm wearing under it is a stretchy lace bralette. "I want to see you. I want to suck on you and make you come so hard you see stars. Do you want me?"

I gasp, and he takes this as a yes. It's more than a yes. It's an I'll-die-if-you-don't. Maybe there's something chemical between us, because my craving for him is stronger than anything rational. Elias's fingers pull the neckline down, so my stretchy top frames my breasts, lifting them and squeezing them lightly together.

Holy shit.

I'm reminded then that Elias is much older than me and far more worldly than I am. He's a big, rough super-star who, as successful as he is, has a rebellious side to him. Maybe it's one he hasn't had a lot of opportunity to explore, but I can feel it now.

"*Look* at you," he groans. "You're a fucking goddess. I need to taste you now, my gorgeous girl. Are you ready for me?"

It seems strange to me that I'm already so addicted to him. If he doesn't touch me and feed more of his effect into my quivering, half-naked body, I'll go mad.

"Tell me what you want, Zara."

"*You,*" I manage to moan. "*I want you.*"

"You want me to touch you like this?" He touches a finger to my taut, hyper-sensitive nipple and I'm losing my mind.

He takes my breasts in his huge hands so my nipples are both close to his mouth. He watches my eyes as his breath strikes my skin.

"You want me to suck on these sweet, juicy little nipples?"

My body struggles and arches up to him. I genuinely try to fight my frenzy. I shouldn't *love* how he feels and he looks and how he's about to do things to me I've never, ever done.

"Say it. Tell me what you want."

"*Do it,*" I whisper, and I don't even know who I am. I'm lust-crazed and feral. The anticipation is killing me. I want to cry and tell him to hurry up.

"Are you sure?" He's teasing me, those blue eyes dark with fire.

"*Yes. Please.*"

He touches his tongue to my nipple and I moan. He does it again, licking softly, drawing a circle with his tongue. Playing me. Sucking me deeper into his mouth. Each lusty pull sends a channel of warmth straight to my pussy. As he does this, Elias's thumb finds the wet spot between my legs, gliding over it, drawing a tiny, pressing circle around my clit. At first he does this over the laughably skimpy fabric of my practically-nonexistent panties. But he's getting closer...and closer to direct, slippery contact.

And there he is. His thumb feels so good, teasing my clit, that I'm about to die from the building overload.

Elias's teeth gently *bite* and I'm so close to the crazy edge there are tears in my eyes. He sucks on my other nipple and twirls the slick wetness he left on the first one between his fingers.

He's less gentle now, totally in control. Playing my body like he owns it.

I want him to own it. It's his already. It's all his.

He snaps my G-string, tossing it away. Then Elias easily lifts me, laying me back. "I'm at your mercy, angel. I don't fuck around with consent. But I'm hooked. Just tell me what you want. Or tell me to stop. I'm going to make you come, but only when you're ready. Are you ready for me to eat that sweet little pussy until you scream my name?"

Eat?

Oh my god.

He kisses me again, longer this time, giving me time. Every taste, every stroke of his tongue sends a fresh wave of warmth to my core. He nips at my lips, then his mouth moves to my neck. "Is that a yes, Zara?"

Elias licks the delicate skin below my ear. Every nip of his teeth on my skin sends a dart of pleasure to my pussy, which feels slippery and needy, making me squirm.

"Or a no?"

He's still fully clothed. *"Yes."* God help me. *"Yes."*

"Good girl. Say 'please, Elias. Eat my pussy like the starving maniac you are'."

He pulls off his shirt and—*whoa.* I take a few seconds to just appreciate all that, fascinated by the roughness of him, the broadness of his shoulders, the intricate play of muscle and sinew beneath his bronzed skin. Such a masculine creature, hard and angular. So different to my own pale curves.

Our breathing is heavier now.

He sucks on my nipples and the throb inside me swells. I can feel my soft, slick inner muscles quivering as he kisses his way lower, across my stomach. "Let's find out what you like, little angel girl."

Elias lifts my skirt and I'm already almost coming. I don't even care that he can see me. *All* of me.

"*Holy fuck*. How can anyone be so perfect? *Look* at you, so wet and ready for me."

My sister dragged me along with her to laser hair removal treatments before she left for college, insisting it was a bonding sisterly activity. Hannah's hair is darker than mine and she wanted to be thorough about it. At the time I went along, grateful for the distraction and glad to spend some time with her before she left for California. I sometimes wonder now if we went overboard. I don't have a single hair left on my body that's not on my head.

Elias seems almost crazed at the sight of me. "Zara. Oh fuck, Zara. Hold still, baby girl. You have to let me taste heaven. I'm so fucking hungry. Let me."

He pushes my legs wider with brutal strength, holding me down, dominating me easily. And then his tongue licks into me, circling my clit slowly. He growls something that sounds like "*Mmmm. Fucking yum. Mine.*"

Nothing has ever felt so good. I moan, the sound echoing in the room one I hardly recognize.

Elias laughs softly, sucking my clit into his mouth, feasting with hungry, messy adoration. His rough, careful fingers are insanely intimate, sliding through the moisture. Opening me. Touching me like I've never been touched.

His hot mouth closes around my pulsing nub. He sucks on me as his fingers curl and slide. His mouth and his fingers work together. The pleasure peaks and holds, searing my senses with such an ecstatic overload that I cry his name. Pleading. Digging my fingernails into his skin. The shimmering peak fragments, pleasure and heat surging lushly through my body and soul. I can feel my pussy clenching tightly, spasming and squeezing as he feeds on me.

It lasts a long time. My body goes limp as Elias kisses and licks my pussy, until another deeply pleasurable wave washes through me.

When the bliss slows and I start to return to myself, I feel like a different person.

A very *crazy* person. Who has just broken, smashed and trampled Rule Number One.

Holy hell, Zara. You just let a football player give you your first orgasm. Not just any football player. The best one. The only one.

And it's still happening.

The clenching rush goes on and on.

When I finally come down from all that, Elias rolls onto his side and props up his head with a bent elbow. His mouth is wet with moisture and he looks so smug I can't help but gaze back at him.

"Well, it's official," he comments lazily.

I almost don't want to ask. "What's official?"

"I'm addicted, obsessed and completely lovestruck."

This is not good. This is very, very bad. There are so many things wrong with what we've just done. Including how *fast* it all happened. How fast it's *still* happening.

If it's so wrong, why does it feel so damn good?

I notice then that, somewhere along the line, he unbuttoned his jeans.

Oh.

My.

God.

I mean, no wonder he had to unleash it. It looks downright painful. Hot and engorged and sort of... *insanely* big and hard. The hormone-crazed female in me is shocked and also downright beguiled.

So the star quarterback is killing it in every conceivable category. His cock is so big it's sticking thickly out of his jeans, laying at attention halfway up his washboard abs.

I mean, I'm not *that* naïve. My sister has filled me in on most of the information a girl needs to know. In detail. But nothing really prepares you for the real thing.

The round head is glistening with a slick of wetness.

I really want to taste him.

Hell, I've already broken a long list of rules. I might

as well be thorough about it, since I'm this far into it. Besides, no craving in my life has ever prepared me for what I'm feeling now. Biology is some powerful shit.

I don't just want to taste him, I *need* to. Like the future of humankind depends on it. I guess that's why we're wired the way we are, who knows. I'm hardly going to analyze human sexuality 101 right now. I'm busy.

Elias kisses me and it's the most outrageous thing, to taste *myself* on his lips.

I'm shy but hungry. Once you get a taste of hot alpha male, it's hard to control yourself, go figure. "Can I kiss you?" I whisper.

His blue eyes get dark and he kisses me again before he lays back to let me look at him. And explore him. Giving me full access to bad-girl heaven. "I'm all yours, dirty girl. Kiss me. Taste me. Put that sweet mouth on me. Don't be scared of me."

God.

My mostly-naked body still hums with the after-effects of my orgasm. Softly, slowly, I run my fingers over the tattoo on his shoulder. It's a hawk. "The Hawks were my high school team," he explains.

Across his chest is a tattoo of a panther. It's eerily similar to the painting I was just working on. It kind of brings home the fire we're playing with. He loves his team. He's tattooed its symbol across his heart.

He reads my thoughts.

"Oh no you don't. Don't you dare pull back from me

or run from me. The only thing you need to worry about is how you feel, Zara. Let me worry about everything else."

Another kiss obliterates my control. And the fact that he's pulled me closer, laying back with his knees spread so I'm practically on top of him. His cock surges and another gush of moisture seeps, wetting my stomach.

And I can't resist.

So I do it. I ease my hand around the thick length of him, pushing his unbuttoned jeans lower.

Elias groans.

I slide my palm gently along his solid length, fingering the ridge of the crown and the slippery slit.

"Oh fuck."

I lean forward and touch my tongue to the moisture, licking lightly.

His head falls back.

So I lick him again. I put my lips around the broad end and take him deeper, sucking on him carefully.

"Zara," he's moaning. "Zara."

I suck harder, putting some effort into it.

That's when it happens. His cock starts to jerk. Warm, milky liquid floods into my mouth in jetting bursts. Hannah actually told me about this part, but I never imagined there was this *much* of it. I try to drink some but there's way too much. It spills down my chin and wets my naked breasts.

I love how *I* did this to him. Elias is groaning my name like his heart is breaking.

More cum pumps out of him as I hold him and lick him. I can sense that this is more than something dirty and forbidden we're doing right now. It's a sticky bond. A dangerous one. But one I can't get enough of. I drink more, almost perversely thirsty for him.

Whatever power Elias O'Shea has over me is profound. I can feel his addictive power inside myself, feeding me with a kind of awe that almost feels like love.

13

Zara

My eyes blink open, then close again. I'm so comfortable I snuggle deeper against the very warm, very big...*holy shit!*—quarterback. My eyes are suddenly wide open. His gigantic, muscular body is wrapped around me in a bearhug.

Oh my god.

It all comes flooding back to me.

We're in my studio. I can tell by the light outside the window that it's just before dawn. A throw blanket covers most of us.

We must have fallen asleep.

After he gave me several orgasms by eating me out like some kind of starving magician.

And then I proceeded to return the favor.

Very thoroughly.

Swallowing mouthfuls of his...yikes.

Wow.

Holy fuck.

We got very, very carried away, is what it boils down to.

And I can't stop the foghorn that's currently trumpeting the reality of this situation behind my brain: *it should never have happened. It can't happen again.*

I lost my mother. I lost my sister, who loves California so much I can't ever see her moving back to the east coast. I can't lose my dad too.

And I can't be the reason Elias O'Shea gets kicked off the team, with the season just starting and the NFL draft picks looming.

I'm not *that* obtuse when it comes to football. I'm aware that Elias has a very good shot of getting some seriously good offers from the NFL. Which is, of course, a huge deal. It's every football player's dream to go pro. It's the pinnacle, where you hone your skills and showcase your talent on the world stage, while meanwhile getting paid astronomical amounts of money.

Something I possibly should have thought about a little more carefully last night, instead of getting completely swept away by the dreamboat elite athlete whose strong arms are still slung protectively around me, even in his sleep.

God, he feels good.

He tasted good too.

Goddamn it!

Very carefully, before he can zap me with his lust wand again or lull me into a sexy stupor with his poetic soliloquies about undying love, I slide out from under his toned, muscular arm. He stirs but doesn't wake.

Not bothering to search for my shredded G-string, I grab a hoodie and my bag and slip out the door.

But not before giving him a long, last glance. He's even more beautiful in his sleep, if that's possible, his handsome face relaxed, his off-black hair an unruly mop, his massive bronzed, sculpted chest rising and falling gently with his breath.

It was the most beautiful night of my life, O'Shea, but there's too much at stake here. I refuse to be the cause of your downfall.

Silently I pull the door closed behind me.

Thankfully, the art building is quiet and empty. I pull my phone out of the front pocket of my bag to check the time as I make my way quickly down the stairs.

4:51.

There are a bunch of missed text messages.

From Isla, late last night.

> Where are you?

> Everything okay? Text me back when you get this.

> I'm hoping you went home for the night, roomie. Hope you're okay. Call me!

From my sister.

> Yesterday might be the first day of our lives we haven't talked to each other. Ever! I miss my little sister. Love you, Z. I hope you're busy getting laid by a hot bo-hunk with killer abs and a great sense of humor [eggplant emoji, splashing water emoji]

Those emojis are giving me flashbacks to his—*no. You're no longer allowed to go there.*

And one from my dad.

> Hi, punkin. Just wanted to let you know I'm proud of you. Hope you're having fun with your new friends. Make the most of every minute. Love, Dad.

My dad always signs off, like he's not sure I'll know who it's from.

And it brings me back down to reality.

I shouldn't have done what I did but I can't bring myself to regret it.

Of course I can't. *Those flaring blue eyes. That ruthless male beauty. That mouth and what he could do with it.*

The only regret I feel is the one where I know for a fact that it can't happen again.

I wish it could. Tonight. Now.

I only hope he hasn't already ruined me for anyone else.

Too late.

I wish I could call my sister. But it's three hours earlier

on the West coast. And I know what she'll say if I tell her about this. I've broken Rule Number One, which goes against the grain of our entire upbringing. Dad's already had his heart broken and she's worried about the state of his health. I can practically hear her scolding me from afar. *Run wild and sow your oats, Zee, hell yes—as long as you're doing it with literally* anyone *but a football player. You know better than that.*

Shoving my phone into the pocket of my sweatshirt, I let myself into my dorm, using my fob to unlock the door, I wave to the night security guy, who's built like a weight-lifter, then I take the elevator up.

I try to close the door quietly but Isla wakes when I come in. "Zara?"

"Yeah. It's me. Sorry to wake you. Go back to sleep."

"Where were you?"

"I fell asleep in my studio. It's got a window seat that's almost as big as a bed. It's a little too comfortable."

"Have you heard from Elias?"

I freeze for a second. "Um…why?"

"The guys couldn't get a hold of him. They thought he might be with you, but they sounded worried."

I don't want to lie to my new roommate. My brain is busy trying come up with an excuse that doesn't quite do that. But my hesitation gives me away.

"Holy shit, Zara. You *were*?"

Damn it. I sit down on my bed and hold my head in my hands. I'm suddenly feeling overwhelmed. But I'm used to that feeling and I manage to shake it off before it comes across as melodramatic, I can only hope.

I need to tell someone before I either burst into tears or spontaneously combust from the sheer overload of what just happened to me. It was more than just intense, it was life-changing.

I just had my first kiss with a hot quarterback, which then quickly devolved into having my first, second and third orgasm—from his mouth, which he knows how to use like some kind of orgasm wizard, which then led to blowing said quarterback like I was a worldly and experienced groupie who knows exactly how to swallow like a pro, and I'm feeling a few things. Like happiness, because I finally understand how lust can connect you to another person in a way you weren't expecting. Like not-quite-embarrassment because I turned into a raving nymphomaniac as soon as he touched me.

"Zara. Come here. Get in with me. Tell me what happened."

It's exactly what I need right now. I'm used to confessing my innermost emotions. It helps.

I climb in with her and she pulls the covers over both of us. "Did you have *sex* with him?"

"*No.* I mean…no."

"But you were together last night?"

Tentatively, I confess. "He came to my studio and we talked for a long time. And then…"

"Did he kiss you?"

And then some. "Yes."

"Was it…good?" she whispers.

I glance over at her in the low light of dawn and she's got this dreamy look on her face. "Was what good? The kiss?"

"He's a hot football player, Zara. A quarterback. The *starting* quarterback. A senior. A reformed player, according to my brother. I know for a fact he would have…you know. Don't torture me. I just want to know if orgasms live up to the hype."

I laugh. At least I'm not the only late bloomer. I smooth a strand of her blond hair out of her eyes. "Orgasms more than live up to the hype."

Her eyes get wide. "They do?"

I bite my lip, nodding.

"How…many?"

"Three," I whisper.

She squeals and scrunches her face up, kicking her feet under the covers. "I *knew* it! I'm just pissed off you beat me to it."

We laugh and it feels good to have shared my dirty little secret a.k.a. the best thing that's ever happened to me in my goddamn life. Even if it was a one-off. "You can't tell *anyone*, Isla. Not a single word about any of this. Promise me."

"Of course I won't."

"Especially not Gabriel."

"As if I'm going to discuss orgasms with my brother," she scoffs, mildly disgusted.

"Or Jake," I add.

"As *if*." She rolls her eyes, but the dreamy look is back.

"It can't happen again, Isla. My dad will literally kick him off the team and possibly get him thrown out of Hawthorne altogether. No one can find out about this."

"Your secret's safe with me, Zara. For real."

"Thank you."

"Are you sure you can't see him again? Would you want to?"

"I don't know." *Of course you would.*

She reads my thoughts. "We have to tell each other the truth. We're roommates. It's our word and our bond. Now tell me. Would you?"

I shrug. Then I grin despite myself. "He really is hot."

We fall into fits of laughter and it's cathartic. "Hotter up close and personal, I bet," she says, when we can finally breathe again.

"I've never met anyone who's so…ideal. There's not a single thing that's not buff and hot and perfect about him. Except maybe that he's wildly romantic, in a really over-the-top kind of way."

"Like how?"

"He's just…nice. He told me I was his dream girl."

Isla stares at me, half-shocked and half-swooning. "He *did?*"

"Yeah. Crazy, right? We only met each other, like, two days ago. At first I thought it was just a line but…the way he said it…I don't know."

My heart literally aches and it takes me a second to figure out why.

I miss him.

She's watching me, still starstruck by my confession. She's tuning into the fact that my entire space-time continuum has shifted. You don't experience something like that without reaching a kind of enlightenment. The colors of the early morning seem brighter. My body feels fully, feverishly alive.

I lay back and stare up at the ceiling, focusing on a red Wildcats banner Isla stuck up there. Not the reminder I need right now. "Either way, we can't be together, even if we wanted to be. My dad is ridiculously overprotective. And he's always told me that football players—especially his—are a total no-go zone."

"Surely he would approve of *Elias*, though, wouldn't he? He's the kind of guy every parent dreams of for their daughter. Loaded, successful, an elite athlete and probably on his way to the big leagues. What's not to like?"

"I guess my dad's spent too much time watching players sow their wild oats. He doesn't think they're good boyfriend material. In fact, he's so bull-headed about it, I know he'd do something…drastic, if he ever found out."

"You think he'd he be mad at you, Zara?"

"Yes. I also think he'd take it out on Elias."

"But Elias is too valuable to kick off the team, isn't he?"

"It's the one thing my dad won't tolerate." I think

about not telling Isla this story because it's sort of a secret. But she knows a few of my secrets already and she's promised not to tell, so I decide to confide in her. "My sister once had a fling with a football player." Hannah and I never talk about this because she felt so traumatized by it after it happened. But it's the reason Rule Number One is such a big deal to her and my dad. "She met him when she was a sophomore in high school and the guy was a junior in college. She was fifteen. He was a hotshot Wildcats wide receiver and she met him at a friend's party. He kept calling her and a few weeks later she lost her virginity to him. But the very next day she saw online that he was in bed with two other women. My dad found out about the whole thing and gave the player his marching orders on the spot. The guy came begging to my sister to convince my dad to let him stay on the team but my dad wouldn't budge. And he wouldn't put in a good word for the guy so he ended up transferring schools but he was second string on his new team and never got his momentum back or got anywhere near the NFL, even though everyone thought he was headed that way before all this happened. He was really bitter about it and it caused my sister a lot of angst. She always saw herself as the cause of his downfall and she felt really terrible about that. And it sort of came between her and my dad for a while, even though they worked through it. So my dad sat us down and said never again. And we agreed to it. It's kind of like our pact."

"Okay. But that was a long time ago now, right? And this is different, Zara. You're in college. You're a fully fledged consenting adult if you want to be."

"I know. But my dad still sees it in black and white. He's been through so much and this season is such a big deal to him. I just don't want to rock his boat."

She nods. "I get that. But I'll just say in Elias's favor that I sort of know him and I don't think he would do anything like…what happened to your sister."

"I don't think he would either. But I'm not completely naive. I just googled him, Isla. His playboy status is all over the internet."

"That's old news, Zara. He hasn't been with anyone for a while. My brother mentioned it before school started. Gabriel was starting to worry about him. He said Elias has become like this lone wolf who doesn't hook up anymore. Something about how he could never find the girl he was looking for."

I'm in this deep, so I confide in her a little bit more. "He said he's been…lonely." I hear the emotion in my own voice.

And so does Isla. Her eyes round, like that emoji people use when something is cute or deeply moving. "Oh my god. You're in love with him."

I huff an incredulous laugh. "I'm not in *love* with him. How can I be? I just met him."

"You are. There was more to it than just a kiss. For both of you."

"I don't know." *But I do know.*

My phone vibrates in my back pocket. I reach for it, pulling it out.

We both stare at the screen, which beams out the name that's now etched onto my soul forevermore.

Elias.

"It's *him*," Isla gasps. "Are you going to answer it?"

"No. I can't."

"What did you say when you left him?"

"I didn't say anything. He was still asleep."

"Answer it, Zara. I can wait outside in the hall if you want some privacy. You should talk to him, at least."

"Stay here, Isla. Can you stay?"

The phone is still vibrating in my hand.

"Do you really think I should answer it?"

"Yes," she whispers.

So I swipe the button, holding the phone to my ear, taking a deep, silent breath. "Hi."

"Hi." He sounds irritated and I guess I can't blame him.

"How are you?"

"How *am* I? If it wasn't for this little scrap of lace in my pocket that I tore off you last night I might have thought you were the most beautiful dream I ever had. And now I'm wondering why you ran out on me."

"I didn't run out on you."

His silence isn't silent at all. He's outside somewhere

and there are people in the distance. He's breathing sort of heavily. "Are you in your room?" he asks gruffly.

"Yes."

"Are you okay?" The question is so protective, so sincere, my yearning flares and my eyes sting with tears. *Fuck this whole situation. Why does the perfect man have to be delivered to me in the form of the one thing I can't have?*

"I'm fine, Elias. Are *you* okay?"

He exhales an irritated laugh. "No, Zara, I'm not okay. I'm definitely anything but okay. I'm on my way to training, then classes, then practice. But I need to see you tonight."

"I don't…" I waver. *Damn it,* I have to be strong about this. For *him*. If I give an inch, I'll totally crumble. So I steel myself and tell him what he has to accept. "No, Elias. I can't see you tonight. I…I had a fun night with you—

"Zara—"

"It can't happen again, Elias. You know that. I don't want you to contact me. I'll come to the game on Saturday but I don't want you to come find me. I mean it. It's better this way, we both know that. You have too much to lose and I refuse to be the cause of it. I'm sorry. I have to go."

"*Zara,* don't you dare—"

I end the call, powering off my phone.

Then, for the first time in two years, I cry my heart out.

14

ELIAS

I IMMEDIATELY CALL HER BACK.

The little minx doesn't answer. It rings ten times then goes to her voicemail. The sound of her banal little recording pisses me off even more.

Hi, it's Zara. Please leave a message.

She sounds so fucking cute I want to punch my fist into the nearest wall. *Don't call me? I had a fun fucking night with you? I don't want you contacting me?*

There's a beep. "Zara. I told you to leave it to me and I meant that. *I'll* handle your dad. I'm coming to your studio tonight and I want you to be there. We can figure this out. I'll figure this out," I say again, like a fucking lunatic. "You have to trust me——" There's another beep, cutting me off.

Fuck.

I call her again. "I know this sounds…intense. And it

is. Last night meant something to me. It was the best night of my life and I fucking *mean* that. I need to see you again. Be there when I come to your studio tonight—" *Beep.*

Fuck!

I punch the call button. "Come on, Zara. Answer your phone. Don't regret anything that happened last night. It was too good to regret. You know that. We both know that. You should have woken me up, baby. I would have convinced you not to run from me—" *Beep.*

Fucking fuck. I call her back.

"I'm fucking addicted to how good you feel. And the way you *taste*, holy fuck, Zara. I need to see you. Tonight. Please—" *Beep.*

I'm seriously about to smash my phone into smithereens. I just left a string of desperate messages on her phone, which is not only pathetic but also a stupid fucking thing to do. Not that Coach would have access to Zara's phone, but still. I need to be smarter about this.

I grab a fistful of my hair. Shoving my phone into my pocket, I count to ten as I walk toward the stadium with ground-eating strides.

Calm the fuck down.

I know how to center myself. I mastered the art of self-control a long time ago—when it comes to fucking football.

Zara Fox is another matter altogether. I don't know how to control what I feel for her.

How the fuck did this happen?

How can I have fallen so fucking *hard*, already?

I'm tempted to turn around and storm over to her dorm, forcing my way in. But she lives in one of those Fort Knox freshman girls' dorms. They'd call security and drag me away in handcuffs, possibly. Which won't help me get closer to her.

I get to the locker room where Jake, West and Gabriel are waiting for me.

All three of them watch me walk in. All three of them have the same expression on their faces. Pissed-off concern. "Where the fuck were you last night, Chief?" Jake asks.

"You know where I was."

"Dude, we were about to file a missing person's report," West adds. "And why didn't you answer your phone—wait, don't tell me, you were busy getting down and dirty with—"

"Finish that sentence and I'll be forced to rearrange your face, Hawkins." I can hear the crazy edge to my voice. "It would be a shame to mess up those pretty-boy looks, so my advice to you is to shut the fuck up." I grab my shoulder pads and pull them on.

Gabriel's voice is low. "You spent the *night* with her?"

"I'm not talking to you about it."

"Are you insane?" Gabe asks. "Are you trying to throw away your entire future?"

"No," I seethe. "I'm trying to make a future. She is my future."

They all go sort of wide-eyed at that one.

"Oh shit," West groans. "This is so much worse than we thought."

I spend the entire training session getting told off because I'm over-exerting myself. It's the only way I can cope with the replays of her angel's face and the post-orgasm glow warming her cheeks. The way she *tasted*, like literal nectar of the gods, is messing with my sanity. The way she *felt*, the awkward, shy but greedy exploration of her cool hands and her insanely-sweet mouth.

You have too much to lose and I refuse to be the cause of it.

I'm in hell.

15

Zara

It's been several hours since my meltdown and I've learned something new about myself.

I'm good at tuning out emotions that are hard to think about. It's what I've been doing for years, after all.

"You did the right thing, Zara," Isla assures me, weaving her long blond hair into a braid. "You can always get together after he graduates. Once he's in the NFL and your dad is no longer his coach, then it won't matter. You'll be free to date him, if you still have feelings for him. Come on, I'll walk with you."

I guess that logic is helpful enough. *If he hasn't moved on by then. If he doesn't forget about you after he's drafted and living the high life in some faraway city. If life doesn't steer you in opposite directions.*

Maybe it's for the best.

Then why does it feel like my heart is beating somewhere outside my body?

I go into autopilot mode as we head across the Green. I go to my classes. Art History 101 with Professor Jenkins is interesting enough but I've already read about all the artists she's talking about. I mean, come on, I've been obsessed with the Impressionists since I was five. I know more about them than she does.

In English, we're given a reading comprehension test, which we have to complete within the ninety-minute class. It's a good distraction.

Maeve is in the class too and, as I'm leaving, she comes over and walks with me. "Hey, Zara, I saw the light on in your studio last night when I was leaving. It was late. I was going to knock but I figured you might be in the zone and I didn't want to disturb you." *Yeah, you could say that.* "Did you sleep there?"

I try to sound as breezy as I can. "Oh. Yeah. For part of the night. I fell asleep."

"I'm right down the hall from you, in room 320. Have you finished your painting for the freshman exhibition?"

Her expression is open and genuine and she doesn't seem to be aware that I had...company. *Thank you thank you thank you.* "I think so."

"You're lucky. I still have work to do on mine. I some-times wish my style wasn't so incredibly labor-intensive. Photo realism is tedious."

"Well, for what it's worth, I think you're the best painter in our class, Maeve. You're so talented."

"Thanks, Zara. You are too. God, wasn't that crazy when the quarterback randomly showed up in our class the other day? That guy is ridiculously hot."

My stomach sort of swoops at the mention of the one person I'm trying to banish from my brain and having zero luck doing it. "Yeah, I guess so."

"Football players are *so* not my type," she laughs. "But I'd make an exception for that one. Listen, I've got to head this way, to grab my laptop before my next class. Are you going to be in your studio tonight?"

"Um…no. I've got an essay to write. I'll be in my dorm, probably."

"Oh, well, I'll see you in class, then."

"See you, Maeve."

I head toward my next class and my phone rings. I hesitate before pulling my phone out. Elias left twenty or so messages earlier this morning but I haven't listened to any of them. I can't. He's clearly my Kryptonite and I know that if I listen to him, my self-control will melt like ice under his fully blazing sun.

But he hasn't called in a few hours. Which is good. It's a sad but real relief. Maybe he's accepting that one beautiful night is all we can have together.

You don't believe that. Not for one second. You know you're both addicted.

I mentally push my little devil mermaid off my shoulder before pulling out my phone. It's my dad.

"Hi, Dad. Everything okay?"

"Everything's fine, sweetheart. How are your classes?"

"They're good."

"Listen, honey, I've got a meeting with some scouts on Sunday afternoon in Boston, both this weekend and next weekend. I tried to get them to come to me but they weren't able to do that this time. So I'm not going to be able to do dinner those two nights. Can I take a raincheck on that lasagna?"

"Sure, Dad. I'll come another night and cook for you."

"Great. You doing okay?"

"I'm good. I'm coming to your game on Saturday. With some friends."

"Oh." He sounds surprised. It's been a long time since I came to one of his games.

"I told you my roommate Isla has a brother on the team. She really wants me to come with her since she doesn't know anyone else yet."

"I can get you tickets, honey. You know that. Any seat in the house."

"Oh, we've got seats. She organized it." I hate telling him white lies but he really doesn't need to know the truth.

"Okay. Any time you want to come just let me know."

"Thanks, Dad."

"Remember what I told you about football players, Zara."

Here we go. "I know, Dad."

"They'll break your heart. It's what they do."

"I *know*, Dad." *He already has.* "Good luck on Saturday. I'll be cheering for you."

"Love you, punkin."

"Love you too, Dad."

Just as we end the call, it rings again.

Still not Elias. It's a number I don't recognize. "Hello?"

"Is this Zara Fox?"

"Yes."

"Hi, Zara, this is Imogen MacBeth from the Sea Glass Gallery in New York City."

"Oh. Hi." *The Sea Glass?* Imogen MacBeth is one of the most respected art dealers in the country. It's been my dream to work with her for a long time. She's also the one that sent me the rejection. "I got your letter."

"Yes, about that. I'm calling because some new information has come to light and we've changed our minds. We got an email from a certain…quarterback, apparently. Just a few hours ago. He sent us a link to his Instagram, which he said has a post of one of your paintings. Did you know about it?"

I'm not sure how I could have forgotten about that, but it's true I've been distracted…by the very same quarterback she's referring to. "He did mention it."

"It has over three million views, he said, and there are quite a few expressions of interest for the painting. Extremely generous offers, in fact. Have you seen those offers?"

"Um…no, not really."

"If you agree to sign with us, Zara, we could help you navigate those offers. It's what we do for our artists and we pride ourselves on being the best in the business. Zara?" If I'm not mistaken, she sounds hopeful.

"Yes?"

"May I ask, is the painting still available? The one the quarterback posted?"

"Yes. Yes, it is."

Her excitement beams itself through the airwaves and it's a strange turn of events, having *Imogen MacBeth* relieved to hear that my obscure little hidden-away painting hasn't sold yet. "I'm very happy to hear that. Do you have…*other* paintings, Zara?"

"Yes. I do."

"How many, would you say?"

"How many paintings?"

"Yes."

I think about this for a second. "Maybe two hundred. Probably more like two fifty."

"Two *hundred?*"

"Maybe even closer to three hundred."

There's a breathless delight in her voice when she continues. "Zara, we'd be very interested in viewing those paintings. And we'd like to provisionally offer you an exclusive exhibition here at the Sea Glass."

"Oh." *Wow.* Even my mother didn't get exclusive until later in her career. "I would absolutely love that."

"Is there a date and time that would be convenient for us to come view your work? Do you have time, say, next weekend? How about two weeks from Sunday?"

"That sounds perfect. How's five o'clock?"

"Five is perfect. Is the address the same as the one I sent your letter to?"

"It is."

"Wonderful, Zara. We'll see you then."

16

Zara

Of course I'm beyond thrilled. But I'm also furious.

I'm half irate that he would dare to take this kind of liberty. I'm also half in awe that he would be nice enough to basically launch me into the stratosphere using his gigantic platform.

Thank you thank you thank you.

Not for the off-limits part of the equation. Or the part that means I've been swept away by the absolute apex of what I'm absolutely forbidden to have. But for everything else.

For the memory of his kiss. The way his mouth felt on mine. The soft, worshipful exploration of the dark-eyed golden boy's tongue. The hot, insatiable hunger.

I decide to check my messages. There are a lot of them, all from Elias. The first few are from this morning, just after I turned my phone off.

Before I listen, I need to prepare myself. I do my best to put up an invisible forcefield between me and what I wish I could have. The choice I wish I didn't have to make.

Carefully, like it might burn me, I push the button to play back his messages.

Zara. I told you to leave it to me and I meant that. I'll handle your dad. I'm coming to your studio tonight and I want you to be there. We can figure this out, Zara. You have to trust me—

The recording ends but it rolls over to the next one.

I know this sounds…intense. And it is. Last night meant something to me. It was the best night of my life and I fucking mean that. I need to see you again. Be there when I come to your studio tonight—

Come on, baby. Answer your phone. You can't avoid me. I know what you're thinking but it was too good to regret. You know that. We both know that. You should have woken me up. I would have convinced you not to run from me—

Zara, I'm fucking addicted to how good you feel. And the way you taste, holy fuck, baby girl. I need to see you. Tonight. Please—

I take a deep breath. And I save each message. I should delete them, of course. They're evidence. But it's not like the freaking FBI are going to tap my phone or somehow hack my voicemail. No one else knows. Just us.

And Isla.

And possibly Gabriel.

And maybe Jake and West.

Shit.

The rest of the messages are more recent, from less than an hour ago.

Hey, angel girl. I was just thinking about you. He sounds calmer. His voice has a soulful husk to it. Which in some ways makes the yearning even more acute. He sounds sad. Which is ten times worse than mad because now I want to comfort him. *I know I'm going to get cut off so I'll just keep calling back until I can tell you what I want to say—*

So, I was thinking about how you're the most beautiful girl I've ever seen. Did I tell you that? I'm still having a hard time believing you're not some perfect, crazy-ass dream. I mean, fuck, Zara, how can you just step out of my wildest fantasies and straight into my life like this—

And then you walk away? You can't just give me a taste and not give me more, baby girl, you just can't. You'll drive me over the fucking edge. It's the memory of you that's keeping me sane at this point. Knowing you're here, so close, it's torture. A beautiful, insane kind of torture—

Zara, don't get mad. I've done something I hope will help you fast track the path you're already on. It's not me that's going to get you there, it's all you, but if I can help you then I'm going to. The post I put up of your painting is up to three million views—

I figured it would be a shame to waste all that exposure. So I emailed the Sea Glass. You told me the name of the gallery you were going for, remember? Don't be pissed off. You sent the letter, so you can't say you don't want this. There's yelling in the background of the call. Someone's calling his name. *So, they emailed me back and they said they're interested—*

They said they're going to call you. Just say yes. Say yes to everything. Say yes to them and say yes to me. When you think about it, giving me what I want is a better option than having your dad's playmaker completely lose his shit before the opening game of the season, right?—

Just talk to me, Zara. We'll figure this out. Be there tonight. That's an order from your quarterback. I have to go to practice now. See you later, angel.

Wow.

I save those messages too. And I happen to know he'll be at practice right now. I also know my dad doesn't allow the players to have their phones anywhere near the field. So I call him.

"Elias, I just wanted to say thank you. The Sea Glass called me and I'm going to meet with them. They changed their minds because of the post. It was a nice thing to do. But please don't post anything else about me or my paintings, okay? I don't want you to take risks like that for me. As I told you, I want you to play football. I want you to win all your games and get to the NFL and have all that hard work pay off for you. I'll be watching from the sidelines. Good luck on Saturday. Bye, Elias."

Rule Number One. Rule Number One. Rule Number One.

Do not ruin his chances of going pro by complicating his relationship with his coach.

He'll break your heart. It's what they do.

I end the call.

17

ELIAS

"LET ME IN, KIT." I've known Kit Peyton since we had a freshman economics class together. She was one of the first people I met at Hawthorne. She and Gabriel and I sat together and we became friends. We spent a lot of time studying together freshman year. She's one of the few women friends I have, as a relationship that never evolved into anything physical. Possibly because she's always had girlfriends. "You have to buzz me through."

It makes me think for a second about what I would seem like to Coach—to a father who's worried about his innocent daughter being corrupted or used. I get that. I know I have a reputation as a playboy, and it was true enough for a long time. There's no point regretting it now, and I don't. It got me here, to the point where I know for a fact that none of them were the one.

Because she is. The gorgeous little artistic genius with the green eyes and the holes in her heart the same shape as mine.

This feels like more than chemistry, it feels like fucking quantum physics—the kind where the universe decides that your DNA is a perfect match and until you make it happen, you're going to crave her with an obsessive, relentless madness.

Every cell in my body felt it the second I saw her. And I'm not entirely prepared for the gargantuan shift my life has taken since then. The craving that feels like I'll die if I can't be near her. The overload of need that's a desert thirst for more of the taste and scent and sight of her. I want to drink in every piece of her.

It's fucking intense.

"Elias, I can't do that. You know I can't do that. I would definitely lose my job and possibly get arrested. We sign *contracts*, Elias. People choose this dorm specifically for its air-tight security and they take that shit seriously. Besides, this position actually pays well. I can't afford to lose it. Who are you trying to see, anyway?"

"I'll pay you. Name your price."

"Elias, I *can't*."

"I'll double whatever they pay you for a month. For six months. For the whole year."

I try the door that leads to the elevator lobby, rattling it, trying to break the fucking thing, but it won't budge. Of course it won't.

"There are cameras on you right now, by the way, Elias. Why are you acting like this? Who is she?"

"I'll get you season tickets. I'll get you an executive box."

Kit gives me a look. "I already have season tickets. And since when are you *this* desperate, O'Shea? You're chasing after freshmen now?"

"Just let me in, Kit." Zara wasn't in her studio. And she's not answering any of my calls. She left me one message, a sort of formal, dismissive thank you, but she's deluded if she thinks she can avoid me or get rid of me that easily.

Kit picks up her phone. "I'm calling Gabe. He can deal with you. I'm not letting you in. I'm sorry, Elias."

"Forget it." I start heading for the door. "I'll find another way."

"Why don't you just call her?"

"She won't answer my calls."

"Wow," Kit muses. "I never thought I'd see the day when the hotshot quarterback is getting turned down by a freshman."

"Yeah, well, this time it's different."

Kit smiles sympathetically. A part of her is enjoying this. "You okay, O'Shea? You don't seem yourself. Is the stress getting to you?"

"You could say that."

"Do you want me to page her? Who is she? What's her name?"

"I'm not telling you that." I head toward the door. "I'll find another way in."

"Don't try to, Elias. I mean it. I'll have to call security if you do."

Fine. I'll climb the walls then. Or find a back door. "I'll see you later, Kit. Thanks for nothing."

Kit calls after me but I'm already out the door.

Outside, I scan the front of the building. It's four stories. I don't even know which floor she's on.

There's an open window on the second floor. And a drainpipe that runs the height of the building. Thick ivy clings to the brick. It might be sturdy enough to take my weight. Or it might not. I guess I'm about to find out.

But before I can get a reliable hold to pull myself past the ground floor window, I hear familiar voices behind me.

Damn it. That was fast. Kit must have told them it was urgent.

"Step away from the freshman dorm or we'll be forced to shoot," West calls out, and I guess I can be glad it's not an actual cop.

Fuck.

"He's losing his mind," I hear Jake say. He's not wrong. He grabs my shirt. I like to think I could take Jake in a fight but we'd be evenly matched. He's strong as fuck and he easily yanks me down.

Jake slings his arm around my shoulders. I try to pull away from him but the three of them pull me in the direction of our house and I finally let them. Fighting with my teammates when I'm this fired up would only injure one of us. Scaling the building probably also isn't the best idea, especially since I would have had to climb in some random freshman girl's window. Which probably wouldn't have gone down that well with the local authorities.

"We need a plan," Gabriel says. "We need to get you and Zara together so you can talk this through before you get fucking arrested."

"Good idea," I growl sarcastically. "I wish I'd thought of it."

"We'll get Isla to bring her over to our place," Jake suggests, "so the two of you can talk this through without distractions and you can get your head back in the game. No one else has to know about it."

"She won't come," I tell them. "She won't answer my calls. I've left shitloads of messages. She's refusing to talk to me."

"We'll ask Isla not to tell Zara where she's taking her. We'll set it up so Zara doesn't know."

"We'll ambush her," West says, enjoying this.

Gabe, not so much. "We'll do whatever it takes, Chief, to make sure Coach has no idea whatsoever that you're obsessed with his daughter."

At this point I'll agree to anything as long as it means I can see her again.

18

Zara

THE SKY IS clear and blue. Fall leaves are glowing with the kind of light you can only find in the golden hour on a September afternoon in New England. There's a soft coolness touching the edges of the sunlight's warmth, like summer and fall are wrapped in a slow, erotic dance.

Get your head out of that loop of slow, erotic dances, girlfriend.

It's game day.

Even before we get anywhere near the stadium I can feel the excited rumble of 75,000 cheering fans. The marching band is playing, the sound almost drowned out by the noise of the sold-out crowd.

Isla, Mollie, Lauren and I hold hands as we make our way inside, so we don't lose each other in the seething mass of humanity. I tried to suggest to Isla that we get the seats my dad offered instead of taking the box Elias reserved for us, but she wouldn't hear of it.

It seemed kind of wrong to use it when I've basically made it clear to him that we can't...*do what we did.* We can't see each other again, when we're clearly like magnets that can't resist each other's pull. Especially with all that's riding on the season.

"If the quarterback gets you a fully catered executive box, then you take it," reasoned Isla. She also insisted we paint our faces with stripes of red and white across our cheekbones. We're dressed head to toe in school colors, just like the rest of the stadium.

People are waving red feathers and wearing the trademark cat's ears headbands. Thousands of red flags are flying. A group of girls are wearing skin-tight red catsuits with *Marry Me, Elias!* written across their chests.

I ignore the flash of jealousy. My little devil-mermaid whispers, *You know what he tastes like when he comes.*

Yikes.

And the angel on my other shoulder whispers back, *Maybe they do too.*

I try to distract myself from thinking about him, but it's impossible. The entire stadium is cheering for their star quarterback. Homemade signs and banners are waving through the sea of red and white, most of them dedicated to him. *I love you, Elias!! Take us all the way, O'Shea! Elias, I want to have your babies!*

People are wearing hats and red t-shirts with the logo they've created for him: a Superman's S but with an E in the middle.

The rumbling underfoot grows to fever pitch as the loudspeakers start playing *Wildcats Forever*, the team's theme song that's always played as the players enter. People stomp their feet in rhythm to the blaring music, creating an exhilarating thunder, like the collective heartbeats of 75,000 fans are in sync. I can feel the pulse of excitement in my bones.

In the middle of all this fervor, I notice an older couple, wrapped in a red blanket, holding hands. And a family, with a starstruck little boy wearing his Wildcats shirt and being held by his strapping probably-alumni father. It reminds me that this football team is bigger than just a one-off sporting match. It's a legacy that runs deep and wide. These little snapshots of a shared love for the game and this team reminds me that it would be selfish for me to gamble with that. The last thing this campus needs is for its coach and its quarterback to be at war.

The crowd goes absolutely nuts as their players run onto the field. We get to the box and I'm glad for it now, for the sake of my eardrums. I close the door behind us and the noise is immediately less deafening, but not by much.

"Wow, this is incredible," Mollie exclaims, her eyes wide as she takes in the lavish setup.

It *is* incredible. It's a plush little football-themed haven, with an expansive view of the field, a bar area with every variety of food on platters you could ever want, all laid out for us. There are drinks on ice and a standing glass-fronted fridge with more of them. The view of the field is framed by four flat-screen TVs, each showing a different angle of the game. One of them is showing a close-up of Elias as he walks to the center of the field for the coin toss.

Seeing him on the screen, his dark hair lightly wind-blown, his eyes a vivid blue on the high definition screen, shocks me a little. I'm not sure why it would. Maybe because I'd almost forgotten the extent of just how damn beautiful he is. *I want him so much and I can't have him. He's theirs. He belongs to everyone in this stadium.*

One camera angle cuts to several women swooning. Then it pans back to the two captains. The Falcon's captain calls the toss but I can hear through the commentary that they lost. Elias chooses to defer. The crowd cheers as he walks back to the bench and the other team take to the field.

"Oh, they're deferring," Mollie says. "That's good. If they start the game on defense it means they can start the second half with possession of the ball." Mollie's a life-long football fan with two older brothers who all played throughout high school, she told us. Part of the reason she chose Hawthorne is because of the football team.

Isla notices me staring at a screen that's honing in on Elias. She puts her arm around me, offering me a Coke, pulling me gently over to the impressive spread of food before I make myself too obvious. She starts piling her plate. "Girls, let's feast. Zara, your dad wasn't joking when he said the box was catered." It's what we decided to tell Lauren and Mollie, to keep my cover: my dad got us the box. It's believable and it keeps things simple.

Isla piles her plate full.

Lauren laughs. "I don't know how you eat so much junk food and look like that, Isla." As a dance major, Lauren is all about eating the kind of unprocessed food that will hone her body into a specimen of fitness, strength and health. She doesn't eat anything that might have a preservative as an ingredient. She loads her plate with fruit, cut vegetables and nuts. "You and your nachos are a love story for the ages."

Isla shrugs. "What can I say? I'm just making the most of a free meal."

I help myself but there are too many butterflies in my stomach to eat much.

"Oh, shit, they've scored," Mollie says. "That's the downside of deferring the coin toss. If the other team scores first it can set the tone for the rest of the game." It's handy having Mollie run the commentary for us, since she's so informed.

"No way." Lauren is fully embracing Wildcats mania. It's impossible not to in this setting. "The only tone that's been set is the one where the Wildcats make a huge comeback and annihilate the Falcons."

We go back to our seats as the Wildcats' offense gets into formation. For a brief moment, Elias looks up. Directly at me. I don't know if he can even see me from where he is, but as he gazes up at the window, he places his hand on his heart.

Anyone else might not even notice it. But I do. And I remember what he said to me. *You're my dream girl. If I know you're watching, I'll play out of my skin.*

He's so freaking glorious it's hard not to get as swept away as everyone else. The entire stadium goes ballistic as Elias nails pass after pass. He moves with the kind of grace that's riveting to watch. The excitement reaches fever pitch as Elias passes the ball to West, who runs it ten yards before he's brought down by three very large Falcons defenders, causing a collective groan.

Some of his teammates help West to his feet and he waves to the crowd, which erupt in cheers. There are plenty of fans in the stands who are here for West, Jake, Gabriel and their other favorite players. But it's Elias who has this entire stadium at his feet. He's wildly impressive. His talent and precision are spellbinding. He's tall. Toned. Agile. His muscles as he moves are coiled and sculpted.

"God," gushes Mollie. "Our quarterback is *so good*. He never misses."

"He's not hard on the eyes, either," Lauren giggles. "That guy is on a different level."

I can hardly blame them for noticing how good Elias is. *Or* how hot. There are 75,000 people all around us who are deeply immersed in their own thoughts about the exact same thing.

Isla nudges my arm, her whisper playful, "Eyes on the ball, roomie, not the player."

I offer her a half-hearted glare. "Impossible," I whisper back.

Her laughter is soft and empathetic.

Elias pivots and throws with an elegance that leaves us all breathless. The ball arcs through the air, landing securely in the outstretched arms of Gabriel, who scores a touchdown. Isla claps her hands together, exhaling with relief. "*Yes*. That's my brother, y'all."

"Your dad is obviously a really good coach, Zara." Mollie's eyes are glued to the game. "These players are talented but you can also tell they're well trained." It's a moment of pride for me. My dad's dedication to the team is unwavering and it shows. He's put so much work into this team. Pouring his heart and soul into it after my mother died was the only thing that kept him going.

Lauren is observant. "You okay, Zara?"

"Just thinking about how much effort my dad has put into preparing for this season. I hope they go all the way, for his sake."

"If they play like this all season, they'll have a damn good shot at it," Mollie offers.

We're on the edges of our seats for the next few quarters, along with the rest of the stadium. Some of our less experienced players are making too many handling errors. It's the first game of the season so maybe that's to be expected, but it must be worrying my dad. And the other team gets lucky. A small but fast running back juggles a badly-thrown pass, scoring a touchdown at the end of the third quarter.

"Damn it," Mollie groans.

The other team is leading by one point.

75,000 people are on edge, pinning all their hopes on the star player. I can almost feel the weight of his burden. The pressure is *so* intense. But Elias is level-headed and cool. This is what he's worked his entire life to do and you get that feeling. His innate confidence calms us.

Elias's pass is perfection. But the wideout is one of the younger guys and he can't hold onto it, fumbling at the crucial moment. I remember the name Mitch Logan from my dad's conversations. He's a sophomore and I feel sorry for the guy. It's a crushing mistake and the crowd is unforgiving, wild with desperate hope and edgy frustration.

There are less than two minutes left in the game.

"I can't take this!" Lauren groans. "They're *so* close. They *need* to make this touchdown."

My dad calls a time out and the players huddle, then break into formation.

Elias glances up at our box and I can't breathe. His hand holds his face-mask for a second, sort of contemplatively. Then he points two fingers directly at me. *I see you,* that little signal says.

Isla gasps. "Zara," she whispers.

My heart is in my throat, for ten different reasons.

Elias gets into position.

The ball is snapped. Elias is deep in the pocket. It's a moment of sheer terror for everyone watching, and also pure beauty. Elias calculates the distance while simultaneously dodging an offender.

"Where's the offensive line?" Mollie shrieks. We're all on our feet.

Then, with the kind of awe-inspiring genius that can only come from an exceptional player, Elias sidesteps another attack as he makes the pass. The ball's spiraling arc floats gracefully over Gabriel's head, almost seeming to wait for him as he catches up to it. It lands securely in Gabriel's arms and he dances past two defensive players almost playfully, running over the line in the last second of the game.

Touchdown.

We won the game.

The stadium erupts.

I watch on screen as the team gathers around Elias, patting him on the back with relief and pure joy. Elias pulls off his helmet. His smile so genuine and full of life I really have no choice but to fall in love with him, if I hadn't already.

I lean back in my seat, my emotions a whirlwind. I'm proud and happy for my dad. I'm in awe of Elias. And our secret bond feels more magical but also more unlikely than ever.

How can he want *me?* And *why?*

If only I could have him.

Isla places a reassuring hand on my arm. "I hope you don't have plans tonight, roomie."

"Why?"

She gives me an enigmatic answer. "Whatever happens, Zara, remember that what you feel is real. And sometimes, real is messy."

My eyes are still fixed on Elias. "Yeah," I whisper. I shouldn't be, but what I'm thinking is that sometimes real is worth fighting for.

19

———

Zara

PEOPLE ARE STARTING to leave the stadium, rowdy from the win. Mollie and Lauren have plans to meet up with Mollie's brother, who's visiting with some friends for the weekend. They're here somewhere, down in the stands.

"Come with us." Mollie's eyes are bright. "We're going into town to get some dinner."

"We would but we already have plans," Isla tells them. "But we'll see you back at the dorm later on."

"What plans do we have?" But my question is drowned out by the noise of the crowd and Mollie's distraction as she answers a call from her brother. They hug us, then disappear into the massive crowd.

I let Isla lead me down the steps toward the back entrance of the stadium. "What plans do we have tonight, roomie, and why are you being so cagey about it?"

Her smirk is just a little bit guilty. "It's a surprise."

We're shuffled through the crowd, which is noisy and pushy, so it's a few minutes before I can question her. "What kind of surprise?"

"I'm not allowed to tell you. You'll just have to wait and see."

We're out the door now and I can guess what she's up to. "Isla—"

"Here it is. This must be our car."

There's a nondescript black sedan with tinted windows waiting by the curb. It looks like the kind of car people get kidnapped in, except that the guy leaning against it, waiting for us, is a fully decked-out Wildcats fan. Maybe a senior or a grad student. "Are you Isla?" he asks.

"Yes."

He opens the back door for us and Isla slides into the back seat, pulling me along with her.

"What is this, some kind of heist or something?" I'm confused. "Have we joined the mafia?"

"Not exactly."

"Where are we going?"

Our driver closes the door. There's a tinted window between the back and front seats so we can't see him as he gets into the driver's seat, but it's only moments before we're pulling away from the curb, slowly making our way through the traffic. The radio is turned up in the front seat, blaring football commentary, but the sound is muted back here.

"I want you to know this wasn't my idea," Isla tells me. "They really felt like the two of you need to talk."

"They? Who's they?"

"Gabriel and Jake. And West. They wanted to make sure you got delivered to the back door, so no one knows about it and there's no hassle."

"So this is about Elias." I've kind of figured that out by now.

"Of course it's about Elias. He knew you wouldn't come unless we roped you into it."

"We? You're in on this?"

"I'm sorry. But they were very convincing, Zara. He's going crazy. He tried to scale the walls of our dorm last night. They got to him before security arrived, but it was a close call. They had to take shifts last night keeping an eye on him so he wouldn't leave the house without them knowing about it."

"It's a bad idea."

She eyes me, and I appreciate that she's genuine with her question. "You really don't want to see him?"

"I mean, of course I *want* to. But I *can't*, Isla. It's…" It's hard to explain.

"You two can just talk to each other and maybe it'll help him calm down a little. That's what they're hoping."

It's very unlikely Elias and I can just calmly talk to each other. I vividly remember how entirely…irresistible he is. *How his crazy man-effect turned me from a shy, reclusive virgin into the kind of girl who thinks she knows how to…swallow.*

We went from zero to sixty so fast it made my head spin. In fact it's still spinning.

Our car is pulling out of the crowded parking lot now, taking a left. We turn the corner to a street that's only one block away from our dorm. We're pulling up behind the kind of villa-style house that's popular with the fraternities. The car pulls to a stop and our chauffeur jumps out to open the door for us. "Here you go."

Isla thanks the guy and we climb out. I allow her to guide me toward the house, despite my hesitations. "We're doing this because they're worried about him, Zara."

Half of me wants to make a break for it because I know that what I'm about to do isn't something I can come back from. I can't tread lightly when it comes to Elias O'Shea. I'm already head over heels in love with him. How can I not be? It's the first time I've admitted that to myself and even though it's happening at lightning speed, I forgive myself. Because no matter what happens here tonight, my heart's going to get broken into a million tiny pieces either for one reason or the other.

I follow Isla to the back door, which is already open. Music is coming from inside the house. They're having a party. I guess they have a lot to celebrate.

And they're expecting us. Gabriel's standing in the doorway. He waves to the driver, yelling something about Venmo before following us inside. "Don't worry, Zara. It's only us."

Which is exactly what I need to hear right now. Maybe it's still possible to keep this little rendezvous between our group of insiders. No one else has to know.

"Hey, Pix," Gabe says to Isla, closing the door behind us.

She kisses him on the cheek. "Good game tonight, bro."

He grins but his gaze is on me. "Hey, Zara."

"Hi, Gabe. Well done on those touchdowns."

"Thanks."

I feel like I'm entering a portal into The Realm of Bad Decisions. At least I can console myself that there are probably multiple orgasms waiting for me on the other side of those bad decisions.

Stop it right now.

And there he is.

Leaning against a counter in the kitchen as West tells some animated joke to him and to Jake, who's sitting at the table. It's almost like West is deliberately distracting Elias from something.

They all look up as Isla and I walk into the kitchen.

"Hey, pixie girl," greets Jake. "Hey, Zara."

Isla helps herself to a chair. "You guys need to stop calling me that."

"Never."

Oh hell.

I barely hear the conversation going on around me.

The look in those stormy blue eyes instantly melts every barrier I might have hoped could withstand him.

All he's wearing is a pair of worn, low-slung jeans.

And nothing else.

No shirt.

No shoes.

Just jeans. Showing off those sun-tanned, inked muscles. His corded neck that's so fascinatingly male to me. Mussed-up dark hair, still damp from a shower. Clenched jaw. Abs that could be classified as the Eighth Wonder of the freaking World. Stern, sexy eyebrows. Had I noticed before how sexy his eyebrows are?

Get a grip!

For a second I wonder what I must look like to him. I'm still dressed in my white mini-skirt and the red Wildcats jersey that matches Isla's, Mollie's and Lauren's. We bought them yesterday at a stand in the Green. Apparently girls try to outdo each other in the sex appeal department at football games and these tight-fitting tops were the consensus of my friends. Lauren thought they'd look good in an Instagram post. My face is still painted with the red and white stripes across each cheekbone and I feel flushed from the excitement of the afternoon. And now this, coming face to face with the one person in the world who makes me feel both crazily alive and totally out of control.

"Hi, Zara," says West. "Look, Elias, it's your good luck charm."

"Hi, West." I barely even glance at him. I'm too locked in a heated staring contest with the brooding quarterback.

Elias's expression is dark but there's relief there too. He walks over to me and takes my hand in his, lacing his fingers through mine in a grip that's somehow gentle and vice-like at the same time. "You and I need to have a little talk." He pulls me toward a door that leads into a wide hallway with a staircase. Over his shoulder: "Thank you, brothers. And little sister."

"Am I doomed to spend my entire college experience as 'little sister'?" Isla grumbles.

"Yes," confirms Gabriel.

Oh god. We're going to be alone?

The squeeze of his strong hand is enough to kickstart my pulse, until it's doing that thing it seems to do whenever he's near me. Thrumming its little drumbeat in the most intimate places imaginable.

He leads me up the stairs to his room. All my alarm bells are clanging loudly. *Do not go into Elias O'Shea's bedroom under any circumstances whatsoever. You'll be cashing in your V-card before you can say 'virgin nymphomaniac goes wild'.*

But it's too late.

He closes the door behind us, letting go of my hand to lock it.

Help.

But then I'm distracted by his room. The space is a man cave on steroids. It's cluttered but also organized.

There's so much to look at. This is the sanctuary of a college football legend, but one who's grounded and disciplined. And awe-inspiringly good at what he does.

It's a shrine to his legacy. The walls, painted a muted shade of gray, are a backdrop for framed jerseys, some showing visible signs of wear from particularly intense seasons. Professional photographs capture heart-stopping moments on the field. The ball leaving his outstretched hand. A sprint. Triumphant touchdowns. Championship wins.

His king-sized bed is made, a plush black comforter laid over the top. There's a small, scribbled note pinned to the wall above the bed that says *MAKE YOUR BED.* Maybe from his dad or some coach who taught him about the importance of consistency.

At the foot of the bed is a wooden chest full of footballs. Some are signed by teams, others are scrawled with hand-written notes of motivation or gratitude. Probably game balls from particularly memorable victories. My dad has a similar collection in his home office.

On the left side of the bed is Elias's desk. There's a MacBook, a stack of well-worn playbooks, textbooks, a couple of speakers and a few football-themed coffee mugs. Even his lamp is a football player, offering the only low, golden light in the room.

The desk's chair is piled high with a stack of boxes labeled with familiar logos. Gifts from sponsors or companies who want his endorsements, is my guess. Some of them haven't even been opened yet.

A built-in bookshelf takes up one entire wall and is filled with trophies, plaques, awards and photographs. A corkboard is overflowing with practice schedules, play formation sketches and a few photos. There are some with his friends and teammates. One with Jake after a win. One with an older guy who must be his dad. The look on his dad's face is one of pure, ecstatic pride.

This room says a lot about him. He's a football god, which I already knew. But it's the personal touches that hint at the deeper complexities of his character. He takes his studies seriously. He cares about the people in his life. He values his relationships. He's careful about what endorsements he chooses to put his name on.

I notice then a photograph of a young woman with dark red hair. She's achingly beautiful and I know who she is immediately. I can tell by the shape of her eyes.

I do it carefully. I know how this feels. "Is this your mother?"

He leans a brawny shoulder against a wall, shoving his hands into his pockets as he watches me with a surly but beguiled absorption. "Yes." Elias O'Shea has the ability to make me feel like the most beautiful thing in the world, just with the intensity of his fascination. No one's ever looked at me the way he does. I think if everyone had someone to look at them the way Elias looks at me, there'd be no need for therapy in this world. The low-key adoration washes away insecurities. It plants little seeds of happiness that grow every time he does it.

And it's entirely too addictive. I should leave before I get in too deep.

But I can't.

Not yet. This new addiction—which I'm trying like hell to control—holds me in place. I feel too good with him to walk away, it's as simple as that. "She had red hair," I comment.

"My dad's is black. I take after him."

"I can see her in your eyes."

Her memory has softened whatever aggression was in him before, but not by much. "I'm not happy with you," he accuses gently.

"I came to the game, like I said I would. Thanks for the box seats, by the way. We made the most of the all-you-can-eat buffet."

"Ignoring my calls? Not showing up when I told you to meet me at your studio? What the fuck, Zara?"

I turn back toward the bookshelf, perusing some of his trophies, trying to keep this light. "You know why." I pick up a small box. It's an actual action figure of him, unopened. "You played really well. You definitely live up to the hype. But I knew that already." I place the box back on its shelf. Am I being bitchy? He's hardly Prince Charming himself tonight. Our tensions are too high.

His warm hand slides over the skin of my wrist and his grip shackles me gently. "It was all for you."

I laugh a little, waving over my outfit. "You're just saying that because I dressed up for you."

His gaze drags over my bare legs, to the tight fit of my top. "If you're trying to torture me, it's working."

I look up into his smoldering sapphire eyes. "I'm not trying to torture you, Elias. I'm trying to save you from yourself. We can't do this."

His other hand eases around the nape of my neck, gripping not-quite-but-almost painfully. "Oh, we're doing this, angel girl." His eyes challenge me to stop him.

But for reasons known only to my little mermaid-devil, who's gleefully leaning in, that's one thing I don't seem to be capable of doing.

It's the insanely alluring scent of him, like firewood that's been warmed by the sun. I don't know why I say that. He triggers a memory. Of a weekend trip up to the Adirondacks with my mom and my sister, to meet up with my mom's old college roommate. It was late September, maybe five or six years ago. I remember the name of the lake too, because it perfectly summed up how I felt about the whole experience: Paradox Lake. I hadn't wanted to go. I'd wanted to stay home with my dad, and paint. He couldn't get away because it was football season. But my mom talked me into it. She was excited. She wanted me with her, "to make memories together," she'd said at the time. There'd been a neatly stacked pile of wood near the cabin, like a big rectangular puzzle, each log fitting happily against the others. We swam and splashed and laughed in the water that was so clean and icy it made you feel like you were being reborn when you got out, and it ended up being one of those weekends that stands out as a treasured jewel that you revisit so often it becomes like a dream. The Adirondack chair I'd lazed away an afternoon in, reading, overlooking the lake, happened to be right next to this pile of wood. And it was sunny. And sometimes a red or orange or maroon maple leaf would flutter down and land on this sun-warmed puzzle of a woodpile, or onto my book, or onto the artistic layer accumulating on the grassy ground. This is what Elias smells like. That wood, and that sunny afternoon by that paradoxical lake, and those colorful leaves. And it suddenly feels like all my best memories are tied up with his scent.

He kisses me like I'm the air he's been missing, capturing my mouth hungrily. Elias's tongue slides against mine and a warm wave of lust floods my body, licking me like liquid flames.

If I thought he smelled good, his taste is something else altogether. Mint. Man elixir—I don't freaking know what to call it. All I know is that the feverish, perfect taste of Elias O'Shea fires up a sweet obsession that digs into my soul.

He's so big. So *hot*. My body is humming with his warmth.

As I know by now, in situations like this, with a rugged quarterback feeding his taste and his scent into my parched, partly-naive but fully alive body, I'm consumed by a need for more, craving him like a drug.

"Don't run from me, Zara," he growls. "Don't fucking stonewall me."

I blink up at him, mesmerized, like always, by how ridiculously good-looking he is. But a glance at the photo of his proud father on the wall behind him convinces my sane mind to make one last attempt to slow this down.

I step away from him—which takes every single one of my powers of resistance. "You wanted to talk, Elias, and so do I. Let's talk." It already feels like we're in this, deeply. The reality is, we hardly know each other. I can jump into bed with him any minute—and probably will, who are we kidding. Before the night is over, odds are I'll give him all the firsts he hasn't already taken. But I don't know the first thing about him, except that he's good at football, he says nice things to me and he looks like he just flew down on his Pegasus from Mount Olympus.

He lays back on the bed, a burly arm crooked behind his head, which is propped up by pillows. His long legs are spread and his jeans are low on his hips, revealing that muscular V—my sister once called it an Adonis belt and now I know why—and the quilted eight-pack of his abs. Not to mention the *gigantic* straining ridge inside his jeans. I try not to stare, but it's hard not to when it's snaking thickly to one side. "Okay. Let's talk."

There's nowhere to sit since the only chair is piled

high with boxes and a football jersey with his number: 12. Probably the one he wore tonight.

I pick it up. I'm tempted to hold it to my face and take a deep breath.

"I want you to have that. If my lucky charm wears my lucky jersey, maybe it'll help me win every game. I'll wash it first."

What I'm thinking is, *I don't want you to wash it.* And it's a good place to start. Holding his jersey, I walk over to the other side of the bed. I lean against the pillows, curling onto my side to face him. But I leave some distance between us. "You really want me to wear it?" I happen to know that athletes are some of the most superstitious people on the planet. So are their coaches.

"I already told you you're my dream girl, that we're destined to be together and that I haven't been with anyone else for a long time. What do you want? A ring?"

I stare at him for a long moment. "What? You mean…"

"Marry me, if that's the kind of assurance you want."

"Very funny."

His eyes are locked on mine. "I get it, it's too soon. But here you go: I want you. I know we're taking a risk, but to me it's worth it, Zara. I know the situation is complicated. I know we'll probably have to deal with the consequences of that at some point soon. I'm ready to. I don't want to wait. The last thing I was expecting was for you to wander into my life and grab me by the fucking heart with both hands. And that's exactly what you've done. I know it's crazy. But I'm not letting you slip through my fingers because I didn't try hard enough to keep you. I would regret that a hell of a lot more than taking a risk for you."

"It's a big risk," I whisper. This room is full of reminders of all he has to lose.

"And we're ready for that. I can't be casual about this, Zara. My dream girl is real. When that happens, you don't just let her go and know she's wandering around out there for any asshole to look at and lust after. Don't ask me to fucking do that. I can't."

He sounds like he means it. "Okay."

"The only way I'll be able to concentrate on football is if you're *with* me. I need to know you're okay. I need you safe at all times. I need you to be happy. And if you're not, tell me so I can fix it."

Okay, I'm curious. "How would you fix it?"

"Fix what?"

"What if I'm not happy?"

His finger twirls a ringlet of my hair. "Then I'll fucking cook you breakfast or fly you to France or call your friends or give you the best orgasm you've ever had. Whatever it takes."

I blink at him for a few seconds. "Damn you. You just did it again."

"Did what again?"

"Said the nicest thing anyone has ever said to me."

"This is what I was born for." He exhales a low laugh, at the intensity of his romantic tendencies, maybe. "*Fuck,* Zara." He has such amazing eyes. Dark-rimmed and lightning bright and so full of awe I can't help but…well, fall deeply, irrevocably in love with him. *Thank you thank you thank you.* His rough-edged fingers draw a line along the tender skin of my cheek. "I like the face paint, by the way."

"Just supporting my quarterback."

"It's a good start." He's quiet for a few seconds, drinking in the sight of me in that enthralled way he has, watering those little seeds of blooming connection he's so thoroughly planted in me.

"We could wait until after football season, you know." My voice is soft, and careful. "I'd wait for you."

"And I'd wait for you. But what if something tears us apart before then, for whatever reason? What if something happens that we don't see coming? We both know time isn't something you can take for granted. That feels like a bigger risk to me."

"But what if it gets you——"

He places a finger over my lips. "Stop protesting and trust your quarterback. We're exclusive now. Or I'll be forced to hunt down every man who glances in your general direction and beat him to a bloody pulp. Like that little fucker in your art class. So—please—for the sake of my team, don't run from me."

"Elias, it's for your team that I *should* be running from you."

"I've just explained why it would be worse for us if you did. I want you at every game, wearing my jersey. I'll deal with the fallout."

"We'll both deal with it," I remind him gently. I think of the risk I'm also taking. But you can't live your life tied up by other people's ironclad rules that don't actually apply anymore, even if that person is your own dad and you cherish your relationship with him above almost anything.

Things change. Things *have* changed and Elias is right. It feels like a bigger risk to let him go than it does to keep him. My mother ran out of time. So did his. I think both of us are too deeply aware of that to waste it.

We'll just have to fight for each other when our decision catches up with us. And we both know it will, probably sooner rather than later.

His thumb brushes over my lips. He's watching my mouth and his breathing is heavier now. "You told me I was all your firsts. Does that mean…" It almost seems like he's bracing himself. "You've never been with anyone before me? Before the other night?"

"No. Of course not."

"Not at all?"

"Not even a single kiss. I guess it's sort of pathetic."

"It's not pathetic. It's meant to be." The blue-ember

burn behind his eyes is quietly, deeply relieved. There's a thread of wild emotion in him. "Mine."

I think it's been true since he was standing there, lost for words and more gorgeous than anyone I'd ever seen, on that very first day.

His nearness is affecting me, like it always does. My pussy is warm and wet, pulsing with soft, sweet heat. But there's so much I want to know about him. I need more information about the guy I'm now apparently exclusive with. *Before I very thoroughly cash in my V-card with him.* I know that as soon as he kisses me, neither one of us will be able to stop, and neither one of us will want to. "What's your middle name?" I ask him.

"Joseph. It's my dad's name. What's yours?"

"Adelaide. After my mother."

"My mother's name was Amelia."

"I love that name." It's hard to talk about them but it's a bond we share. It's hard for both of us, which somehow makes it less hard. And this is good. It's only a matter of time before I'm closer to Elias O'Shea than I've ever been to anyone. We're starting to get to know each other along the way. "What's your favorite movie of all time?"

"Of all time?"

"Yeah."

He thinks about it. "What's yours?"

"Hmm. Maybe Sweet Home Alabama."

"I've never seen it."

"Really? Never?"

"Never."

"I've seen it around a hundred times."

"I think I need to see it, then."

"Maybe we can watch it together sometime."

"We can watch it tomorrow. We don't have practice. We're getting a rare day off."

"You still didn't tell me yours."

"Maybe Raiders of the Lost Ark. Or one of the Star Wars movies. The earlier ones. Bo used to watch them and whenever he'd put them on we'd always end up watching the whole thing."

"Bo?"

"He's a friend from home. We played football together all through high school. We've been friends since we were kids."

"Bo McCabe? The quarterback who went viral for falling in love with the girl from the Jumbotron?"

"You heard about that?"

"I think everyone heard about it. My sister told me about it, and she lives in California. It was so romantic, that he could just fall for her like that and not even know who she was. Are they still together?"

"She moved in with him."

"Wow. So I guess that proves it. Love at first sight is real."

"I already knew it was real."

"Have you ever been in love?" I ask him.

The smile lingers. "Is this a trick question?"

"No. Answer it."

My sassiness is getting a reaction. His dark eyes flash and his smile is hot. "Yes."

"How many times?"

He's playing my game, making me wait. "Once."

I guess I know what he's implying but it's still hard to grasp that this literal superhero is somehow convinced *I'm* his star-crossed soul mate, when it's been less than a week since we randomly met in the middle of the stadium.

I want to test him. I want him to somehow prove that all this lovestruck stuff is for real. "What did she look like?"

Elias leans back, humoring me. A thick lock of his hair partly obscures one of his blue eyes. Carefully, I smooth it back.

"Her eyes are green," he tells me. "But not your ordinary kind of green. They make her look like there's magic going on inside her soul, like it's all glittery in there and if you can only get close to her, it'll rub off on you. And you *want* it to, so fucking bad. Your craving to have some of her fairy dust sprinkle itself onto your life is so intense it makes you do crazy shit, like scale the walls of her dorm just so you can get close to her."

Elias O'Shea is a romantic—like me, even though I never knew it until now.

"And her hair is so shiny and soft-looking, with all these different colors of blond weaved through it that catch all the light of the sun, which seems to follow her wherever she goes and land directly on her, even in the dark, like now, that it almost seems as though she's made of silk and starlight."

Turns out, Elias is *very* good at humoring me. He leans his big, buff body toward mine and we're sort of gazing into each other's eyes now. His warm, jean-clad thigh rests against my bare skin. "How did you know it was love, as opposed to…before?" I sound like an investigative journalist but I don't care. *When you were with all those others girls* lingers in the air, but I don't say that part out loud.

His eyes glimmer with both humor and something more like agony. "It just landed fully formed in my head as soon as I saw her. *I want her*, is what I was thinking. And I couldn't question it because it was so fucking sure of itself. And then when I tasted her, that's when I knew for sure that I was ruined for anyone else. Because her lips are perfection. And her pussy tastes like the sweetest honey on earth."

I feel myself blush. Lying here in this locked, private haven, feeling less alone than I ever have in my life, I'm still aware of my own inexperience.

His eyes are watching mine and they're so spellbound. So vividly blue.

His hand smooths a strand of my hair back from my face. "You blow my mind every time I look at you."

It's as though he's seeing me like I see him: flawless, even though there's no such thing.

We lay there like that for a while, just staring into each

other's eyes and it's the most connective experience I've ever had. Like our souls are melting into each other's, merging and entwining.

He brushes his lips over mine. "You're worth the risk, Zara. And so am I."

And so I go with it, because I don't have it in me to resist him.

"Do you trust me?" he says.

"No," I whisper.

He laughs again, reaching down to unbutton his jeans. I glance down and—*holy hell.* His huge cock lays taut against his hair-dusted stomach, glistening with moisture. At the sight, a warm pleasure-throb softens my pussy. My nipples bead against the thin, soft fabric of my Wildcats shirt. "I could barely throw the ball in the right direction tonight because I'm so obsessed with how fucking gorgeous you are and how good you taste, baby girl. All I can think about is eating your sweet pussy like the starving man I am until you come all over my face."

I'm blushing and I can feel that my panties are saturated. But he's gruff tonight, and bossy. I want to challenge him. "It looked like you were throwing it in the right direction to me."

His smile is cocky and heartbreaking. "It's the best I've ever played."

"Really?"

"That's why they were you calling you my lucky charm."

I don't want to think about anything outside this room. I've become molten and liquid, hot beyond belief.

"Are you ready for another kiss?"

"Almost."

He smiles, his lips brushing against mine. "I'm going to take all your firsts, angel girl. Every single one of them, in the best possible way. That's my mission in life now. But I'm not going to rush you. We'll go as slow you want."

But we're not going slow. His kiss turns greedy and desperate, claiming me as our tongues tangle and slide.

His fingers graze my nipple, which goes taut and softly electric.

"I'm going to take this off you now, baby girl. I want you naked for me, okay? I need to taste you. You can tell me to stop anytime and I will. I'll only do what you beg me to do."

Oh god. "Okay." I'm nervous, but not unsure.

Elias pulls my shirt up, unclasping my bra and easing it off. Then he takes off my skirt, hooking my panties with his thumbs and pulling those off too.

"You're so fucking beautiful it hurts."

Elias kicks off his jeans and—*oh, sweet Jesus.* I mean, I've seen him…and *sucked* on him—with gusto, let's call it like it is—but the thought of taking all that *inside* me is daunting, to say the least. How will it even…*fit?* I mean, of course I know how everything works but this is next level.

He seems to read my mind. "I'm going to get you nice and soft and ready for me. It'll feel good, trust me."

Elias lightly circles my nipple his rough fingers, teasing me. Each squeezing pull sends a current of pooling need deep into my body. He leans closer, drawing the sensitive bud into the hot fire of his mouth, sucking hungrily until a melting warmth builds in the core of my body. It feels *so good*. He moves to my other breast, feeding there like he's starving, drawing with his mouth until the melting warmth inside me gets hotter. And deeper. And higher, reaching an excruciating peak and then tumbling over it. I moan as the pleasure-surges clench voluptuously inside me, over and over.

Holy fuck.

"Good girl. You're so fucking hot, Zara. Let's see how many times I can make you come."

He takes his time, lazily licking and sucking until I think I might be about to come *again*, but then he starts kissing a line down my stomach. His tongue dips into my belly button which makes me squirm but he holds me down, roughly pushing my legs apart.

I can feel the hot strikes of his breath on my clit and fresh wetness coats my pussy. "You're so wet for me, baby. How bad does my dirty girl want me to eat this perfect pussy? You want to come again, baby girl?" Elias touches his tongue to my clit and I moan. "That's my girl. Fuck, you drive me crazy. I can't sleep. I can barely play football. I'm fucking obsessed with you. I'm addicted to this wet, pink, perfect little heaven on earth." He eats into me like I'm a ripe, juicy fruit, dipping his tongue inside me. "You taste so fucking good."

His mouth fixes on my clit and he sucks on me in deep, rhythmic draws. My body goes limp. Where his mouth is latched becomes the center of my universe. The pleasure radiates in slow-moving waves. He slides his fingers barely inside me, pushing the burn deeper as his mouth feasts and pulls. The feverish pleasure consumes me in a tidal surge. I'm writhing against his mouth. Wave after wave of pleasure throbs hotly through my entire being as my pussy clenches, over and over. I hear a low sound and realize it's me, moaning his name.

"Elias," I whisper, after the waves calm.

He takes his time, licking me clean, murmuring dirty words about how he'll never get enough. It's so deliciously carnal, another deep ripple of bliss breaks my heart, because I'll never get enough either. Then he climbs up my body, laying himself over me.

I weave my fingers through his hair. I need him. I'm riding some crazy rush and I need him to anchor me.

Elias's enormous cock is pressing hotly against my stomach. He shifts his weight, and his rigid length slides against my still-spasming pussy.

"Maybe you've had enough for now. I don't know if you're ready for more."

I glare at him in a daze, gripping him more tightly. I gasp something that sounds like, "I *am*."

"We can take it slow."

"*No*."

He laughs, even though his eyes are so lusty and dark, he almost looks dangerous. In a good way. In exactly the kind of way I need him to be right now.

"Elias?"

"Yeah?"

"I'm on the pill." It's fairly obvious that this night is quickly shaping up to be another one of my firsts. A gargantuan one. "My sister sort of insisted, before I started college."

"Remind me to thank her." The head of his cock rubs against my slick, hyper-sensitive clit. "Are you sure you're ready for this? Tell me to stop."

"*No. Don't stop*." Because if he keeps doing that I'm going to come again. And I *need* to come again. So fucking badly I'm holding onto him for dear life, trying to keep him pressed against me. I don't even mean to squirm but it's like my supple body has a mind of its own. *I want to get closer. I want him to push that huge cock inside me.*

"This will be a first for me too. I've never had sex bareback before. I want you to know I'm good to go. It's been a while and we get regular tests as part of our health checks."

"You've really never…?"

"No. But this is *you*, Zara. My dream girl is real. I want to fuck you with no barriers, baby girl. I want to *feel* you. Are you ready for me to fuck this tight little pussy that's all mine?"

His cock is there, pressing thickly against the sweet coil of pleasure that's still rippling through my core. "*Yes.*"

"All right, then. You'll take it like a good girl, won't you? Wrap your legs around me and hold on tight."

He pushes his thick length against my slippery pussy, opening me. I'm tight but so wet he slides in a little. *God, he's so freaking big.*

"*Oh, fuck,*" he growls, taking my mouth in a ravenous kiss.

Elias's thumb glides over my clit while his other hand grips me. He's so strong I think he might leave bruises. I'm glad. I want him to mark me and claim me as his. He forces his thick cock barely inside me, pushing me toward the edge of a mindless bliss that's edged with star-studded pain.

"You ready, angel girl?" he murmurs against my neck.

"*Oh.*" I can't deal with how much he hurts and how good he feels.

"Is that a yes?"

"*Fuck. Yes. Do it.*"

I can *feel* more than hear his low laughter as his gigantic cock slides deeper. My silky body stretches to accommodate him and the pleasure-pain becomes a dizzying tsunami riding a crazy-high crest. My whole body is throbbing with desperate need. It's happening.

His thumb rubs against my clit and it's enough. The

wave crashes. The clenching spasms pull Elias's massive cock deeper. He's gripping me, sliding thickly into the rapture. There's a flash of pain somewhere inside this wall of pleasure and I cry out as he thrusts hard and deep, until he's fully rooted inside me. His hands grip me in lusty fistfuls, ensuring total possession.

All I can feel is Elias. *He's so big and so deep.*

"You feel so fucking good baby. I'll never get enough of you." He's kissing me as he fucks me with his whole body, giving me his tongue as he thrusts in punishing drives.

The pain only compounds the bliss. I'm coming hard. My pussy is milking his huge, hot bulk in tight, compressing squeezes as I suck gently on his tongue. He groans as his cock jerks inside me. The jets of his liquid heat find some perfect trigger, setting me off again. My inner muscles work him as we come together in some kind of mindless, gripping, grinding frenzy.

His body lays heavily over mine, his thickness still throbbing hotly, wedged deep inside me.

My arms and legs are wrapped around him, my core rippling around him almost lovingly.

"You've melted my bones," I whisper.

I can feel his lazy smile against my neck.

This is nothing like I was expecting. I thought my first time might hurt, emotionally as well as physically, like I was being used, or broken. I never expected that losing my virginity would make me feel like a freaking goddess warrior. The warm, pleasure-heavy flood of him is empowering me. *This is what I was born for,* he told me. And it's weirdly true. Our bodies and souls are feeding off of each other with a desperate, enthralled madness that feels more like true love than anything ever has.

My heart is beating in sync with his. Our bodies are still locked in a secret, pulsing rhythm as he kisses my face. My lips.

Elias O'Shea is a part of me now. I want to keep him close to me, inside me, always, just like this.

"I LOVE THIS MOVIE," he murmurs in my ear. We're in his bed, watching Sweet Home Alabama on his laptop. I'm curled up on my side with my knees pulled up. Elias's big body is wrapped around mine as he spoons me.

And fucks me.

From behind.

Slowly, like he's dreaming me.

We took a shower together. He washed me, making me come with the relentless, clever curl of his fingers. And was fascinated by the power my careful, soapy hands have over him. He came so hard he had to wash me all over again.

He made me breakfast in bed. His cock was so painfully hot-looking and perfect as he fed me French toast, that I sucked on him until he came again in milky mouthfuls.

I've given up trying to slow this down or resist him. I can't, it's as simple as that. And I don't want to. He has the power to pull me completely out of my shell, until I'm drinking him and offering myself to him like I already know how.

We've hardly disconnected. When Elias said he was obsessed, he wasn't kidding. He's been kissing me and feasting on me like he's starved for it. He's lost all control and doesn't care. Maybe we're making up for lost time. Or maybe we're desperate to make the most of this avalanche of beauty sparking between us, because we can. And because we know that there are things that will happen after we leave this little bubble of lust and connection that are going to try to tear us apart.

He's come inside me more times than I can count. My body *loves* this. I've turned into a vessel of squirming, primal need. My little devil-mermaid is having the time of her life.

And he's about to do it again.

I arch my back, taking him deeper, giving him everything.

"You okay, baby girl?" I can already tell by the rasp of his voice that he's close.

"*Oh*," I moan, and it sounds almost like *ow*. I am, in fact, *very* sore. He's trying to be gentle with me but he's too feral. "Look," I gasp. "You're missing the best part. This is where she tells him she can't marry him. Because she gave her heart away a long time ago. And she never really got it back."

Elias's fingers glide across my clit, gently squeezing as his cock thrusts deep inside me. "I can relate. I gave mine away on a sunny afternoon in the middle of a stadium, and now I'm so fucking in love it's killing me."

His next thrust unravels me, shattering me into a million tiny pieces of raw, pain-edged bliss. I'm writhing, squeezing him with my body, instinctually working his pleasure until he gives me what I want. The warm, thick pulse of his essence. His surrender and his gift.

I don't know how it happens. How you can transform, like a chrysalis bursting wide open, finding out that you're actually the most beautiful butterfly. I don't know how you can fall in love over the course of a single weekend, with both yourself and the one who feels like he was sent to you from the universe as some kind of cosmic perfect match. All I know is that I have.

20

ELIAS

"WHAT KIND OF CAR IS THIS?"

"A Corvette Stingray."

"Oh," she says.

I kiss her for the thousandth time, helping her get into the passenger seat. Once she's in, I close the door carefully. Then I get into the driver's seat, start the car and start backing out of the driveway. It's the slowest I've ever driven. I don't want her bounced around too much by the speed bumps.

"This thing is like a spaceship."

"I wish it was. Then I could fly you up to Mars and keep you all to myself until the end of time."

Zara smiles, but then she's distracted by her phone, ringing in her pocket. She pulls it out to check the number. "It's my sister. She wants to FaceTime. She's left me a zillion messages. I can call her back. We usually talk every day."

"Answer it. She's probably worried."

She hesitates, then answers. "Hey, Han."

"I was about to call the freaking cops, Zee. Why haven't you answered your phone in two days? Dad hasn't heard from you either."

"I've…been busy."

"Doing what?"

"Doing exactly what you told me to do."

"What did I tell you to do again?"

"Have fun, remember?"

"Oh yeah. Where are you?"

"I'm just… with a friend. I'm on my way to class."

"What friend?"

"Um…" Zara glances over at me, then does her best to change the subject. "How are you, by the way? How's your new job?"

"What kind of *car* is that?"

"It's…a Corvette Stingray."

"Whose is it?"

"Listen, Han, we're almost there so I'm going to have to call you back a little later—"

"Have you met any guys? Are there any hot freshmen in your classes?"

"Uh…no, I haven't met any hot freshmen yet." Guiltily, she bites her lip. Just the sight of her little white teeth sinking gently into her plump bottom lip gets me going again. My cock thickens as I remember how fucking sweet she looked with those pink lips wrapped around it, *swallowing my overflowing cum as I came harder than I ever have in my life. Until the next time with her.*

Fuck.

How am I going to handle being separated from her? How am I going to get through the day and casually act like everything is normal when my addiction is on overdrive?

She ends the call as I pull up in front of her dorm and kill the engine. We sit there for a while, not wanting our time together to end.

I hold her face in my hands and kiss her, tasting her, drowning in my obsession for her. "Zara?"

"Yeah?"

"I know it's fast. I don't want to scare you or rush you or freak you out. Don't say anything when I tell you what I'm about to tell you."

She's quiet, blinking up at me with those colorful green eyes, which are so star-flecked and filled with light, they *do* make her look like there's magic going on inside her soul.

"I'm fucking head over heels in love with you," I tell her. "You're beautiful. You're—"

She holds a finger to my lips. Then, softly, she kisses me. "I had a good time. I don't regret anything. You're all my firsts, Elias O'Shea."

"I want to be a million more of them."

It's incredibly fucking difficult to leave her.

"Answer my calls." I kiss her again. I don't want to let her go. Here, inside my car, I can control whatever influences will try to keep us apart. Out there, there are too many forces at play that will try to do exactly that. "When can I see you again. Tonight?"

"Okay. Tonight. I'll be in my studio."

She opens the door and gets out. It's early morning but there are a few people around and we're taking a risk. "See you tonight, then."

I watch her go into her dorm, then I drive over to the gym. Noah, Mitch and Jared are always here first, trying to prove to Coach they're dedicated. West is just arriving. He checks to make sure no one else is within earshot. Then he punches me lightly on the arm. "Was wondering if we were going to see you this morning, QB. I'm guessing you had a better weekend than I did."

She feels far too sacred to talk about. "Don't even go there, Westie. Unless you want your face rearranged."

He laughs but there's genuine sincerity in him. "I hope it was real for you, brother."

The way he means it is almost touching. It's probably the nicest thing he's ever said to me. "It was."

Grinning, he climbs onto the leg press machine. Jake and Gabe arrive and the place gets crowded.

Two personal trainers who work specifically with me start running me through a series of lateral raises, front raises and side planks and it helps take my mind off how far gone I am and how much I miss her. An hour passes. Then two.

We're almost done when I look up to see Coach Fox and Coach Warren, one of the offensive line assistant coaches, standing near the machine I'm working on. Coach Warren is holding his phone and both of them are staring at it grimly.

Whatever they're looking at is deeply concerning to them. Coach's agitation is easy to read.

"O'Shea," Coach says gruffly and I don't like the edge to it.

I climb off the machine. Coach Warren holds his phone out. "What the fuck were you thinking, Elias," he murmurs, shaking his head. It's not a question. It's a warning in slow motion. It's the writing on the wall. I take the phone from him. My blood ices in my veins, but I have no regrets. How can I when she's so fucking perfect?

It's a photo of Zara and me. We're in my car and I'm kissing her. *Really* kissing her. My hands are weaved through her hair, which is an adorable riot of bed-head curls. It's obvious that we've spent the night together, especially since the post states clearly: *Two hours ago.*

It's barely seven a.m.

I steel myself for what's coming, but I wouldn't change anything, even if I could.

"That's my daughter." Coach's voice is graveled with rage.

"I know that, sir. Zara and I are—"

"She's a *freshman*. And completely off limits to you and everyone else on this team! You *knew* that! Get out of my goddamn gym."

"Coach, I'm in *love* with her." It sounds wildly unrealistic, blurted out like that in front of the entire team and all the coaches, even if my voice sounds resolute as fuck.

"How *dare* you! You don't even know her!" Coach's outrage is unchecked, but he catches himself, trying to control his temper. Even so, each word is dripping with fury. "I've seen the carnage you cause, O'Shea. I've watched you play the field every goddamn night for the past three years. How many naive hearts have you broken? Hundreds? *Thousands?* It's what you do! You play games and you destroy lives. That's *all* you've done since the minute you stepped foot on this campus. Players like you don't deserve—"

"I'm not playing *games* with Zara, Coach. I'm fucking *serious* about her!" He's furious and so am I. I can't give her up. I'll die if I have to give her up. "I *mean* that, Coach. This is different."

"You're goddamn right it's different! It's different because *this* time it's cost you your place on this team. Now get the hell out of my gym before I call security."

"Coach, I'd never hurt Zara. She's—"

"You're damn right you won't!" He's absolutely seething. "Because you're never to see her or talk to her again! Stay away from my daughter. And get the hell off my team before I do something I'll regret." With that he turns to leave, barking orders at several of the other coaches. "See him out. Get him out of my sight." The cold venom in his tone doesn't leave room for negotiation.

"You're not even going to give me a chance to *prove* myself? You won't even let me *try*?"

"Oh, you've proven yourself, O'Shea! You've *proven* that you're capable of preying on freshmen girls who are too innocent to see you for what you really are. You can go do it somewhere else from now on. Out!"

Coach Warren and a few of the other assistants grab my arms but I shake them off, heading for the door as my team watches me leave, with varying expressions of disbelief and confusion. Gabriel and Jake are in shock. "Good luck," I tell them.

They try to follow me but they're called back by Coach Warren. I can hear his low warning.

I get to the locker room, fury and anguish warring inside me. How dare *I*? How dare *he*? He wouldn't even fucking *listen*! So the fuck what if I have a past, who doesn't? Does *he*? I'd bet a million fucking dollars that his own past probably looks a lot like mine, before he met the wife he was devastated to lose.

I'm not losing Zara.

Fuck it. I'll play football somewhere else. I'll start talking to the scouts who have been in contact.

Coach's warning echoes in my head. *I think we both know that scouts are rarely interested in players whose coaches have issues with them. My feedback plays into their decisions, as you're well-aware. If any information comes across as negative, then more often than not those players are removed from the value boards. Am I making myself clear enough?*

My phone rings in my bag. I pull it out, thinking it might be Zara. If I have to leave, I'll convince her to come with me.

Would she? Would she chose me over her father?

But it's Bo.

Why would Bo be calling me? Some sixth sense gives me a dark, sinking feeling that grips my heart in its fist. Bo's been my best friend since junior high and he was on the football team with me all the way through high school. He checks in on my dad once a week for me, and keeps in touch with the home help I hired. "Bo."

"Elias. Listen, I wish I didn't have to tell you this, but…it's about your dad."

"What about him?"

"He's dead. It just happened. I'm sorry, man. The nurse called me a few minutes ago and the ambulance is already here. It was a massive heart attack. There was nothing they could do. I'm so sorry, brother."

21

Zara

"Wake up, Zara. Zara, wake up."

Isla's sitting on my bed, shaking me gently.

"What time is it?" I ask, groggy.

"Zara, it's Elias."

I sit up a little. "Is he okay?"

"He's off the team."

"What? *No.* Oh, shit. Isla. I have to find him."

"He left a note for you. It's downstairs. Kit said the entire lobby is filled with flowers. He sent you, like, a hundred bunches of flowers. He told Gabriel to arrange it when he was leaving."

"Where is he?"

"Don't freak out, but there was a photo of the two of you online. Someone saw you getting out of his car."

"*Oh no.*"

"Whoever it was posted the photo online and it's… well, it's sort of…gone viral."

Isla hands me her phone, showing me the photo. It's a zoomed-in shot of me and Elias. He's holding my face in his hands and he's kissing me. We both look completely lost in the moment. I have to admit, it's a good photo. You can tell it's us. Besides, his car is hardly subtle. It's blue and more fancy than any car I'd ever seen. It's not hard to guess how we spent our night. My hair's a mess. We look…like we just had hot, passionate sex and lots of it.

"It's all over social media. Someone recognized you. They found out you're the coach's daughter. It got back to your dad and he kicked Elias off the team. Then, five minutes later, Elias got a phone call from home. His dad died. They found him this morning. It was a heart attack."

"Oh my god."

"And now he's gone."

"Gone? Gone where?"

"He told Gabriel to tell me that he'd be back for you."

"Where is he?"

"He went home to Michigan."

I jump out of bed, handing her phone back to her. "I have to go see my dad. I have to call Elias."

"None of the guys can get a hold of him. His phone just goes straight to voicemail."

I find my phone and I check my messages. There are a lot of them. But none from Elias. And none from my dad. I hit the call button. Isla's right, it goes straight to voicemail.

So I leave him a message. "Elias. I just heard what happened. I'm so, so sorry about your dad. I hope you're okay. I'm going to go talk to my dad and everything will be okay with the team, I'm going to make sure of it. I'll fix this. I'm so sorry." The message beeps and cuts me off.

Fuck.

I go into the bathroom, brushing my teeth in a rush. As I do this, I find some jeans, a sweater and a pair of sneakers, yanking them on. I grab my keys and my bag.

"I'm coming with you." Isla follows me. I jab the elevator button but it's too slow so we run down the stairs down to the lobby.

It looks like a convention of florists went wild down here. There are dozens of vases of stunning red roses. Their perfume has infused the entire room. They're covering the entire desk. And the tables. There are some on the floor.

Three very large security guards are standing inside the locked front doors, facing a crowd of people outside. Some have microphones with news channel logos on them. When they see me, they start pounding on the glass, taking photos and yelling my name.

Kit rushes out from behind the desk. "Zara. I've left

you, like, twenty messages. Here." She hands me a small white envelope with *Zara* written on the front of it. "Those people are the press. Fucking CNN is here. You don't have to talk to them, Zara. They won't get in here."

I open the envelope and pull out the note.

> To my absolute perfection.
> I'll come back for you.
> Everything will be okay.
> Don't ever doubt me.
> You're the one, Z.

"This is all my fault." There are tears in my eyes. "I have to find him."

"Zara, you can't go out there." Kit is frantic. "The back door is just as bad."

"I need to see my dad." The thought of walking across campus is daunting, with all these people chasing after me. I go up to one of the security guards. "Can you help me get to my car? It's just over there, at the edge of the parking lot."

"Sure thing, miss."

Isla's holding my arm. "I'll come with you."

We get outside and literally hundreds of people swarm around us. They're taking photos and pushing their microphones in my face, yelling questions all at once.

"Did you spend the weekend with Elias O'Shea?"

"Did you know Elias is off the team?"

"Are you and Elias together?"

"When's the last time you spoke to him?"

"Do you feel responsible for getting Elias O'Shea kicked off the Wildcats? Do you think you've hurt his chances of going pro?"

The security guards do their best to make a path for us and we finally get to my car. Isla and I jump in, fighting to get in and close the doors. I click the lock and start the car but I have to be careful not to run the assholes over.

"Fucking hell," Isla gasps. "These people are rabid."

"They're right though, Isla. It *is* my fault."

"It's not your fault, Zara. Don't say that. None of it's your fault."

"I should have left when I had the chance. I should never have gone there in the first place."

"If you're going to blame anyone, blame me. *I'm* the one who got talked into dragging you over there on Saturday night."

I'm trying to keep my eyes on the road and not get freaked out by the cars that are obviously following us. But I need to tell someone. I need to let it out. "I love him."

I glance over to find her staring at me. "You *do?*"

I laugh weakly, swiping away a tear. "Am I going insane? I lost my virginity to the hot quarterback and meanwhile fell head over heels in love with him over the course of *one week* and now I've fucked up his entire life."

"You haven't. Your dad probably just lost his temper. It'll blow over. He'll come to his senses."

"He has no sense when it come to this particular topic."

"Just give it some time."

"And now Elias has lost his dad. God, he'll be so devastated. His dad was all he had."

Until now. Now he has me. If he still wants me after I've cost so much.

"Zara?"

"Yeah?"

"Are you okay? Did it...hurt?" Her golden eyes are wide behind her little round glasses.

"You mean...?"

"Sex. Your first time."

"No. I mean, it hurt a little. But it was...a good kind of pain. It was the best thing that's ever happened to me. All of it. It was just...intensely beautiful."

She sighs sort of dreamily. "You're so lucky. I hope I fall in love."

I'm still trying to figure out if she's got a thing for Jake or not. It definitely seems that way. I don't even know if she realizes it. "Do you have someone in mind?"

"No," she says lightly.

I pull up in front of the players' facility behind the stadium. There's another smaller crowd of reporters gathered outside the doors but they must realize there's no way they'll be allowed in.

"Go to your class, Isla. I'll be okay. I don't know how this is going to go."

"Are you sure, Zara? I'll come with you if you want me to."

"No, it's fine." I give her a heartfelt hug.

"I'll let you know if I hear anything."

"Thanks, roomie. You're a true friend."

She grins at me. "Besties for life."

I get to the door and show my ID to security. They immediately let me through.

My dad is sitting at his desk, talking on the phone. I close the door behind me. When he sees me come in, his expression is stormier than I've ever seen it. I've seen sadness and I've seen a whole lot of grief, but this is different. He's livid. Even worse, he's disappointed. It's a weird thing, to face your dad when you both know he's thinking about the fact that you're probably no longer a virgin.

But that's life. Most people get to do things like that without their dad knowing about it. And it almost pisses me off that the two of us have to be *this* in tune. I can make my own choices, and I have. I don't regret anything except that my dad has to know every freaking detail.

"Clayton is with the coaching staff now," he says into the phone. "I need to call you back. Something urgent's come up." I know the name Jared Clayton. He's the second string quarterback.

My dad ends the call.

I launch straight into it. "I need you to put him back on the team. Right now. It's not his fault. It's mine."

"I asked one thing of you, Zara. *One* thing." He hardly ever calls me Zara. It's always "punkin" or honey or sweetheart. I don't think I've ever seen my dad this furious. He gets up out of his chair and he starts pacing. His face is red. "It had to be one of my *players*? Out of the thirty-five thousand students at Hawthorne, you had to pick *that* one?"

"When you know, you know."

He stops pacing to glare at me. It's cruel of me, maybe, to reference his own connection to my beautiful lost mother, the love of his life. But then I realize that I'm entitled to one of those too.

"Daddy, I love you. I always have and I always will. But my personal life doesn't have to involve you."

"It does when it's one of my *players*, Zara, damn it! You *know* that." He's pacing again. "Of all the people you could have chosen, you had to go for my *starting quarter-back*? Do you know where this puts our team? Did you *think* about that before you—" He can't bring himself to say what he's thinking. He doesn't have to.

"I didn't '*go*' for your starting quarterback, Dad. I met him and we…" How to say this? "We have a connection."

"How much of a connection can you have with someone you've known for a goddamn *week*?"

I hate that I'm crying. *I'm* mad too. All Elias ever did

was care about me. "You said you met mom and you knew instantly. You've been telling me that my whole life. What if *I* knew? What if I *know*? You should be *glad* he's the starting quarterback! At least I chose the best of the best. You shouldn't hold that against me. And you definitely shouldn't hold it against him! I want you to put him back on the team right now. You have to. You have to call him up and tell him that as soon as he gets back from dealing with what he's dealing with—which happens to be losing his *own* dad—that he's back on the team."

"He knows the rules and so do you. I don't make exceptions."

"God, Dad! Why are you being so stubborn? He's *good* to me. He's not seeing anyone else. He's—"

"Of course you'd believe that. They all do. I've seen it a hundred times and he's no different. Zara, you are *not* to see him again. I mean that. You're to stay away from him and that's final!"

It's the first argument I've ever had with my dad. Ever. We've always gotten along amazingly well. But his old rule doesn't make sense anymore. And I refuse to be shackled to it. "You're wrong. This *is* different. And if it isn't, then I'll make my own mistakes." I take a deep breath and try to calm myself. "I want you to think for a second about how much you loved her, from that very first day. How much would you have risked for her? How far would you have gone to keep her?"

He's breathing sort of heavily as he glowers at me, but he doesn't answer me.

"The rules don't apply anymore, Dad. I get to make my own now. If you can't forgive him for me, do it for her."

My heart feels like it's breaking, but I turn from him and walk out the door.

22

ELIAS

I PLACE the last of the boxes in Bo's huge attic, brushing the dust off my hands. I'm covered in dirt and drenched in sweat from lugging thirty years' worth of boxed-up shit from my dad's house over to Bo's. "That's everything."

"You could rent the house out for a while, Elias. That would give you time to adjust and think about what you want to do."

"I know what I want to do."

I've spent the past ten days going through everything my parents ever owned or accumulated. Which, as it turns out, was a fucking lot. My dad was a borderline hoarder.

"I offered to buy him a new house a few years ago," I tell Bo. "After I got the Nike deal. I offered him three million dollars to buy any house he wanted. But he refused to leave my mother's memories. That's what he said."

"You should be glad. If he'd had a ten bedroom house, he probably would have filled it with Wildcats merch."

I laugh but there's no humor in it. "True."

Everything in that house was in some way related to me. Hundreds of newspaper clippings, all my childhood trophies, medals and certificates. School report cards. MVP awards dated all the way back to my Pop Warner days. My old baseball glove. Football helmets I wore in junior high. My old Hawks jersey. I wore the same number then as I do now. Every bookshelf was dedicated to showcasing all the early achievement of my life. A thousand photographs, mostly of me. Graduations. The day I became starting quarterback. The ones of my mother that have sat in their same positions for as long as I can remember, gathering dust.

I take a swig from the half-bottle of whiskey I found wedged into the chair my dad always sat in, which the removal company took away today, along with a truck-load of other stuff I just don't need to haul along with me through life.

But I feel weirdly untethered. Like all the ties that kept me grounded are suddenly gone.

"This is a lot to deal with at once, Elias. You're allowed to take some time for this stuff."

"I don't need time." Time, in some ways, has always

been something to fight against. Or fight for, who the fuck knows.

I boxed up everything I wanted to keep. The pictures. Some of the trophies. But a lot of it was just stuff that's lost its meaning without my dad's die-hard enthusiasm.

Do I even want to play football anymore?

"Of course you do. You've always played just as much for yourself as you ever did for him."

I didn't even realize I'd said that out loud. Maybe because I've drunk my way through seven or eight shots of whiskey. Maybe nine.

Bo closes the attic window and turns off one of the lights. "Besides, your coach will probably come crawling back to you any minute. Your team just lost their second game without you, 37-3."

Shit. Our QB2, Jared Clayton, just doesn't have enough experience to handle the pressure. He has a long way to go when it comes to precision. He's young, green and crumbles too often when he's feeling the heat. Throwing him in at the deep end will help him learn, but it might take him all season to get there.

No doubt he'll be taking it hard. And the rest of the guys will be seething with disappointment.

"Come on," Bo says, "we're done up here. I'll put some steaks on the grill."

Bo's house is a modern mansion built on its own estate that's surrounded by high stone walls. His parents, who both died six or seven years ago, were loaded. His dad was eccentric and extremely good at making money, and his mother was a designer and an artist. Bo's oldest brother Gage lives in Chicago and his other brother Caleb recently got back from a tour of duty in Afghanistan. Caleb's living in the other house on the property that's down by the lake. So Bo had been living here alone, until Millie moved in with him. Tonight she's visiting her roommate.

"Maybe I'll buy a sailboat and sail around the world," I mutter.

"You don't know how to sail."

"So? I could learn."

"Have you heard from any other teams?" He's careful with the question.

"Yeah. Five or six, last time I checked. And I've been offered a shitload of new endorsement deals. Why would they want me now?"

"You're all over the internet. They're saying that if you were willing to sacrifice your career for love, it says something about your character."

"Yeah. That I'm a fuck-up."

"No. That you're a romantic. People eat that shit up. Trust me, I know."

Bo's game room looks out over the Olympic-sized pool and a swanky patio. It's got a pool table, pinball machines, a poker table, giant leather couches, a 98-inch flat screen and a full bar. He pours us both a beer from one of the taps. He's wearing an old Hawks t-shirt and his hair's a little longer than he used to wear it. We're around the same height and lot of people used to tell us we look like brothers. "Have you talked to her?"

I told Bo about everything that happened with Zara. Well, most of it anyway. I told him because he gets it. He fell just as hard and fast for Millie. Luckily for Bo, he didn't have to get kicked off his team to keep her.

"No." I chug half my beer, setting up a game of pool. But there are double the number of balls. "You know what my coach told me?"

"What?"

"He said he's watched me cause carnage in the lives of every girl I've been with over the past three years. I use them, steal their innocence and break their hearts, according to him. To tell you the truth, I never thought the guy was that fucking observant. Apparently, he knew about all the one night stands—which is all I've ever had. He must have had scouts planted all over campus, watching and reporting back."

I finish my beer, and realize I'm in the process of becoming seriously fucked up.

Good.

Just what the doctor ordered.

I haven't slept in a long time. I've spent the week planning a funeral, working out at night like a maniac in Bo's home gym because it's the only thing that takes the edge off, and packing up three lifetimes' worth of memorabilia into thirty or so boxes so I can get rid of the rest.

"What if he's right?"

"He's not right, Elias. It's just bullshit he would have said in the heat of the moment. So what if you played the field for a while? You just hadn't met the right person yet. You had no reason to be faithful before. Now you do. Don't take that shit to heart."

I'm trying not to, but Coach's words cut deep. Unfortunately, I respect him. If Zara and I are going to have any kind of a future at all, it would be nice if her father didn't consider me the lowest form of pond scum in the history of humanity.

This is where Bo and I are different. For reasons that go back to some promise he made to his own mother on her death bed, he saved himself for the real thing. So, when he found it, he wasn't carrying all the baggage I'm carrying.

"I'm meeting with the real estate agent before the funeral tomorrow," I tell him.

"Are you really sure you want to put the house on the market so soon?"

"They're both gone now. There's no point hanging on to it. I need a clean break. I need to figure out why I played the game of football to begin with and if I even want to keep playing it."

"You do want to keep playing it," Bo insists. "You're too good to quit, just because of a misunderstanding between you and and the love of your life's bull-headed father. Trust me, he'll come around. He needs you. He just hasn't admitted that to himself yet. But he'll be realizing it pretty fucking quick as he stares up at that scoreboard."

Is she there? Is *she* staring up at the scoreboard, wearing my jersey when I'm not even there? What do I have to offer her now?

"I'm going to fly back there tomorrow after the funeral and take her. I don't care what they say." I sound drunk. "We're going to sail the world together. Fuck football."

The room is spinning so I lay back on one of the couches for a minute, to give it a chance to even out.

I fucking miss her. "She's the best—and worst—kind of addiction, you know what I mean? Dangerous and so fucking sweet she's impossible to get enough of."

"I get it, man."

So this is what it feels like to lose everything.

I'm so fucking tired.

"That's because you haven't slept in a week, bro," Bo says, and he's sort of gentle about it. He tosses a blanket over me and I can hear him outside talking to someone on his phone before I get pulled into a deep and dreamless oblivion.

23

Zara

I'M IN MY STUDIO, trying to paint my emotions onto the canvas in front of me. So far, it's entirely black.

This used to work. It used to help. But tonight, all I can feel is a manic kind of worry and a double-edged heartbreak.

I've left a few more messages for Elias but so far he hasn't answered or called me back. I know he's dealing with a lot, so now I'm just trying to give him some space. He knows how to get in touch when he's ready to. But it's hard to wait.

What if he doesn't want you anymore? What if he's told your dad that he's choosing football? It's the logical thing to do. He's worked too hard and too long to give up on it, just for you. He barely even knows you.

Unfortunately my subconscious makes a good point. Of course he should choose football. He's too good and too valuable to throw it all away just because we happen to have shared a moment.

An unbearably hot, beautiful, life-changing moment.

But still, maybe it isn't enough for him to really know.

Don't ever doubt me. You're the one, Z.

I touch my fingers to the note in my pocket, holding onto that assurance with everything I've got. *Thank you thank you thank you.*

Please please please.

My phone rings. I check the number before answering it. I've had non-stop phone calls from reporters and paparazzi and media people who want my story. As soon as that photo of us went viral, the whole thing completely blew up.

I just hope Elias has some sort of buffer from it. I hope he's okay.

It's not Elias's number but it's got the same area code. I answer it on the first ring. "Hello?"

"Is this Zara?"

"Yes."

"Zara, it's Bo McCabe here. I'm a friend of Elias's." Bo McCabe. Elias mentioned him. A friend from home. Another quarterback, famous for bringing a game to a standstill to stare up at the girl the Jumbotron had zoomed in on. He couldn't stop staring at her and everyone was looking for her because he'd been saving himself for true love and there she suddenly was. The hashtag *#JumbotronAngel* was trending for weeks.

And now there's a new one. *#SaveElias*

I think I like Bo's hashtag better. Save Elias from who? Me?

"Is he okay?" I ask. *Please be okay.*

"I wondered if you could come out here to Michigan."

"I…yeah, of course I can. When?"

"The funeral's tomorrow and he's talking about leaving directly after it so he can see you. But I think he needs more time. To decompress. He's been sort of… manic. Could you come tomorrow afternoon and maybe spend a couple of days with him here? It might help him clear his head so he can figure out how to handle everything that's happened. I think it would help."

"Of course I'll come."

"Great." He sounds relieved. "What's the name of your dorm?"

"It's Carrington Hall."

"I'll send a car to pick you up at ten o'clock and take you to the airport. A private jet will be waiting for you. And then a driver will bring you to Elias. Can you be ready by ten?"

First a Corvette Stingray and now a private jet? I sometimes forget that these elite players live in a different world. "Yes, I'll be ready."

"Thank you, Zara. He's going to be very happy to see you."

24

Zara

I LAND at the small Michigan airport and, just like Bo said, there's a car waiting for me. Not just any car. A sleek black stretch limo. I'm kind of wondering if this is really necessary but I'm too strung out to give it too much thought. The chauffeur takes my bag and opens the door for me.

Wow.

Two full sized couches face each other and there's a table, small fridge and tinted windows, including one that separates the driver from the back seats.

I check my phone. As I was waiting for my flight to leave, I sent a message to Hannah. She's heard about what happened, of course, and she's frantic with worry and with a rabid need to know what's going on. She's left me dozens of messages. She even threatened to come home. I told her I'm okay, that I broke Rule Number

One, that I'm on my way to Michigan, and that she absolutely shouldn't come home right now. I told her not to worry about me, that I'll call her and tell her the entire story as soon as I get a chance. I can only hope it has a happy ending.

I also sent a text message to my dad, telling him I was leaving and I wasn't sure exactly when I was coming back. I told him I loved him. And I told him I hoped he'd changed his mind.

There's a text from him.

> I'd like to meet with both of you.
> Together. As soon as you can get back
> here. Don't be gone too long, honey.
> Love, Dad.

Okay. I guess that's progress.

Another text comes through from Hannah.

> I'm calling you now. ABSOLUTELY DO
> NOT IGNORE MY CALL THIS TIME.
> ANSWER YOUR PHONE!!!!

Shit.

My phone rings.

I take a deep breath. "Hey, Han."

"Zara Adelaide Fox, have you lost your freaking mind? What the *hell*, Zee? You broke *Rule Number One?* And now dad's starting quarterback is off the *team?* Are you *crazy?* Do you know what a big deal this is, for everyone who's involved with that team? Do you realize you've just ruined Elias O'Shea's entire *career*? What were you thinking?"

Damn it. My sister is right. It *is* my fault that Elias is off the team. I *have* ruined his life. Not just that but I've probably screwed up the entire season for my dad, all the football players and hundreds of thousands of fans. And now I'm here and I'm only going to be making it worse. "I'm in love with him," I sob.

My sister hasn't heard me cry in a long time. We've talked about this. We cried so much when we lost our mother that our tears dried up and neither one of us thought we were even capable of crying anymore. Like we broke the mechanism or something. But now, here I am crying again. "Zee," she says. Patiently. With empathy but also harsh logic. "You've known him for a *week* or something. Get real. You're *hot* for him, that's a very different thing than falling in love."

"I'm hot for him *and* I'm in love with him."

"Oh, shit. Did you *sleep* with him?"

This is not going to go down well. "Yes."

"*What?* Holy shit! I told you to have *fun*, not go totally insane!"

My breathing is jagged and my face is wet. "I know."

"What did you do, meet him, fall under the hot quarterback's spell, then five minutes later jump straight into *bed* with him?"

"Pretty much."

"Zara, *why?* Please tell me you at least used protection."

"I'm on the pill. I started taking it, like, a month ago. I told you that, remember?"

"And that's *it?* What about a condom?"

"He said…" Crap. I don't want to tell her all this.

But she's not having a bar of my hesitation. "He said what?"

"He hasn't been with anyone for a while. They get checks and so on."

"And you *believed* that? He's a major *player*, Zee. He's *famous* for it."

But her question shifts something in me. Because I did believe him. With all my heart. I *know* he was telling me the truth. I could see it and I could feel it.

I take a deep breath. I wipe my eyes. I pull myself together as much as I can. "Han. I love you. And I get why you're upset. *I'm* upset too. I'm upset because I'm so sure of this and because it's caused so much pain for a lot of people, but mostly for Elias. I'm going to fix it. I'm going to talk to Dad and convince him to put Elias back on the team. Because we want to be together and we should be allowed to be if that's what we decide. It's not up to anyone else. It's not up to Dad. It's not up to you. It's up to us."

Hannah's quiet for a few seconds, which isn't like her at all. "You really are in love with him." Like this is exceptionally bad news but also something to be marveled at. I happen to know my sister has never even remotely been in love. But she has slept with a lot of men that never make her happy.

"Yes." The limo is pulling into a cemetery. "And I have to go now."

"I'm coming home, Zee. You need someone to talk some sense into you. One week of college and you've totally lost your mind."

"You don't need to come home, Han. I'm in Michigan. I don't know how long I'll be here."

"Zee, *please.* Be reasonable."

"I love you, Han. I'll call you back. Wish me luck."

"Zara, wait. Please be careful."

"I will." How can I explain to her that it's impossible to fall in love carefully? I guess that's why they call it falling. You can't control how fast it happens or how you're basically throwing yourself off a cliff and hoping he'll catch you. All I can do is have faith in him. "I'm hanging up now, Han."

"I'm so furious with you, Zee. And I love you so much."

"Love you too. Bye, Han."

I end the call.

The limo pulls up behind a long row of parked cars. I can see a small crowd of people dressed in black. Some are walking away from the gathering, heading back to their cars.

They must be finished.

The chauffeur opens the door for me.

"Can you wait here for a minute, please?" I ask him.

"Of course, Miss Fox." It gets my attention that he knows my name, but it's not surprising. Bo would have told him. Or maybe it's because Elias and I are trending on social media in ways I don't even want to think about.

I'm wearing a little black sleeveless dress. My hair is long and loose, hanging down my back.

He's standing with a group of people. They're talking to him and he hasn't seen me yet.

I'm nervous. Does he really even want me here?

He's at least a head taller than everyone else. The only other person who comes close to his outrageous physicality is another guy who's also built and dark-haired. I'm guessing that must be Bo.

But all I can see is Elias. He looks sad. His hands are shoved into his pockets. He's wearing a suit and I can't help notice…*damn*. He definitely knows how to fill out a suit. He's so beautiful it takes my breath away.

That's when he looks up. And he sees me.

He's in shock for a couple of seconds. Bo notices this and turns. And smiles. He holds up a hand and I wave back. Then he pats Elias on the back and gently pushes him in my direction.

My heart's beating like a hummingbird's wing.

Elias is walking toward me now, his expression full of so much relief and love and heat and emotion, I'm already crying. He scoops me into a bearhug and I wrap my arms and legs around him, not caring about anything else in the world but how good it feels to be with him again.

He presses his face into my hair and inhales deeply. "Zara. Fuck, I missed you so much."

He kisses me, carefully at first, like it's the only time he might get the chance. His kiss deepens, desperate and full of hunger. Bo was right, there's a manic edge to him. If there was ever anything about him that was unsure or was holding back because of the nature of our situation, it's gone.

Holding me like I weigh nothing at all, he pulls a roll of hundred dollar bills out of his pocket and peels off a few of them, handing them to the driver. "Drive us around for a while, will you?"

"Yes, sir, Mr. O'Shea."

Elias glances back at Bo, who gives us a grinning thumbs up. Then Elias pulls me into the limo and the driver closes the door behind us, sealing us into the luxurious privacy.

He positions me on his lap, so I'm straddling him. He holds my face between his hands. "Your smile is saving my life, angel girl." His heated body is humming with tension. "I need you," he murmurs between obsessed kisses, licking into my mouth like he's gone too long without the taste of me. He's gripping me like his life depends on it.

"Shhh." I hold his face close to mine, trying to calm

him. "It's okay. You're okay. I'm yours." But he can't be calmed. He eases my dress down my shoulders, lowering it over my breasts. I give him everything. He pulls the flouncy dress to my waist, ripping my panties easily.

I'm still kissing him but I murmur, "You're going to need to stop doing that or I'll have none left."

"Then stop wearing them."

He unfastens his pants and I touch my fingers to his hard, silken length but he's guiding his thickness into me, aggressively. I don't know how I'm already wet for him.

"I need to feel you come around my cock."

It hurts a little, his forced, sublime possession, and tears wet my face. He's hurting and I don't want him to hurt. I want to fix him and take all his pain away.

"It's all right," he's whispering, wiping my tears with his fingers, kissing my face. "You're all right, baby girl. I'm here now. We're together now."

I slide onto him, taking more of him, until he's fully, deeply inside me. Elias takes my breasts in his hands and guides them to his mouth, sucking one flushed, sensitive nipple, then the other. He's panting lightly, groaning each time I grind my hips against him and squeeze him.

"I won't be apart from you again. I fucking can't. We'll figure it out. I'll figure it out."

I'm coming, despite the pain, and because of it. The ache is laced with shards of longing. The clenching spasms of my release are manic and wild, drawing him deeper into my body. Elias's growl is agonized as his cock pulses inside me, filling me with liquid warmth, setting me off again into long, shimmery waves of pure pleasure.

"Zara, I need you. Fuck, baby, I *love* you."

I writhe, clinging to him, kissing him as yet another orgasm floods through me.

We both understand, mindlessly losing ourselves in each other like we'll never get close enough, that we'll do anything. That we're falling in love with more than another person, we're falling in love with the tears and the laughter and the broken pieces that hold us together.

I'll do anything, if it only means I can keep him. This kind of perfect desperation isn't something we can either escape from or take for granted. It's a wildfire that will burn us to the ground if we don't let it consume us.

25

Zara

WE PULL up in front of my house. It's late afternoon and the first leaves are starting to fall. My house is a big old rambling Victorian four-bedroom with a wraparound front porch. The kind with lots of stories and nooks and is always in need of a paint job. It's white with dark red trim. Wildcats colors, I only realized a few years ago. We moved into this house when I was three years old. It's where practically every memory I have was made. It's the home base of my soul. Mostly because my dad is in it.

I can only hope this goes well.

After the crazy and unforgettable limo ride, we went back to Bo's to get a few of Elias's things. I got to meet Bo, who lives up to all the hype. And I got to meet Millie, who's one of the nicest people I've ever met. She's got an edge of bruised vulnerability to her but is smart and sort of wise beyond her years. If we end up as sisters, I know we'll become close. And it was entertaining to watch, how besotted Bo is with her. She said the same thing about Elias.

I showed Elias the text from my dad and he didn't want to wait any longer to meet with him. So we didn't stay with them long. Elias got the limo driver to take us to the airport.

"You ready?" Elias asks me.

"No."

His slow smile helps. "Whatever happens in here, Zara, we're together. I'm all in."

"I'm all in too, Elias."

"Good. Come on, then. Let's get this over with."

Elias holds my hand as we walk up the front steps. I texted my dad and told him we were coming. By the time we get up to the front door it's already open my dad is standing there. He watches us, taking it all in. The two of us together. My hand clasped strongly in his best ever football player's.

He doesn't look mad. He looks sad. And tired.

I walk up to him and give him a big hug. He hugs me back and we just stand there with my dad holding me in this big, comforting dad-hug, the kind that's so familiar and restorative it makes you sigh and brings tears to your eyes.

Then he releases me and holds my shoulders, looking at me. *Really* looking at me. He's looking at me like he can see my mother in me. He's looking at me like he missed me terribly. "I'm not going to lose you, punkin. You and that crazy Californian sister are all I've got."

"You could never lose me, dad. I'm too hard to get rid of."

My dad looks at Elias, and I hope he can see him as I see him. Tall. Brave. Glorious. How could he not? "I'm sorry to hear about your father, son."

"Thank you, Coach. He respected the hell out of your coaching. He was always glad I chose Hawthorne." *It was good he never had to know I got kicked off the team.* I don't even know if Elias is thinking that. But I am. And my guess is my dad might be too.

My dad heads for the door. "Come inside, you two. I have some things I want to say to you both."

So we take a seat together on the couch in the living room. The place is a little messier than usual, but just in the area around my dad's chair. His papers, notes and playbooks are stacked in mid-flow piles.

My dad sits in the chair opposite us. There's a change in him. There's a defeated edge to him that's new.

"Can I speak first, Coach?" Elias says.

"Go right ahead."

"I know this might seem incredibly fast and it might be hard for you to accept, but I'm in love with Zara. I'll ask her to marry me when she's ready, if she'll have me. You should know that I can provide for her financially, even without football. I have a few very lucrative endorse-ment deals in place and a portfolio that's managed partly by Gabriel that's been growing exponentially. It was always my plan to finish my business degree as well as to play in the NFL, so I'll have that too to fall back on if I need it. I know that half my life will be lived after football so I plan to finish it, wherever I have to do that." He glances at me and squeezes my hand. "From the very first second I saw her, I knew she was the one. I don't know if I even believed love at first sight was a real thing, except for my parents, who'd been telling me their story their whole lives. I didn't think it could happen to me. But it did. I want you to know I'll take good care of her. Everything I have is hers. She's my reason now and I know that sounds intense and lightning-fast but when you find absolute perfection, there's no point in slowing it down. When you meet the one person who's everything you thought you might never find, you really have no choice but to fight for her with everything you've got, even if she is off-limits. *Especially* if she's off-limits. I'll play football again, with you or without you, sir, and I'll be doing it for Zara, for building a future together with her, and for my dad's memory. But I'll be doing it for myself too. I *do* want to play football. I want to finish out this year strong and give it everything I've fucking got. I want to get to the NFL and make a stellar career out of it. And the way I'd like to do that is with you as my coach, because you're the best one there is. I just wanted you to know that. I'm for real, Coach. I'm all in."

My dad's quiet for a few seconds. His voice sounds

scratchy with emotion when he finally speaks. "I guess it can be hard to teach an old dog new tricks. But for Zara, I'm willing to learn as many as it takes. She's one thing I'm not willing to lose." He glances at me, and the way my hand is still firmly clasped in Elias's. "You sure about him, honey?"

"I'm sure, Dad." I look up at Elias and fall even more deeply. "I love him." It's the first time I've said this and Elias's eyes get very blue.

"Well, then, I guess there's only one thing to do." My dad stands up. "Since it looks like you two aren't going to budge on this, you give me no choice." I don't know if my dad is pausing for effect just to prolong our agony because we've put him through hell, but if he is, he's doing a damn good job of it. "The thing is, I know what love at first sight feels like. I've said it before and I'll say it again: when you know, you know. So I'm rewriting Rule Number One. It's now: only date one football player for the rest of time and make sure he's my starting quarterback." Gruffly, he admits, "We need you, son. We've lost both games—badly—since you've been gone and we need our play-making magician back on the field."

My dad offers his hand and Elias stands up to grasp it. "Thank you, sir. You won't regret it."

"Treat her right, O'Shea, or I'll be dusting off that sawed-off shotgun I keep in my gun closet."

"*Dad,*" I scold.

The doorbell rings. Once. Twice. A third time. Whoever it is, they're insistent.

"Are you expecting someone, Dad?"

"No."

I go over and open the door. A woman is standing there. She's wearing trendy black-framed glasses and has brown, wavy hair that hangs to her shoulders. She looks like she might be in her early forties but she could pass for younger. She's dressed in a very fashionable outfit with an eccentric, artistic twist. Her dangling earrings are little paint palettes. "Can I help you?"

"Are you Zara?"

"Yes."

"Zara, I'm Imogen MacBeth from the Sea Glass Gallery. We have an appointment."

"Oh. Of course. Please, come in." With everything that's been going on, I'd completely forgotten that we'd arranged for her to come to my house today. "Ms. MacBeth, this is my dad, Jack Fox. And this is Elias O'Shea."

Her eyes get wide. "Oh. You're the quarterback." Her cheeks get pink. "The one who posted Zara's painting. Which is now up to seven million views. Please, call me Imogen."

Elias shakes her hand.

So does my dad. Her cheeks get even pinker and the two of them hold eye contact for a fraction longer than they need to.

Hang on.

But then Imogen turns to me. She's brimming with anticipation. "So, Zara, you said you have some work to show me. Possibly…a lot of it? Would you be willing to show me where you keep your paintings?"

"Of course." I'd planned to bring the best of them downstairs and create some kind of display, to show them off as impressively as I could. But it can't be helped. She'll just have to view them as they are. "They're upstairs. Please, follow me."

So I lead her toward the staircase. Elias follows, and so does my dad.

We get to the fourth floor and I'm glad I cleaned and tidied it before I left for school. It smells like paint but I guess Imogen wouldn't mind a detail like that.

My room is the attic and takes up the entire fourth floor of our house. It's got my bedroom area on one side, where two sash windows offer early evening light. But the entire south side of the room is dedicated to art. There's a long rectangular paned window seat with its faded green cushions my mother made, years ago. Dozens of easels are set up, most with finished works or works in progress. Tables are full of paints, water jars, paintbrushes and palettes, mostly organized, but as I look at it now, the busy space is almost like an art installation itself. Every inch of wall space is covered with hung paintings, sketches, quotes, articles, photos and ripped-out pages of inspiration. My studio is full to bursting with ideas, memories and, most of all, art.

Imogen actually gasps. "Oh my." She's quiet as she walks though my studio, taking her time. She stops in front of one of the paintings. "Here it is."

It's the one I showed Elias the photo of, that very first day we met. The one he posted on Instagram that got all the views and the attention of the Sea Glass. My only self-portrait, painted in a grief-heavy moment when I wondered if I would ever find a way out of it.

It could be a painting of my mother. My father is also staring at it and his eyes have gone sort of bloodshot and shiny. I think he's a little bit shocked by how many paintings are actually up here. He never comes up here. It might have been years since he ventured into my zone. He knew I needed space and our two obsessions didn't have a middle ground, so he left me to it.

Imogen turns to face me. "Zara."

"Yes?"

"I'd like to offer you a solo exhibition at the Sea Glass. We're booked for the next few months but we could schedule it for December. Would that work for you?"

Wow. Even my mother didn't get a solo exhibition until she was well established. "Yes."

"As part of our representation," she says, turning back to the painting, "we also provide a social media manager for you. I looked at your Instagram this morning. I noticed you haven't posted in a while."

"I don't really post very often."

"You have an impressive following."

"I do?" I've only posted twenty or so times, mostly photos of things like a red leaf on green grass or a flower in the sun. Just slightly-banal images that catch the light in a certain way or somehow seem photo-worthy. Last time I checked, maybe a month or so ago, I had around two hundred followers.

But now I'm curious. I take my phone out of my pocket and bring up my Instagram account.

"What the…?" *Three million followers.* "When did this happen?"

Imogen's looking at my dad again, stealing little glances. "If I had to guess, it's probably because…well, that photo of you and Elias went viral. And once people knew that the two of you were together, they did some research and it wasn't hard to find out that you're the coach's daughter and also an art student. And that one of your paintings is going to be included in the freshmen art exhibition. And that the styles of that painting and the one from Elias's post were very similar. And that, of course, your mother was Adelaide Fox. So they figured out the painting from the post was yours."

Whoa.

"Have you checked the comments section of Elias's post lately, Zara?" Imogen asks me.

"No."

"The offers are up to one million dollars for the painting. And people want to know if you have others. We can make sure we showcase your work to the highest possible standard. I'll go through our partnership terms before I leave tonight, but I'm confident we can offer you a very generous package. I can leave it with you, so that you and your advisors can look over it. You could let me know in, say, a week?"

"That sounds perfect."

"Elias can take a look at it," my dad says. "The kid obviously knows his way around a spreadsheet."

Imogen giggles lightly and it's not the sound I would have expected from the cut-throat pinnacle of the New York art scene, but she's obviously elated, possibly for more than one reason.

"Why don't you stay for dinner, Imogen," my dad suggests. "We can talk more about it over some lasagna. I bet you're parched after your trip from New York. How about a drink?"

"I'd love one."

"We'll be down in a minute," I tell them, as the two of them head back downstairs.

We wait until the sound of their voices disappears down below and into the kitchen. "If I didn't know better, I'd say Imogen MacBeth was flirting with my dad."

Elias closes the door and locks it. "Nothing wrong with second chances." He takes my hands and leans down to kiss me. "I told you everything would be okay."

"I should always listen to my quarterback."

Thank you thank you thank you.

For bringing me a burly lovestruck romantic.

For my dad's change of heart.

For Imogen MacBeth.

Elias takes my bottom lip between his teeth, biting gently. His tongue slips into my mouth and I'm dizzy from the sublime taste of him.

"I love you," he whispers. "I'm going to make all your dreams come true."

"I think you already have," I whisper back.

He licks my neck in a slow, sexy claim. Then he drops to his knees and pushes my skirt up. "I'll see those dreams and raise you one killer orgasm."

"Elias...*oh.*" I grab handfuls of his hair as he licks me in an open-mouthed kiss.

"Give me five minutes. And then give me a lifetime. You're the one, angel girl, and I'm going to prove it to you every day for the rest of time. Starting right now."

And that's exactly what he does.

EPILOGUE

Zara

Six weeks later...

"Did you see that pass?" Hannah squeals. "That was genius!"

"Touchdown!" Mollie screams.

"That's my brother," Isla says proudly.

"They're on *fire* tonight," Lauren adds.

We're in our usual box, watching the Wildcats absolutely clean up the visiting team. They're leading by 21 points. Elias has led them to four consecutive wins since he's been back on the team and tonight's game will be their sixth win of the season.

Like he does after every touchdown, he puts his hand on his heart and looks up at the box. He says he can see me up here. The crowd goes wild when he does this.

They know the story. We ended up giving an interview once the news broke that Elias was starting quarterback again. There was so much buzz and speculation on social media that we wanted to make sure we told the story as it actually happened.

#ZaraSavesTheWildcats was overstating things just a little but at least it was better than the last trending hashtag.

I'm not sure I could ever get used to "trending" on social media but it seems to happen all the time these days. For some reason, people are interested in our story. I've gotten a lot of messages from people who follow me, saying they never believed in love at first sight until they watched it happen to us.

Elias now has two hundred million followers and has just signed three new endorsement deals that are worth an eye-watering amount of money. He and my dad have been meeting with NFL scouts and there's no doubt that Elias will go high in the draft.

Last time I checked I had around twenty million followers. Which is insanely crazy. I've started posting pictures of my art, mostly the pieces that will be included in my Sea Glass exhibition in December. Imogen decided that we'll run the show as a sort of auction over the month, to see how high she can get the prices to go. The offers we've already had are mind-bogglingly high.

She's already talking about another solo exhibition, maybe in March.

My path is very different to my mother's path to fame. I still have to pinch myself sometimes when I read reviews of my work in the art magazines I used to read religiously during high school. There are some that are critical. But Elias says that's true of everyone who's ever put themselves out there. He's right, of course, and I don't take those too much to heart. My mother's art didn't please everyone either. Neither do Elias's passes. Or my dad's coaching calls.

So I focus on the reviews like: "*Zara Fox shines with her own artistic style.*" And: "*She's every bit as good as her mother and just as original.*" And: "*Imogen MacBeth is about to make Zara Fox exceptionally rich.*"

Elias's Instagram post has changed my life so much it's practically unrecognizable.

As for Elias himself, all I can say is that he's transformed me, body and soul, into someone who feels more loved than I sometimes know what to do with. We're together as much as we possibly can be. And since we can't keep our hands off each other, we spend most of our time having hot, very orgasmic sex. I literally can't get enough of him. To say he feels the same way would be an understatement.

Isla wasn't happy that I spent so little time living at Carrington Hall. I moved in with Elias the night we got back from Michigan. On the evenings I work late in my studio, he stays there with me. But he's cleared out some of the stuff in his room to make space for my things, including an easel, which he put next to the window.

Isla spends more and more time at the house too. She and Jake still haven't admitted to themselves that they share something more than an old friendship. But the sparks between them are practically electric. I'm waiting for new developments…

Hannah's working on her thesis, which she can do remotely, so she came home soon after we got back from Michigan to check on me. When she met Elias, she was totally, comically starstruck and once she saw the two of us together, she fully agreed that Rule Number One needed a major overhaul.

Two weeks ago, she met a graduate student named Oliver who used to be a Wildcats player but injured his knee junior year and is now studying finance. She's been on three dates with him and last night she told me she's thinking about moving back to Massachusetts after she graduates.

My dad is happier than I've seen him in…well, years. He loves having the house full of people. He loves having both his kids living nearby or, in Hannah's case, back in her old room, at least temporarily. And, of course, he loves that his team is on a winning streak. Once he made his mind up about Elias, he treats his star quarterback like he walks on water. Elias and I go over and cook my dad dinner every Sunday and it's nice to be a family again… plus one. And sometimes plus two, when Imogen is in town. And now, plus three, since Oliver is coming next Sunday.

Imogen has visited several times to work through the paintings we'll be showing in the December exhibition. She and my dad went out to dinner one night at the Hawthorne Steakhouse. On an actual date. Now she's talking about opening a second gallery, in Hawthorne. Like Elias said, there's nothing wrong with second chances.

My classes continue to go well and I've made a lot of new friends, including Maeve. She and I have become close. I introduced her to Imogen, who's offered to exhibit one of Maeve's paintings in the February collective exhibition at the Sea Glass.

Christopher was disappointed that Imogen wasn't interested in his work. He's still one of my biggest critics in class, which I don't dare tell Elias. I'd hate to see Christopher targeted by a very grumpy quarterback and his extremely large friends.

Tonight, Hannah, Mollie, Isla, Lauren and I are making the most of the fully catered box as we wait for the stadium to clear out a little, and for Elias and the others to get back to the house. They're planning a small party tonight. I'm not sure why but maybe they just want to celebrate their win.

Everyone on campus is in good spirits. The leaves have mostly fallen and they crackle underfoot as we make our way across the Green. The night is cool and clear, and dusk gives the sky a purple glow.

Mollie and Lauren head back to the dorm and Hannah's got plans in town.

"I'll see you guys later," Hannah says. She borrowed my dad's car tonight and it beeps from the curb as she unlocks it.

She gives me a hug and I can't resist. "Hot date?"

"As a matter of fact, yes." Her eyes are bright. I've never seen my sister this happy about a fourth date before. Her relationships usually fizzle out after one or two.

"Don't forget to use protection," I tease her.

"Thanks for the advice." Hannah gives me a wry look. "Which you didn't even bother following."

"I followed half of it."

She laughs and shakes her head. "See you tomorrow, Zee. Bye, Isla."

"Bye, Hannah."

As we get closer to the house, the lights are on and we can hear music. West's current favorite song. Since I moved in, Elias's three teammates have become like brothers to me and I couldn't love them more. West is always fun, Gabe is smarter than anyone I've ever met, and Jake is grounded and easy to talk to.

We step inside the small entrance foyer, which leads into the open plan living room and huge kitchen. The place is definitely a bachelor pad on steroids but for some reason, tonight, it's full of at least a dozen bouquets of red roses.

"What's this?" Isla asks. "Is someone getting married?"

All four of them are here. West, Jake and Gabe all have shit-eating grins on their faces, like they're bursting with news but playing it cool. "What's going on?" I ask.

Elias comes over to me. Like always, when I haven't seen him for a while, I'm almost shocked by how beautiful he is. I love his face. I love his thick dark hair and the way it flicks in half curls behind his ears. I love that I know how the coarse silk of it feels in my hands…*when he fucks me relentlessly until I come around him.* I love his big, buff body…*and how the hard textures of him feel when I grip him because he's so unbelievably big and he feels so good.* He's wearing jeans and a black shirt. A nice one. In fact, all four of them are dressed nicely.

"Good game tonight," I say, sort of breathless from his effect.

Elias takes my face in his hands and looks down at me with a vast kind of tenderness. "Thanks, angel girl." He kisses me, the kiss erotic in its lightness. "You're so damn beautiful it hurts. I can't believe you're mine."

As much as I love that Elias is a drop-dead gorgeous sex god and an elite football hero, my favorite thing about him is that he's careful with the broken places in me. He *gets* them. And I get his. It's where the cracks are that our love grows the strongest.

And just when I think I couldn't love him more, he'll say or do something that proves me wrong.

Like now.

Elias gets down on one knee.

Isla gasps.

I'm finding it hard to breathe.

Elias is holding a small duck-egg blue box. He opens it, and inside, there's a diamond ring. Not just any diamond ring. The biggest, shiniest diamond ring I've ever seen in my life.

"Zara…" Elias takes my hand. "You're my dream girl. I've been waiting to do this for a while but I know you're young and it's fast and I wasn't sure if you were ready. But I'm ready. There's no one else for me when you exist in this world. I love you. I've loved you from the very first second I saw you. I knew you were the one on that very first day. I want to wake up next to you every morning. I want to build a life with you. I want to give you everything you've ever dreamed of, because to call you the love of my life doesn't do justice to how much I love you. My imagination couldn't have dreamed up this level of absolute perfection. Zara, will you marry me? Please say yes."

I'm crying. And nodding. And laughing *as* I'm crying. I launch myself into his arms. "Yes."

The room erupts and there's the sound of champagne corks popping.

Jake gives Gabe a high five. "The amygdala never lies," says Gabe.

Elias slides the ring onto my finger. Then he holds my face and kisses me.

Falling in love with Elias O'Shea wasn't something I could have planned, or even dreamed. I never knew I was capable of this kind of happiness.

Turns out, my dad was right.

When you know, you know.

Thank you so much for reading **Lovestruck**. If you enjoyed this book, please consider leaving a quick review or rating on Goodreads and Amazon.

Want to see what happens with Elias and Zara five years down the road? Read the bonus epilogue: https:// BookHip.com/XWSGGNC, also available on my website: www.juliecapulet.com

Below I've included the first two chapters of **Hopeless Romantic**, which is Bo and Millie's story. Like **Lovestruck**, it's a tribute to love at first sight and insta-everything (because it happened to me :).

xoxo,

Julie

Please come join my Facebook reader group, <u>Julie</u>

<u>Capulet's Romantics</u>, where I share cover reveals, insider info and we discuss all things romance!

Sign up for my newsletter to receive my free bonus content and get access to sneak peeks and exclusive giveaways!

Visit my website @ www.juliecapulet.com

HOPELESS ROMANTIC

When he falls, he falls *hard*.

Millie Baylin just moved to a new city to start college. Introverted and studious, she plans on spending most of her time holed up in the library working on her novel and keeping to herself. But when she gets dragged along to a school football game by her fun, football-mad new roommate, the hot alpha quarterback almost drops the ball at his very first sight of her.

Bo McCabe is saving himself. A hopeless romantic at heart, he's holding out for the real thing. As soon as he lays eyes on the shy stranger with the striking gray eyes and the angel's face, he'll stop at nothing to find out if she's the one he's been waiting for all along. Millie thinks Bo's insta-obsession is insanity and wants nothing to do with him. But Bo is determined. Because, somehow, Millie has already stolen his heart … and he is now utterly obsessed with winning hers.

Can Bo convince Millie he's the man of her dreams?

Hopeless Romantic is a sexy standalone sports romance starring an obsessed hero and the love of his life (includes two hopelessly romantic HEA epilogues!). This book is a tribute to love at first sight and insta-everything (because it happened to me :).

McCabe Brothers

Chapter One

Millie

The bus drops me next to the front entrance of the university and I walk up to the main admissions building, where I'm given a map and a bag full of booklets and welcome materials. I make my way through the crowd of people on the campus green, keeping my hat low over my eyes, using the map to try to find my way to my new dorm.

I can't believe I'm here.

College.

I never knew if I'd actually get this far. So many times along the way, college had seemed like a place *other* people went, a goal not just up among the stars, but over in someone else's galaxy. But I've made it. This is *real*. My dream, against all odds, has come true.

I graduated from high school more than a year ago, but it's taken me this long to save up enough money to get started. Desperate to get as far away from my hometown in Florida as possible, I applied to four schools. *And I got in.*

This place is like a different world. More than forty thousand students go to this university. It's practically its own city, with top-ranked sports teams, space-age libraries and students from every walk of life you could imagine. It's got an energetic, optimistic vibe to it that's kind of blowing my mind. The autumn air is crisp and cool. People are pink-cheeked, wearing colorful scarves, holding steaming cups of coffee and hot chocolate from a nearby coffee truck. Until two days ago, I'd never in my life been north of Atlanta. Everything about this place feels new and exciting and picture-perfect. I almost feel like I belong here.

Belonging isn't something I've had a lot of experience with. I don't fit in or make friends easily. Not because I intentionally try to be an outcast, but because I'm used to keeping secrets.

But not anymore.

All my secrets have turned to dust.

Here, I'm not the poor kid with a heroin addict for a mother. Or the lonely waif who lives in a trailer park and carries Narcan in her pockets. I'm not the freaky teenage girl who wears hats and oversized jackets in August to hide myself because I live alone, or close enough. My only protector was too far gone to care.

All that's behind me now.

My mother is dead. It feels like a mercy. The needles, the wasting away, the giving up of every shred of herself just to get her next fix. I tried to save her, but she just couldn't be saved. Grief was weaved into the painful fabric of our downward spiral. Which meant that, as soon as she was gone, it was surprisingly easy to walk away. I'd already said my goodbyes to the person my mother was, a long time ago.

Now, I'm *free.* Free of the pain and sadness of my past.

Today, here—right this minute—I can start my new life.

In this mini-city of forty thousand people, I know I can find my own quiet corner, where I'll be perfectly content to watch everyone else having the time of their lives while I get to work and do what I came here to do. Kick ass, in the only way I know how.

It's a strange thing to have a knack for. As soon as I started writing stories, something clicked. When I write, I enter this fever dream that takes me into other worlds. I use writing to crawl inside my own mind. To escape from reality. It helped, when I needed it most.

The coffee-scented air leads me over to the coffee truck. I stand in line. I'm wearing my usual loose jacket and my black sailor's cap that I tuck my hair into.

Because I actually *need* them in this weather, which is a nice change. People still stare at me. I'm used to it. I know what I look like.

Students are clustered into groups, talking to each other, *meeting* each other. I sometimes wonder, like now, what it would be like to be fun and outgoing. The girl behind me in line starts up bubbly conversations with a couple of random strangers, without even a hint of self-consciousness or turning red or stammering over her words, like I would. Shyness is a curse.

My backstory doesn't help, but at some point, you just have to move on. That's why I'm here, after all.

"What can I get you?" says the guy in the truck. He's staring. I pull my hat a little lower.

"One hot chocolate, please."

He smiles, making no move to get my order. "You must be a freshman. I'm sure I would have noticed you."

"Yes. I just arrived." After three days on a Greyhound bus, but I don't bother with the details.

He pours cocoa into a cardboard cup. "I'm Mason."

"Hi, Mason."

I don't offer my name in return. There's a line behind me and I really just want to get my drink so I can go and find my dorm. But Mason takes his time. "And you are?"

I relent. "Millie."

"Millie," he repeats. "I like that name."

"It's sort of old-fashioned, but it works."

His gaze roves across my face, taking its time. "Hey,

there's a party at my place tonight. You should come." He scrawls a number on a napkin and hands it to me, along with my cup of hot chocolate. "Give me a call."

"I'll see. Thanks." I hand him my money card.

"It's on the house," he says. "Really. You should come. It'll be fun. I can pick you up if you need a ride."

"Hey, man," says a guy behind me in line. "How about stop trying to pick up the freshman and make us some coffee instead?"

I take that as my cue. "Thanks, Mason."

"See you tonight, hopefully," Mason calls after me, but I let myself drift into the crowd. I already know I'm not going to Mason's party. I'm not really the party-going type. Besides, I don't have time. Part of being able to afford college came from the advance money for a book I wrote last year, when I was going through the worst of … the worst. By some miracle, I landed a literary agent, who got me a two-book deal with a major publisher. They said my writing was "heartfelt," which is true enough. The money isn't a huge amount, but it meant I could afford to start college this year, instead of waiting another year or two to save. I have no idea how I'll finish the second book by their deadline of January 1st, but I guess I'll figure it out. That, along with the full course load I'll be taking, means I'll basically be living in the library for the entire first semester.

I check my map, pretending I feel confident and ready to take my new world by storm. At least if I *look* like I know what I'm doing, people might actually think I do.

There's a band playing a Fleetwood Mac song in the middle of the green. Nearby, some guys are throwing a football around.

The sky is blue, with only a few high, wispy clouds. It's late afternoon. The leafy trees are vibrant shades of red and orange, with an artful smattering sprinkled across the green grass. Autumn, like I've only seen it in movies. Everything's so colorful and ... *collegiate*. Preppies, jocks, hipsters and academics are mingling seamlessly, all wearing splashes of the same school colors.

Nearby, a cluster of girls are eyeing up the football jocks. These are the kinds of girls who used to make my life hell in high school. The social media-obsessed types who spend hours making sure their selfies are envy-worthy. They hate people like me: people with problems they don't want touching them and their shiny lives. Loners, who—God knows why, since I avidly try to avoid it—take attention away from them. And it's always the kind of attention I wish I wasn't getting.

I do my best to avoid them. Maybe things will be different in college.

I'm mortified when one of the jocks calls out to me and starts walking over to me. He's huge and built like a Marvel character.

I try to steer clear but he blocks my way, so I'm forced to stop.

"Hey," he says. He's literally towering over me. I have no doubt he could break me in half if he wanted to. It's intimidating. "Are you a freshman?"

I just had this conversation and I really don't feel like having it again. I'm not good at small talk. "Yes. And I'm on my way to my dorm, if you'll excuse me."

"You're fucking *gorgeous*," he says.

I don't know how to reply to that so I step around him and keep walking but he walks along with me.

He's persistent. "Where're you from?"

I don't want to chit-chat with this oversized stranger. "A small town I'm sure you've never heard of."

"Try me." He's sort of sweaty and bulging and it's freaking me out.

So I hurry past him. "I'm sorry but I'm meeting someone and I'm late. It was nice talking to you."

"You and me should get together sometime," he says.

That's not going to happen in this lifetime or the next twelve, I don't bother saying. I keep walking, hoping I'm heading in the right direction.

"I'll look out for you," the jock calls after me.

Luckily, unless he likes hanging out in hidden corners of the library, he'll never find me.

My dorm isn't far. It's full of people carrying boxes and saying goodbye to their parents. A pang of something that's not quite sadness and not quite jealousy flutters, but I let it go. It doesn't matter anymore that I'm alone. These people are starting their new lives too, just like I am. Some are already partying. I slide past them and make my way up to the third floor.

My roommate is there, sitting on the bed next to the window that has a view out over the green. She's going through an open suitcase and she looks up when I walk in. She has long hair the color of polished copper and a sprinkling of freckles across her nose. Her face lights up, like she's genuinely happy to see me. "Hey, roomie. I'm Violet."

I smile back at her. It's impossible not to. She's fun and nice, you just get that impression. "Millie."

"Hi, Millie. I hope you don't mind me claiming the bed next to the window. And the bigger closet. Your desk is bigger, though. And you have an extra bookshelf."

"No, that's fine."

"I saw you talking to that football player and his groupies," she says.

"You saw that?"

"I was feeling your pain." She laughs. "Those girls' faces when they saw it was *you* and not them he was chasing after."

"Well, they can have him. I hope I haven't already made a few enemies."

"Those girls will be fine as long as you stay away from the football team."

"You know them?"

"I know their type." She sets a picture of her family on her bedside table. She has a lot of brothers, it looks like. "My brother was the quarterback at my high school in Wilmington. My other brother was a wide receiver. And my *other* brother was a halfback. We had girls like that camping out on our doorstep every night of the week."

"Wow. Well, I'll definitely be staying away from the football team," I assure her. "As far away as possible."

"There's no way we're not going to the game tonight, though. You *have* to come with me. I don't know anyone else here yet."

I laugh a little as I put my bag on my bed and start unpacking it. "I'm probably going to skip the game, sorry."

"No *way*, roomie, you can't bail on me! I refuse to sit there by myself and I can't miss the opening game of the season. My brothers would kill me."

"I'm not really into football," I admit. I've honestly never watched much of it and couldn't tell you the rules if my life depended on it.

"What are you into?" Violet's face is open and sunny, like she's actually interested and not just asking to make small talk. So I find myself telling her.

"I'm a writer."

"That's so cool! Are you an English major?"

"Yeah. How about you?"

"Psychology. I'm planning on becoming a shrink. Believe it or not, it's been my lifelong ambition."

"Wow." I start putting some of my stuff into drawers.

"Yeah, just be careful. I might go all Freudian and start psycho-analyzing you any minute."

I smile without meaning to and it feels good. It's been a long time since I made a new friend. "I'll watch out for that."

"If you ever feel like you might need some therapy, just let me know. You can be my first patient."

I take my hat off and toss it onto my bed. My hair tumbles out and hangs past my shoulders. It's been a while since I cut it.

"Wow," she says. "Is that your real hair?"

I have strange hair. It's a very pale shade of red that's almost blond, but not quite. It looks pink under certain lights. A lot of people comment on it or stare at it or want to touch it, which is why I usually keep it hidden. I cut it shorter after my mother died, in one of those weird moments where you do something and you don't know why. But it's grown back since then. I have bangs and it's angled around my face, unevenly in places, because going to a hairdresser wasn't something I could ever afford. "I'm thinking about dyeing it black."

"Don't you dare. It's amazing."

"So's yours." It really is. It's a coppery red with gold highlights.

Her phone pings and she's busy for a few seconds. "So, what do you say? Kick-off is at four thirty."

"I don't know the first thing about football."

"I'll teach you," she says. "Who knows, you might actually enjoy it."

Chapter Two

I climb out of the pool after doing my daily two hundred laps and grab a towel. My house, as usual, is quiet. It's been a long summer. I was glad to start football practice again, just to get out of my own fucking head. I have plenty of friends, but a lot of them go back to their hometowns for the summers, to hang out with their families. This is my hometown. The only family I have left is a brother who was deployed to Afghanistan eleven months ago and has been through some very real shit, and another brother who lives in Chicago. I don't see Gage that much. He's the CEO of his own investment firm. He also happens to be busy sleeping his way around Chicago most nights of the week. We get along well when we're together but when

I visit, I always feel like I'm encroaching on his bed-hopping schedule.

I have the opposite problem. I grab my bag and put it into my car, driving the short distance to campus.

I could bed hop if I wanted to. Very easily.

I don't, though. For … reasons.

Reasons I prefer not to dwell on.

In fact, the whole topic is one I avoid like the plague.

The problem is, a lot of *other* people seem to thrive on speculating continuously, like they have nothing better to fucking do.

Maybe because I'm the starting quarterback. I'm 6'4" and I work out for four hours a day, so I'm built as fuck. I keep to myself when I'm not hanging out with friends or at practice, so I've been labeled "brooding" and "mysterious." Go figure.

The more I deflect, the more they want me.

Like now, as I park my car and make my way toward the players' entrance of the stadium.

"Hi, Bo."

I turn. It's three girls, hanging out next to a yellow Jeep. It looks like they've been waiting for me. They smile as I walk past. "Hey."

"What are you doing for the next twenty minutes?" one of them asks.

"Getting ready to play a game of football."

"The game doesn't start for two hours," one points out.

I don't feel like having a conversation with these girls. They're dressed in … not much at all. I barely even look at them. That would be a bad idea. "We have warm-ups."

"What about later?" says the blond. "What are you doing after the game?"

"Celebrating, hopefully."

"We could meet up with you. If you wanted to … you know … party."

The redhead is twirling a strand of her long hair around a finger. "That is, if you're *sure* you don't want us to help you warm up a little … *before* warm-ups."

"Yeah, Bo," says the dark-haired one. "We could *all* help you warm up."

I keep walking. "Maybe another time."

My behavior would probably be considered strange to most people, I know that. Most guys would be thanking their lucky stars that every woman they meet is desperate for some goddamn action. My problem is, I can't bring myself to go with it.

Which could have something to do with the fact that my mother died of a particular aggressive form of pancreatic cancer on my fifteenth birthday. A few weeks later, my father hung himself in our garage. He loved her so much, he just didn't want to live without her. On her death bed, my mother's final words to me were … *promise me you'll stay true to your own heart.*

I told her I would.

Which I now regret.

Caleb joined the Marines a few years later and Gage coped by jumping into bed with a long line of willing women, maybe for some kind of comfort or distraction, who knows. As for me, I'm stuck in a zone that's partly about honoring a promise and partly about trying to find a way to respect what my dead parents once had.

I'm not exactly fucking thrilled about any of it, but it's the hand I've been dealt: I'm incapable of letting myself have random, meaningless sex. I'm waiting for the real thing, as ludicrous as that might be.

And, since I've never met anyone who I could potentially see myself falling in love with—not even close—I've been saving myself for some elusive, perfect woman who might not even exist.

Who probably *doesn't* exist, let's be honest.

The whole scenario sucks, some days almost more than I can bear.

I *wish* I could climb into that Jeep and go for a joyride with these girls. I wish I could let off some metaphorical steam all over them. Take out my frustrations in a long-overdue frenzy until they were crying for more than one reason.

But no. I spend every single second of my time mired in a ferocious, feral state of relentless, raging lust. For a phantom lover who never shows up.

I exist in a haze of blazing, pent-up need that has nowhere to focus besides football, which only releases a minuscule fraction of it.

I hang out with my team and my friends, I swim until my muscles are aching, I pump iron until I'm drenched in sweat. But none of it helps.

It's a big fucking problem.

I'm glad the football season officially starts tonight. Now that I can immerse myself in practice, games and my business and finance classes, time won't seem so slow and heavy, I can only hope. Caleb will be home next month. My brother has seen some serious combat in Afghanistan and I have a feeling he'll be a changed man when he gets back. I email him every couple of days to try to boost his morale, which hasn't been great lately. It'll be good to have him home again.

The girls call after me, begging me to come back to them.

I almost turn.

I almost fucking do it.

Promise me … stay true to your own heart.

I am. I said I would. But what if it kills me?

There's more to me than a heart. And everything else about me wants to fuck like a maniac.

I keep walking.

I get to the locker room and toss my bag onto a bench.

Most of the team is already there. Coach is already barking orders. We go through our plays and we warm up. I do what I need to do. I try to focus.

Each day, it's getting harder.

My head isn't straight. My situation is starting to fuck with my concentration. I'm consumed with a raging fever that's becoming harder and harder to control.

As we run out onto the field for kick-off, I can hear the fans chanting my name. We're playing one of our biggest rivals tonight and they'll give us a run for our money, but I'm more than up to it. I can feel the adrenaline pumping through my veins like a drug. The thrill of the game is the only thing that takes the slightest edge off.

I pass the ball to Kirby, who advances twelve yards. It's a good start. The fans go wild. It's our first game of the season and they're feeling it.

I nail pass after pass. By the end of the first half, we're up by fourteen points.

Time does what it always does when I play football. It becomes all about my focus on the game. I don't have to think about anything else and it's a relief, as much as it can be.

It's the physical part of the urge that never really eases. Not even relentless workouts or the intensity of a game can distract me from *that* side of my craving.

I can't go on like this much longer.

I'm going to lose my mind.

Kirby pats me on the back, smirking. Reading my state of mind, probably. "You okay, man?"

"Just get into position." I sound gruff. I should be enjoying my life, for fuck's sake. I just wish I didn't have to break a sacred promise to do it.

"Chief, we're going to have to stage an intervention." He laughs sympathetically but then runs over to take his place. It's sort of infuriating that the entire team—and therefore world—knows the extent of my pain.

Everyone knows I'm mired in the misery of my own fucking "rule." It's all over the internet. I'm the starting quarterback who's saving himself for the real thing. Which makes the whole clusterfuck a million times worse.

Another pass slides perfectly into Kowalski's hands. Touchdown.

We're on a roll.

We score again.

It's deep in the fourth quarter when it happens. Our possession. The score is 38-7. I'm getting into position for the next play when something catches my eye. I glance up at the Jumbotron.

And I stop.

The camera has zoomed in on someone.

At first I think I'm seeing things. Imagining some kind of vision, dug up, maybe, by an agony that's only compounding itself hour by hour.

It's a girl. An unbelievably … *beautiful* girl.

Her face is angelic, impossibly cute, like something out of … a fantasy, maybe.

A fantasy I want to step into and live inside.

She's wearing a little black hat but as I stand there watching her, a gust of wind blows her hat off and her long hair spills loose. Her hair isn't quite strawberry blond and isn't quite white gold but some impossible shade in between, framing her face like a halo. The setting sun catches it. Everything about her shines with a surreal glow. She looks soft and enchanting and somehow shimmery, like a shy mermaid that just wandered onto dry land. You can tell she doesn't know the camera is on her. She smiles sort of self-consciously at something her friend has said and reaches for her hat.

Fuck, she's stunning. She's devastatingly sexy in a dreamy, totally-unaware-of-it way. *Jesus.* I spend most of my time half-cocked but at the sight of this unbelievably beautiful girl, my problem levels up. Just from gazing at the fucking Jumbotron. My lust is already in overdrive and my cock thickens at the sight of the gorgeous little angel on the screen. Which is really not ideal in the middle of a football game.

The camera zooms in a fraction closer.

Her face.

Her mouth.

Someone's yelling at me. A *lot* of people are yelling at me. I can hear their voices, but I literally can't pull my eyes away.

I'm star-struck, like one of those shots in a movie where everything fades out except the object that takes all your focus. My mouth feels parched. And my heart aches as though I've been missing something monumental and here it suddenly fucking is.

Who is she?

I don't even realize I've said it out loud, but Tyler is within earshot. "That's the girl I saw on the green today. *Look* at her, man. She's a goddess."

I feel like lunging at him. Tackling him to the ground and making sure he understands that he can't have her. That if he goes anywhere near her, I'll go fucking ballistic.

But then she realizes she's on camera and her cheeks get pink as she puts her hat back on and pulls it low over her eyes.

The camera pans away, across the crowd, and she's gone.

No.

I scan the stadium but have no idea where she might be.

Coach is yelling from the sideline. He calls a time out. His face is bright red. Hayes and Kowalski and some of the others are laughing. I realize I've been standing there for a while, maybe close to a minute.

"McCabe! What the hell are you doing?" Coach is screaming.

"He's checking out some girl on the Jumbotron." Kirby elbows me. "Does this mean our lone wolf quarterback has finally met his match? Dude, you need to find her."

I know.

My team gives me shit all the time about my lack of a love life. They don't understand it and neither do I.

Coach is about a foot shorter than me, ranting like a lunatic. He's worked up. "If you have any intention of continuing as the starting goddamn quarterback for this team, McCabe, you'll get your goddamn head back in this game, and pronto! You can play the other field in your own time. Is that understood?"

"Yes, sir."

He finishes his rant and we get back into formation. I scan the crowd as subtly as I'm capable of as I return to the field.

I can't see her.

Fuck.

It takes every shred of willpower I possess to keep my focus. Somehow, I do. For the final fifteen minutes, I go through the motions. Bronson's a wild card with occasional flashes of genius. And he's right where I want him. My pass glides into his outstretched hands and he juggles it before securing the ball.

Touchdown! yells the announcer. The crowd goes insane.

The game is over.

I have to stop myself from running up into the stands to search for her. But there are a hundred thousand people here tonight. They're standing up. They're starting to leave.

Where is she?

Who is she?

I have to find out.

I need to see her again, *like I've never needed anything in my life.*

The people around me are cheering, celebrating, patting me on the back.

I barely hear them. All I can think about is the shy, glowing girl and the realization that's hitting me like a ten-ton wall of bricks.

I'm going to search for her until I find her. If it takes me the rest of my life to do it.

I've kept my promise, and now it's time to find out what I've been missing.

To make the most beautiful girl I've ever seen … *mine.*

I want *her.*

ALSO BY JULIE CAPULET

I Love You Series

The Obsession Begins (free)

XOXO I Love You

XOXX I Love You More

Love You the Most (free)

Sexy Standalones

Max

Cowboy

McCabe Brothers Series

Hopeless Romantic

My Hero

Arrogant Player

Music City Lovers Series

Nashville Days

Nashville Nights

Nashville Dreams

Nashville Lights

Hawthorne U Series

Lovestruck

Paradise Series

Devil's Angel

Wild Hearts

New York Billionaires Series

Billionaire Boss

Billionaire Grump

Billionaire Devil

Billionaire Romantic

Standalone Rom-com

Beautiful Savages

ABOUT THE AUTHOR

Julie Capulet is an Amazon top 20 bestselling author of contemporary romance. She writes steamy he-falls-first romance with heart, heat and fairy tale HEAs. Her stories are inspired by true love and she's married to her own real life hero. When she's not writing, she's reading, traveling, walking on the beach and watching rom-coms.

www.juliecapulet.com

9 781968 790127